SAVING ZIGGY

LIVERPOOL BOYS SERIES: BOOK ONE

ALEX J. ADAMS

To Lizzie
Best wishes
Alex

Saving Ziggy

Copyright © 2022 by Alex J. Adams

All rights reserved

No part of this book may be reproduced in any form or by any electronic or mechanical means, including information storage and retrieval systems, without written permission from the author, except for the use of brief quotations in a review.

All characters and events in this book are fictitious. Any similarity to real persons, living or dead, or any companies is completely coincidental.

Editing: Karen Meeus

Cover Art: Wynter Adams

Beta Read: Marianne Krabseth and Joanne Oates

Proofing: Jae Atal

CHAPTER ONE

I stood on the dimly lit street corner, waiting for my next trick to turn up. I'd been here for two hours now, and pickings had been slim. I stamped my feet on the wet pavement and blew into my hands, trying to generate heat, my pink, chapped hands freezing in this weather.

Fuck, but it was cold. November in Liverpool was no fun, especially when all I had to wear was my thin turquoise jacket and red booty shorts. My dirty white over-knee socks were threadbare, but as long as no one looked too closely, you couldn't tell. The pink sparkly trainers I wore had holes in the bottom, and I really needed to buy new ones. The cold and wet had already seeped through; my toes were as frozen as my hands.

But if I didn't score again tonight, there'd be no chance of that happening anytime soon.

I heard a car approach and watched as the others on the street heard it too, all of us turning towards the sound. I reluctantly undid my coat, shivering as I did, and pushed it behind me, placing my hand on my hip. I thrust my groin out, my shorts so small my skinny midriff was on show. The baby-pink crop top barely covered my erect nipples, and it was so fucking cold, I could cut glass with them.

I looked across the road to my friend, Suzie, who was doing the exact same thing, but neither one of us knew which side the punter might go. As usual, it was a case of girls on one side of the street, boys on the other.

"A quid says he's coming my way," she shouted to me, a lopsided grin on her face.

"You're on," I yelled back, laughing at her goofy smile.

We watched as the car turned into the street and swerved over to my side.

"You lose, Suzie." I smirked as the dark-blue BMW slowed down. The driver looked at me approvingly through the passenger window, finally stopping.

I sauntered towards the car as he opened the window, a swing in my step. I needed this one tonight.

"How much?" His voice was velvety soft, and his eyes roamed across my body, taking in my slim physique.

"Depends what you want, big guy. But nothing is over fifty quid for you," I replied huskily. Anything to get out of this freezing cold.

"Do you want to get in?" He leaned across and opened the door for me.

I looked across at Suzie and winked.

"Text me," she mouthed, giving me the thumbs up. I nodded and climbed into the car. The heated leather seat instantly warmed my frozen legs.

I fastened my seat belt before turning to look at my last trick of the evening.

"Hi," I said, "I'm—" But before I could get the rest of my sentence out, he stopped me with a finger to the lips.

"No, no names. I don't need to know who you are, only what you can do, beautiful."

"OK, we can play it like that if you want," I said, pouting slightly at his words.

I looked over and studied him as he drove. His hair was short, neatly cut and black. Jet black. His eyes were as dark and glittered under the streetlights. He was clean-shaven and so fucking good-looking. Maybe my night had just got a whole lot better. I sat back in my seat, feeling smug.

"What will I get for my fifty quid? I want at least a blow job; those plump lips would look gorgeous around my cock."

"But here," he carried on, "let me put the heat up. You must have been freezing standing out there in this weather."

"Yeah, thanks," I replied. "It's no picnic this time of the year, I can tell you."

My fingers and toes started to tingle as they warmed up, but it'd be a while before I was fully warm. This guy seemed nice enough, though, and I thanked my lucky stars he'd stopped by my side of the street.

"Well, you relax, beautiful." He reached across, rubbing my cold thighs with his hand, slipping his little finger beneath the hem of my shorts. "We'll be there soon, and then you can warm up some more."

The heat in the car and his soft touch began to lull me to sleep, but I needed to stay awake. I couldn't afford to miss where we were going; I would need to text Suzie.

"You're very beautiful, you know. I know I keep saying it." I turned to look at him again as he gave me a sideways glance, his gaze flicking between me and the road.

I knew I was nothing special to look at. I had dull brown hair, boring brown eyes and, at the age of twenty, had yet to master the art of growing facial hair. I supposed it made me look a little femme, but I didn't wear make-up; it wasn't my style. I did like to wear pink and sparkly and had been known to wear a skirt on occasion but never heels; I was already close to six feet tall.

I flattened my hair to my head and gave a small laugh, embarrassed at his words. I wasn't beautiful. I was just me—plain old Ziggy.

He lifted his hand from my thigh to stroke my face, and I snuggled into his hand. It was warm against my chilled face, and I almost purred with contentment.

"So beautiful and such smooth skin." His voice had softened until I could barely hear him.

"I'm really nothing special, just me, you know?"

He hummed under his breath but didn't say anymore, concentrating now on the road ahead. We'd arrived at a junction with many traffic lights and road signs, but I couldn't see which way we were heading.

I turned in my seat, trying to see exactly where we were, starting to panic. Mr Velvety-Smooth must have noticed my frantic searching.

"Don't worry. I'll drop you back where we started. We're going to my place in Crosby. It's right by the beach. You'll like it."

His hand was back on my thigh, and he continued to stroke, grazing my crotch as he did so. The action soothed me, and I started to relax again.

"Ok. It's just I normally text my friend to tell her where I'm going. Safety and all that, you know? I just wondered where we were going."

"I understand. Tell her we're headed to East Street, close to the beach. You can text her the number when you see it for yourself. Not much longer now."

He continued to drive, and I stayed silent. I never usually went this far off my patch, but I could hardly jump out of the car, so I sat, quietly watching the road as we drove further and further away from my safe place.

Was I anxious? Of course I was, but I felt safe with him for some reason. His soft voice and gentle touch eased my nerves.

He drove for another ten minutes, rain continuing to batter the windscreen, before pulling into a side street, terraced houses on either side of the narrow road. The houses all looked the same, painted in various shades of white and cream. He pulled up outside of number seventeen, putting the car in park.

"You want to text your friend now? Tell her where you are?" I was so captivated by his smile; I'd be safe with him, I reckoned.

I nodded and got my phone out, sending a quick message to Suzie, giving her the address, telling her I was in for a good night.

"Shall we go?" he asked, and we stepped out into the pouring rain.

Mr Velvety-Smooth locked the car and ran to open the front door of the nearest house, ushering me quickly inside. I stepped straight into a warm and inviting room, an orange glow coming from the lamp in the corner. There wasn't much furniture, a grey, comfy-looking couch almost filling the room with a small table off to the side. With a hand on my arm, he guided me to sit, slowly stroking my face as he walked away.

"Can I get you a drink?" he asked, heading towards a door. "Something to warm you up or water, anything you want." The glint in his eye made me think we were talking about more than just a drink.

Mr Velvety-Smooth or Mr V-S as I was calling him now, because let's face it, Mr Velvety-Smooth was more than a mouthful, was being exceptionally nice, but I still needed to be on my guard. I was in his house, for fuck's sake, and I began to get nervous again, worrying about how I'd managed to get myself into this situation.

I could have kicked myself. I never did this, never! But I'd got swept away by his smooth voice and relaxing demeanour.

"I'm OK, thanks," I stammered as I spoke, my anxiety getting the best of me.

"If you're sure. Let me know if you change your mind, beautiful." He sat down next to me. "Shall we get started?"

He looked me in the eye, taking my hand in his and kissing my palm.

"I can't wait to feel your mouth on my cock. It'll feel so good." He leaned towards me, eyes closed, intent on kissing me, but I never kissed a punter. It always felt too personal, and this was a job, a business transaction.

I moved backwards out of reach, and he opened his eyes, confusion filling them. I slid off the couch onto my knees, feeling the soft carpet beneath them. I was no expert, but this shit felt expensive, plush and thick.

I ran my hands up his firm thighs as he leaned back, and he spread his legs wide, putting his hands behind his head. He closed his eyes again, a soft groan leaving his lips.

"Fuck, feels so good."

I continued to massage his thighs, moving my hands closer and closer to his cock. I watched with wonder as the bulge behind his zip grew to impressive proportions. Mr V-S was definitely going to be a mouthful.

"Oh God. Get my cock out, boy. I need those beautiful lips," He moaned and thrust himself towards me, his big dick straining the dark fabric covering it. I couldn't wait to see what lay beneath.

I undid the button, his zipper loud in the quiet of the house, and I wondered if we were here alone. He hadn't mentioned anyone else, so assumed it was just us.

He put his legs together and helped me as I slid his trousers down his legs, swiftly followed by his underwear, revealing the most perfect dick I'd ever seen.

My mouth watered.

It was long and veiny, thick with a delicious upward curve that would hit the back of my throat as he fucked my face. The foreskin was pulled back, revealing a purple, engorged head, leaking from the slit.

I wanted it desperately and gripped it, stroking my hand up and down the length, feeling the silky skin coating his hardness. I thumbed the precum, and he groaned louder, opening his eyes.

They were even darker than before, almost demon-like in appearance, two orbs of glittering obsidian. I couldn't look away from them; they were hypnotic, mesmerising, but the spell was broken as he thrust upwards into my hand.

"Suck me, lick me. I need it." He was breathless now, panting heavily, and I continued to play with him before sucking and licking around the head. The taste was salty with a bitter tang. I wasn't convinced he'd washed before picking me up, but fifty quid was fifty quid. I'd make the most of it, make him come, collect my money and get him to take me back to Liverpool.

"I don't swallow, just so you know," I said, and he nodded briefly before I continued to suck him, working his shaft. I used my other hand to roll his balls, scratching them gently with my nails, and I felt them tighten beneath my touch. I continued to suck, hollowing my cheeks and humming as it reached the back of my throat.

I hoped he was nearing his release. My jaw was aching as the impressive girth stretched my mouth wide. I loved giving blowjobs but hated swallowing, disliking the taste of come, so I was hyperaware of the telltale signs of an impending release.

Moments later, the grunting became more guttural, and I knew he was close. I pulled off and jacked him with my hand until seconds later, he shot his load over my fist.

"Wow," he managed to croak out. "Amazing, thank you." He handed me some wipes from the table, and I cleaned off my hands, wiping the saliva from my face. I managed to stand and adjusted my own erection. My knees ached, and I backed away from the couch, wanting to be as far away from him now as I could. Once the deed was finished, I was done. I never masturbated and never asked for my trick to get me off. I was there purely for their needs, not mine.

I watched as he cleaned his dick, tucking it into his briefs; even soft, it was stunning. He stood, putting his clothes straight and fastened his trousers. I stood expectantly, waiting for my payment. If he didn't hand it over soon, I'd have to ask, and I hated doing that, but before I could open my mouth, he reached into his back pocket for his wallet. He took out a wad of notes and counted out fifty, handing it to me slowly, grazing my hand with the exchange.

"Thanks," I managed to get out. Now I needed to go home, back to Suzie, back to my patch. I tucked the money into my pocket, zipping it shut so I wouldn't lose it.

"Can we go now?"

He nodded, collecting his keys and opening the front door. We'd been there for about twenty minutes, hardly worth the trip, but at least I'd managed to get warm and earn myself more money. Once he dropped me off, I'd make my way back to the place I shared with Suzie and crash. Tomorrow was another day.

CHAPTER TWO

The journey back was quiet. No talking, no stroking, just silence, and I was grateful for it. I needed to be home. Safe, and I wouldn't be happy until I was.

Twenty minutes later, we pulled up where he'd initially picked me up, the rain having stopped. The street was deserted now, and I knew I'd find the others in the local cafe. I considered meeting up with them, but it would eat into the funds I'd made tonight, and shoes and a roof over our heads were more important than a cup of tea. I decided to call it a night, climbing out of the car as it came to a stop.

"Cheers for the cash, Mister." I could have kicked myself, but I didn't know what else to call him. I couldn't call him Mr V-S, could I?

"Thank you, again, for tonight, beautiful. I know you didn't get off, but I didn't pay you for that. Next time, I might let you." He winked and turned away, ready to be on his way.

I shut the door, a frown on my face as I thought about his comment. I didn't usually have repeats. Most men wanted a one-off and rarely came back for more. Sounded like this guy fancied another go, but I wasn't sure what to think.

He drove away, and I walked home, eager to be in the warm again. Tonight had been different. He'd been different, but I'd made my money and now I was tired.

Several weeks passed and when I didn't see Mr V-S, either on my side of the road or Suzie's, I forgot his insinuation there'd be a next time. I was getting tired, though, tired of the job and tired of standing in the freezing cold just to earn a few pounds.

It wasn't until the end of November that I saw him again. The same thing happened, and I almost said no, but again, the rent was due and we were low on cash. Punters didn't want to come out in the cold and wet to find a willing mouth or hand to get them off, content with sitting in front of their laptops, watching porn, pleasuring themselves, so I was desperate for the money.

We drove to Crosby again and followed the same procedure, him sitting on the sofa and me getting him off with my mouth and finally my hand. This time, he stroked my hair as I blew him, a gentle caress, and I wondered if he cared for me. After all, he'd chosen me again over everyone else. This time, he paid me seventy-five pounds on the understanding I'd buy myself a better coat.

I was still wearing my thin, turquoise jacket, but the colder weather had me abandoning my shorts for a low-slung pair of black skinny jeans and some black boots. I still wore one of my cropped tops, revealing more skin than I would have liked, but times were desperate, and I needed rent money.

"Promise me you'll buy something to keep you warm. I hate to think of you standing there, out in the cold." He handed me the money, his hand lingering, and he stroked my face with his other. Maybe he did care about me. After all, this was his second time with me and he'd paid me more than the going rate. His soft caresses had me thinking things I shouldn't. He put me at ease, and that didn't happen often.

I walked home, still shivering from the cold, thinking of his words. I arrived at our flat and opened the door. It was a small, one-bedroomed place, dingy wallpaper peeling from the walls and the carpet harbouring stains that had been there since we'd moved in. Suzie was in the kitchen area, standing by the two-burner hob, warming up something for our supper.

By the smell, it was a homemade soup. She loved cooking and made most things from scratch. We might have lived in a shitty flat, but we ate well. Suzie would search out the bargains in the out-of-date aisles in the supermarket, expertly whipping up a semi-gourmet meal. She was a godsend, a proper Nigella Lawson.

"How was Mr V-S? Still as smooth as ever?" she asked as she removed the pan from the hob, wiping her hands on a cloth.

I'd told her about him last time, how his voice had been soft and silky, how he'd treated me right and made me feel comfortable and relaxed. I'd still been wary tonight, but not as much as I would normally be.

"Same as last time, but he gave me seventy-five this time. Told me to get a new coat with the extra." I slumped on the threadbare sofa, and Suzie handed me a bowl of vegetable soup. I knew it would taste amazing, and I wasn't disappointed. I hummed with approval as the flavour burst on my tongue and continued to eat, needing the warmth it provided.

"What are you going to do? We need the money for the rent, Ziggy. We need the extra."

I was a little annoyed at her. She'd been out less and less lately, most of our meagre income coming from me.

"I know we do, Suzie, and I probably won't see him again. I'll not bother with the coat, OK? I'm not standing outside for long these days; it's too fucking cold. Everybody seems to be spending time at home the nearer we get to Christmas. Must want to save the money they usually spend on prostitutes to get a lovely present for the wife." I was frustrated, but I couldn't blame her. If I thought I could get away with it, I wouldn't do it either.

She snorted and I laughed. We both knew it was true.

I wasn't bitter about it. I knew many of my punters were in the closet. They wore wedding rings, not even bothering to hide they were married. It really wasn't my problem. As long as they paid up, I was good. But something about Mr V-S was drawing me in, even after only two sessions with him. The way he spoke to me, treated me... It was different.

The closer we got to Christmas, the more Suzie and I struggled to make money. She'd started going out a little more, but the weather was cold and frosty, and they'd forecast snow, deterring any would-be punters. It was unusual for us, living so near to the river, but 'The Beast from the East' was making itself known again.

"We need to get proper jobs if this continues," she said one night as we huddled on the sofa, covered in as many blankets as we could find. The heating in our flat was on the fritz yet again, and no amount of complaining to the landlord had produced any results.

"Can you imagine us working at Starbucks or Costa or some other place where we'd actually need to be nice? Sex is one thing, Suzie, but speaking to people? Not sure either one of us is cut out for that," I quipped.

She sniggered at the comment and snuggled closer to me, but she was right. The money we had stashed away wasn't going to see us very far into Christmas, let alone the New Year.

"Not sure what else we can do," she said with a shrug. "I made two hundred quid last week and not even that this week. I don't see why we should pay the rent until fucking Greg can get the heating sorted. It's like living in a fridge."

I nodded as she spoke. Our landlord knew if he didn't fix the heating, we'd eventually have to move out, which was what he wanted. He hated what we did for a living even though we never brought anyone home with us. We'd only ever been late with the rent a couple of times in the past eighteen months since we'd lived here and had always paid within a couple of days.

"I know, babe, but what can we do? Short of getting a proper job like you said. I don't have the clothes to sell anything but my body at this stage."

"Me either," she said as she snuggled in closer, the blankets wrapped tightly around us.

She was quiet for a while, and I knew what she was thinking. Although she lived here with me, her folks weren't too far away, and she knew she could go back to them at any time. As far as they knew, she worked in a small charity shop in Liverpool. She'd never explained to me why she was selling herself on the streets, and I didn't ask.

We both worked on the premise of 'don't ask, don't tell', and I was more than happy with that. The only difference between us was I had no one. Oh, don't get me wrong. I had family; I just chose not to acknowledge them. There'd be no family at home waiting with a decorated Christmas tree, presents sitting underneath it, but she didn't know that, and I wasn't going to tell her.

Her next words didn't surprise me. I'd been expecting them, if I was honest.

"I might go home for Christmas." She spoke so quietly, knowing I had nowhere to go but here. I'd never discussed my family, and she'd hadn't asked again after the first few weeks we met when I'd refused to talk about them. They were dead to me, and I wanted them to stay that way. I'd been on my own for four years, and they had never once wondered where I was. I was

Ziggy Coleman, twenty years old, and I knew how to look after myself.

"If you're sure," I said, kissing the top of her head. "They'll be happy to see you." I felt a little sad at the prospect, but at least she'd be warm, and she loved her family.

"I know you don't have anyone, Zig, and I feel terrible for leaving you." She paused as if thinking what to say next. "But I'm thinking of going back for good. I'm tired of doing this. Of standing at the side of the street waiting to see where the next bit of money is coming from, not to mention I'm sick of blowjobs, hand jobs and being fucked every way to Sunday."

I was shocked at her words. I'd never once imagined she'd go back home, but it was what it was, and I'd have to deal with it. The only problem, I couldn't make rent on my own. How the fuck was I supposed to keep the flat if I couldn't make enough money?

I didn't want her to feel bad. I supposed if I had someone to go home to, someone who would welcome me with open arms, I would have gone back to them as well.

"It's OK, Suzie. I understand, and I don't blame you. You have your whole future in front of you. What will you do?"

She was silent for a moment, and I honestly thought she'd gone to sleep, but she eventually spoke.

"I've applied to go to college. To do a professional cookery course. I've been accepted and start in the New Year. I didn't want to tell you," she rushed out, "but I can't do this anymore, Ziggy." I heard her voice catch and knew she was close to tears.

"You'll be an amazing cook, Suzie. If it wasn't for you, we wouldn't have eaten half as well as we have these past few months. You were born to do this." I gave her a squeeze. "I'm so proud of you, babe. Not just for getting on the course but for getting out of here, for following your dream. I only wish I had one to follow."

And I wished I did, but my dreams were made up of things I

knew I'd never have, so selling myself for fifty quid a night was the best I was going to do for a while. I knew I didn't deserve anything more.

I was Ziggy. I was nothing special, would never be special, and for the time being, I was OK with that. I just didn't know how long I could continue doing this without hating myself and the job any more than I already did.

CHAPTER THREE

The week before Christmas, Suzie left for good. She packed up her clothes, her pots and pans, and waved as her brother drove her away, taking her to a new future. I cried when she left, but as upset as I was, I couldn't be mad at her for following her dreams. It did leave me in a shitty position. I had no roommate and rent to pay on a place I neither wanted to live in nor could afford.

I had to get out on the streets again as much as the cold was putting me off. I needed to earn more money than I had been. I left the flat and made my way to my usual spot, peering both ways down the shadowy street. There was just the odd one like me with nowhere to go but here, and I waved half-heartedly at the few remaining. I stood in the crippling cold, waiting for someone, anyone, to turn up. I'd be sorely tempted to go home if I hadn't needed the money so badly.

I decided to give it another five minutes. I still hadn't replaced my damn pink trainers nor my coat, but tonight, I wore a sweater and jeans. Not the best for attracting punters, but it was so fucking cold; I might die of hypothermia.

I checked my phone again. One more minute and I was done.

There were only a couple of us here now, most having given it up as a bad job, and I was about to make my move when a familiar BMW came into view. Could it be? Was Mr V-S out on a night like this?

My question was answered as the car drew up next to me, the window coming down as it came to a halt.

"Hi, beautiful. I bet you're freezing. Fancy getting out of the cold?" His soft voice washed over me, and I couldn't stop the smile lighting my face.

"Abso-fucking-lutely." He opened the door for me, and I climbed into the car, feeling relieved at the warmth inside. I rubbed my hands together, blowing on them to try and get the circulation going again.

"Where's your warm coat? I told you to buy one with the money I gave you. Why didn't you get it?" I looked over at him, wondering if he looked as annoyed as his words seemed. There was no way I was taking instruction from a punter, and despite how warm it was in the car, I reached for the door, ready to get out. I'd take my chances out there. Yeah, I needed the money, but fuck him! How dare he tell me what to spend my money on.

"Stop." His voice pulled me to a halt, and I hesitated for a moment. He took it as a sign to continue. "Don't go, please. I'm sorry. I didn't mean that. Let's go back to my place, and we can talk." He held on to my wrist, not hard, but enough to make me stop and listen.

Talk? What the fuck was he on about? I knew from the last two times he'd picked me up he'd be wanting something more than talking. I chanced a look at him and saw he was smiling, a hopeful look on his face. I did need the money, and as much as I warred with my gut on this one, I sat back in my seat and fastened the seat belt.

"I'll let the comment pass this time. But don't tell me what to spend my money on."

"OK, I'm sorry." His apology sounded sincere and, putting the car in gear, he started to drive along the route I now found familiar. Twenty minutes later, we arrived at his house.

He let us inside, and I was surprised to see the small table off to the side set with food and drinks, the usual lamp in the corner giving the room a romantic feel.

"I hope you don't mind, but with Christmas coming up soon, maybe we could celebrate early?" Again with the hopeful look. "I wasn't sure I'd find you tonight. I didn't know if you had any family to go to at this time of year. I thought we could get to know each other a little. I know I said no names, but I've found myself wanting to know more and more about you. It's been hard to stop thinking about you."

He almost looked bashful, glancing down at his feet as he spoke, not meeting my eyes, and if he wasn't the most adorable man.

"I suppose, if it's what you'd like." It couldn't hurt for one night, surely. He looked at me tenderly and gestured for me to sit, grabbing a soft drink and handing it to me. "I wasn't sure what you wanted, but is this OK?" He seemed nervous, and, if I was honest, I was too.

"Yeah, it's fine." I smiled back and took the can from him, watching as he put food on a couple of plates and sat next to me on the sofa. He placed the plate in front of me on a small coffee table, a napkin to the side of it.

"It's true, you know. I can't stop thinking about you." He gave me a sideways glance before continuing. "You've been on my mind a lot lately, so I'm glad I found you tonight. Like I said, I've been around, but you either weren't there or were getting in someone else's car. Must admit, that hurt a little; I didn't like to see it, but I know it's your job. I really do, even if I wish it weren't."

I didn't know what to say to him, feeling a little awkward at his outpouring. I'd heard of this happening before, where punters became obsessed, and I hoped this wasn't the case. Sure I found him attractive; I mean, who wouldn't? He was a gay man's walking wet dream. Handsome, beautiful dark eyes and gorgeous lips, but his words were making me a little nervous, and I edged away from him, trying to gauge how far it was from the couch to the door.

"I'm Damian," he said, closing the distance I'd put between us. "I know I said no names before, but this is our third time, and I can't call you beautiful like I do in my head." He huffed out a laugh, and I turned to face him. No one ever called me beautiful, and I'd said as much to him the first time we met. I was just Ziggy.

I hesitated, not sure if I wanted to play along or not. I supposed this couldn't hurt.

"Nice to meet you, Damian." I held my hand out to shake, and he took it, turning it over in his, stroking the back of my hand. His hand was soft and warm, not pink and chapped from the cold like mine.

"I'm Ziggy, and yes, my mum was a fan of David Bowie." I rolled my eyes as I spoke. My mother had loved him, which was how I'd ended up with the ridiculous name. I hated it growing up, put up with all sorts of bullying at school because of it, but to be honest, it had been par for the course.

"Who isn't or wasn't, I should say now," he replied, still holding on to my hand, and I slowly removed it from his, gripping my drink in both hands.

I wasn't a fan of him, particularly, but it did make me wonder how old Damian was. Definitely in his thirties, maybe older, but I didn't care. A punter was a punter, but tonight, we were straying into different territory. We'd hardly spoken before, and this was new.

"So, tell me a little about yourself. What do you do? Do you have any family? A significant other, maybe?" He sat back on the sofa and crossed his legs, an enquiring look on his face.

"You first," I gestured to him. "I want to know about you first."

I looked him in the eye as I said this, watching him. I wasn't giving him anything. Not yet anyway. I was twenty, not naive. Was that a flicker of annoyance? I frowned, but as quickly as it had appeared, it disappeared. Had I imagined it? I wasn't sure.

"Well, I'm a little older than you at thirty-seven." Fuck, he was almost twice my age, but I didn't let him see the effect his revelation had on me. "I'm single, no partner, no husband or wife." I checked his ring finger to be sure but saw no marks, no sign he'd taken it off for tonight. "There's only me."

He looked into my eyes, and I could see the sincerity of his words. I was usually pretty good at spotting a liar. What was it they said? You can't bullshit a bullshitter, and I was definitely one of those.

I was unsure how much to tell him at this point. He had my first name, and there wasn't anything he could do with that, so I figured a little more couldn't hurt.

"No significant other for me either. Not many would put up with my line of work, so there's just me. I have a couple of friends."

"Ah, yes. The little lady you texted before you came here." He looked at me, puzzled. "You haven't messaged her tonight. Does this mean you trust me?"

I didn't want to tell him Suzie had moved away. I wasn't sure why. I liked him, but I didn't trust him enough just yet. Thinking quickly on my feet, I spewed out the first thing to come to mind.

"Oh, we have a new app on our phones now that tracks each other, so she'll know exactly where I am even though I haven't messaged her. I usually call her when I'm coming home, so if she doesn't hear from me, she'll know I'm with someone."

It was the best I could do under pressure, and I hoped Mr V-S, Damian, believed me. I wasn't sure I would under the circumstances, but from the look on his face, he did.

"I see, I see. Makes sense, I suppose." He gestured to my plate and handed me the napkin. "Eat, anyway. I bought this food for us. I know it's not much, but maybe it would be nice to share something together."

I nodded at him and took a tentative bite from the chicken he'd placed on the plate.

"Go on, eat up. You look as if you could do with fattening up." He motioned for me to eat, and as I swallowed the food, I realised how hungry I was.

With Suzie gone, I was back to eating Pot Noodles and cheese sandwiches. Not exactly nouvelle cuisine, but it was cheap and kept me going. Add in food bought in the reduced aisle, and I was eating like a king, albeit a very poor king with little to no money. Who was I kidding? I was missing Suzie like crazy, not just her cooking but her company and ridiculous sense of humour.

I continued to wolf down the food from the plate, eventually realising how I must have looked. "Sorry, I didn't eat lunch." Or dinner or breakfast, come to think of it, but I remembered my manners and slowed down, trying to not shovel the food in.

"Please, there's plenty of food. Eat as much as you like. Hell, take it home to your friend. I'm sure you'd both enjoy it. It will only go to waste if you don't. Slow down though. We have all evening."

I mumbled a 'thank you' through a mouthful of food, swallowing quickly.

"Of course. It's very kind of you. We'll both enjoy it." I was eyeing the food on the table, wondering how long I could make it last before it started to go off. A couple of days at least. A couple of days when I wouldn't have to dip into my dwindling funds.

Damian didn't say much more, which was odd considering that was what he'd wanted to do. He kept my plate full, encouraging me to eat, but eventually I was full. I sat back on the couch, a satisfied smile on my face. It'd been a while since I'd eaten so much, and I was feeling a little sick, the button on my jeans threatening to pop open.

"I have dessert if you want some," he said, taking my plate from me.

I hoped he wasn't talking about his dick. I didn't think I could give a blowjob without throwing up all the food I'd eaten. Deep throating wasn't on the menu tonight.

He must have read my mind because he laughed, patting me on the knee and giving my thigh a firm stroke.

"No, not that, although I wouldn't say no. I have some ice cream sundaes, but maybe we should leave them until next time."

Next time. Was there going to be a next time? Damian seemed to think so, and I wasn't going to argue. All I wanted to do was sleep. Full of food and with the room being so warm, I was getting drowsy, but I didn't want to stay here. I wanted to go home.

Damian must have sensed a change in my mood because he stood and walked out of the room, returning with a gift wrapped in beautiful shiny paper with an elaborate bow.

CHAPTER FOUR

A gift. He'd got me a gift. What the hell was going on? I looked at him, and I was sure my mouth was hanging open.

"I hope you don't mind I bought this for you. It's not much. Useful more than anything, but I…" Damian hesitated and seemed nervous, his words failing him. He thrust it into my hands, pulling back quickly. I held on to it, feeling the paper crinkle in my hands. The present itself was soft, and I wondered what could be in there.

I felt my eyes filling with tears, and they threatened to spill down my cheeks. I couldn't remember the last time anyone had bought me anything other than the stupid gifts Suzie and I exchanged for birthdays and Christmas, and even then, they'd be edible condoms or brightly coloured dildos.

I looked at the gift, unable to say anything. Should I open it now, or should I save it? I didn't know what to do.

"Open it." He gestured towards the gift, mimicking opening it up. "Go on. I want to see what you think."

Still lost for words, I started to carefully open the gift, first removing the golden bow, then carefully peeling back the tape holding it together. Looking inside, I could see a pair of turquoise woollen gloves, beautifully soft, the colour of my coat. I held them to my face, feeling the softness of the wool, noting from the label they were cashmere.

Fuck, even I knew that shit was expensive. What was he doing buying me gifts like this? There was no way I could accept them. I had to give them back, rude as it might seem.

"I'm sorry," I said, putting them down on the couch. "I can't accept these. This is too much. They would have cost too much." I fucking wanted them, though; they were gorgeous.

Damian's face fell, and I felt awful doing it, but there was no way I could accept a gift from him and certainly not one so expensive.

"Please, I bought them especially for you. The colour reminded me of the coat you wore when we first met, and your hands are always so cold." He looked at me, a pleading expression in his eyes, and I started to rethink my decision. They were lovely and would keep my hands nice and toasty warm. Could I accept them? Should I accept them?

I knew some of the others took gifts from clients, but it felt wrong somehow. Suzie would have had his arm off if he'd given them to her, but I wasn't her. I bit my lip as I considered what I should do. He sat next to me and placed the gloves back on my lap.

"Please, Ziggy. I hate to see you standing there in the cold. At least take these, and I'll know some part of you is warm. It'd make me very happy if you'd take them."

I put them on just to try, loving the feel of the cashmere against my skin. They fit perfectly, like a glove, you could say. I laughed at the absurdity but leaned forward to place a kiss on his smooth cheek.

"Thank you. They're perfect." I looked down at the gloves,

marvelling at the feel of them, stroking and feeling the softness of the wool. They would definitely keep my hands warm. As I peered at him out of the corner of my eye, he sat with his hand to his face, the exact same place I'd kissed him, his eyes closed and a small smile playing on his lips.

As if he felt my gaze on him, he opened his eyes and removed his hand from his face.

"I know this has all been a bit much for you, but how about we pack up this food and I take you home, back to your friend? I'm sure she's been missing you tonight."

This sounded like a great idea, and I stood, picking up some of the plates of food.

"No, let me. Let me do this little thing for you." He gently pushed me back to the couch, patting my knee as he turned away.

Before long, he had everything packed up in plastic take-away boxes, safely stashed in a bag he handed to me. The bag was heavy, packed with so much food. I didn't want to tell him I probably wouldn't eat it all with Suzie now gone. I didn't want to seem ungrateful.

"Thank you for tonight, Ziggy. I know it was a bit of a surprise, but I hope you enjoyed yourself. It was nice to get to know each other. Don't you think?"

It was nice, so I told him as much, and as he drove me back home, parking on the street where he usually picked me up, I knew I had to show him my gratitude even if it meant going against my number one rule—never kiss a client.

I leaned across the console, registering the shock on his face as I placed a gentle kiss on his lips. A small sigh escaped his mouth, but before I could let it go any further, I pulled away.

"This was nice." I removed my gloves and took his hand in mine. I noticed how smooth his was. He clearly didn't do a manual job; there wasn't a blemish on them, and his nails were neatly manicured.

He removed his hand from mine and lifted himself from his seat, producing his wallet from his back pocket.

"I'm not sure how much to pay you for tonight. I know your normal going rate is fifty pounds, but it doesn't seem enough somehow. I appreciated the company, and as much as a blowjob would have been nice, I think tonight it would have ruined it."

He handed me a fifty-pound note, and as much as I needed the money, it didn't feel right taking it.

"How about tonight was on me? My gift to you seeing how I didn't get you one." It was the only thing I could think of, but it felt right. I could see the conflict in his face. He was torn between giving me the money and putting it back in his wallet. I took the decision from him, taking it from his fingertips and placing it in his shirt pocket.

"Happy Christmas, Damian. Save it for the next time." He smiled at me, a blinding flash of teeth, and his eyes shimmered in the darkness.

"Next time. Sounds good to me, and I'll be very much looking forward to it." He lifted my hand to his lips and kissed it gently, a light touch and his paper-like lips tickled my skin. "I'll let you go. It's getting late, and your friend will be wondering where you've got to."

I picked up the bag from the footwell and opened the door, turning once again to place a quick kiss on his cheek. I'd broken my rule once; another time wasn't going to make any difference in the grand scheme of things, and it was just a peck, nothing more.

I watched him drive away, raising my hand in a feeble wave and turned towards home, to my empty, cold flat. Greg still hadn't fixed the heating, and no amount of begging or asking was having an effect.

Three days later, the day before Christmas Eve, and I could hardly stand. I was ill. So fucking ill. I wasn't sure if it was a combination of the temperature of the flat or standing outside in sleet and snow, waiting for business to show, but whichever it was, I was fucking dying.

I felt like death warmed up, and if I didn't get more medication or fluids down me soon, I was going to be in big trouble. I'd eaten most of the food Damian had given me, but some of it had gone bad. My appetite had left me as soon as this flu, or whatever it was, struck.

I stumbled out of bed, checking the time on my phone. It was seven in the evening, and I couldn't remember the last time I'd eaten or drunk anything. My throat was parched, and I felt like I was swallowing razor blades. I hated feeling this way.

I dressed as quickly and warmly as I could, cursing myself for not having bought the coat when Damian had given me the extra cash, but there was nothing I could do about that now. I was still wearing my gloves, though; they'd been a godsend.

I wobbled my way to the door, sure I looked like a newborn calf taking its first steps. I could hardly stay on my own two feet; I was so weak, barely able to put one foot in front of the other, and I practically fell down the stairs and out of the front door.

The wind was biting, but at least the snow and sleet had stopped. A light covering of snow covered the pavement, wetting my feet. I looked down to see I was wearing my light canvas shoes. Who wore those in weather like this? In my delirious state, I'd clearly picked up the wrong pair, but I wasn't going back now. I needed my medication.

I walked to the nearest supermarket and squinted as the harsh lights assaulted my eyes. My headache was thumping like a jackhammer in my brain, my pulse throbbing. I managed to find the pharmacy section, throwing a selection of cold remedies and paracetamol into my basket and wound my way to the self-checkout as quickly as I could, picking up a couple of bottles of water and a Red Bull.

My items beeped as I passed them over the scanner until the red light above my station started to flash. "Please wait. A member of staff knows you are waiting." What the fuck was happening? Why wouldn't this scan?

"I'm sorry, sir. You have too much medication here. We can't let you buy this much. Two packets only."

Struggling to understand, I looked at the young girl standing next to me. She was chewing gum and clearly did not want to be here tonight, but my sick, addled brain was having problems taking in what she was saying.

"I…I need these. I'm sick, ill." I could see her eyeing me sceptically. I no doubt looked like a junkie, bloodshot eyes, hair all over the place and I wasn't dressed for the weather.

"Yeah, sure you do, but you can't have this much paracetamol. You can only have two packets." She spoke to me slowly, as if I was either stupid or high.

"Jesus, love. I just…" I was so fucking tired; I couldn't even finish my sentence, and I felt my strength draining from my limbs. I needed to get back home and into the meagre warmth my bed offered.

I was about to walk away and leave it when a familiar voice rang out across the store.

"Ziggy? Is that you?" I turned and squinted to see Damian striding across the shop towards me. "My God, you look terrible. Are you ill?" He put his hand on my forehead. I was burning up, and I had the shivers bad. Another reason for the store assistant to doubt my insistence I was genuinely sick and not coming down from a drug-induced high.

I smiled feebly at him and all but collapsed in his arms. "Yeah, I'm feeling a little shaky. Not so good, you know." I couldn't get my words out and knew I was slurring. My sight became a little blurry, and I swayed. I was feeling light-headed, and my vision swam.

Ooh, I'd never passed out before, but I supposed there was a first time for everything. Those were my last thoughts as I fainted. I was dimly aware of being surrounded by strong arms and the scent I now knew was all Damian.

CHAPTER FIVE

I woke up not knowing what time of day it was. A feeble light seeped through the curtains at the window. I had no clue where I was either, just a vague recollection of having been scooped up into strong arms and placed gently in the front seat of a car. I'd recognised familiar smells but couldn't pinpoint from where.

And now? I knew I was lying on the most comfortable bed ever. Since Suzie had left, I'd taken over her bed, having previously slept on the couch. It was no more comfortable, and I often woke up with an ache or pain somewhere on my body. This, though, this felt like nirvana, like sleeping on a cloud. The covers were luxuriant, wonderfully soft and freshly laundered.

I hummed my approval and snuggled deeper into the warmth. My mouth felt like sandpaper, but I had no energy to get up to get a drink. I'd wait here a little longer. That was my last thought before drifting back off to sleep, my mind still fuzzy.

The next time I woke, it was darker still, and I had no idea where I was or what time it was. I slowly moved my head from side to side. The pounding in my head had lessened but not yet disappeared.

A glance to the side revealed a bedside table with a glass of water and a strip of tablets with a little note in front of them. I struggled to sit up, eventually managing to get comfortable against the huge fluffy pillows on the bed.

I picked up the note and blinked to try and clear the sleep and blurriness from my eyes. I managed to focus and wasn't surprised to read who the note was from. It was all slowly coming back to me, the shopping trip, Damian and passing out.

"When you wake, take the tablets and drink all the water. I'll be back at around 5 p.m. and explain everything."

Explain everything? What did he mean? There was no point stressing about it now, not until he came back. I popped out two of the tablets and swallowed them down, doing as I was told and finishing the water. My throat felt so much better, and my headache was slowly receding. I was thirsty as hell, though.

My temperature had gone down a little, and I still felt exhausted. I needed to pee desperately and threw back the covers, placing my feet on the carpeted floor.

Shit! I was naked. How had I not noticed until now? I stood up quickly from the bed, wavering as I did so. I obviously wasn't as well as I thought but even so. Who had undressed me? Damian was the obvious answer, but I didn't know why.

I looked around for something to wear, spying a T-shirt and sweats laid out at the bottom of the bed. Hoping Damian had put them there for me, I slipped them on and stepped out of the bedroom, hopping from foot to foot, really wanting the loo now.

Only problem was, I didn't know where it was. I carefully opened the bedroom door, not knowing what I'd find on the other side. I'd never been out of the front room the three times I'd been here, assuming I was in the house we usually came to.

"Hello? Anybody around?" I wondered if Damian was here. He might be able to tell me where I was and what had happened, but I'd called out to an empty house. Definitely no one here.

I stepped back into the room and collected the now empty

glass, needing a top-up. There were two more doorways I could see, and I hoped one of them would be the bathroom. Door number one led to another bedroom with another double bed, all made up. I couldn't see signs of use, so maybe if this was Damian's house, I was in *his* bed!

I'd think about that in a while, but I was desperate to relieve myself now. I threw open door two, heaving a sigh of relief as I stepped into the bathroom. I put the glass on the shelf above the sink, pulling my dick out of the sweats, groaning as I peed like a racehorse. I couldn't remember the last time I'd been, but if the length of time I stood there was any sign, it'd been a while.

I washed my hands and debated going downstairs to grab some more water, but the longer I stood there, the more tired I became. This flu, or whatever it was, clearly wasn't done with me. I filled the glass and gulped it down before filling it again and taking it back to the bedroom.

I undressed again, thinking about whether I should leave the clothes on but decided against it. The bed was cosy enough as it was, and I knew the clothes would only make me hotter. I undressed and settled back into the bed, now thoroughly exhausted after my excursion to the bathroom. The last thing I remembered was the closing of a door, but I fell into a dreamless sleep before my mind could register fully what I'd heard.

When I woke again, I could see the silhouette of a person sitting in a chair off to the side. There was slightly more light coming into the room now, so I was able to see them. They were asleep, but as I moved around in the bed, they stirred, sitting upright.

"Are you awake, Ziggy?" I couldn't mistake the velvety soft voice of Damian, and my heart slowed at his words.

"I am. Still a little groggy. Where am I, and how long have I been here?"

He moved closer, and I could see his normally smooth face had a five o'clock shadow; his dark eyes looked tired. I scooted over a little in the double bed so he could sit on the edge. I wouldn't normally allow people this close to me, but something about this man; his voice, his actions, how he was with me, made me break all the rules I had in place when it came to customers.

"How are you feeling? You gave me a fright when I saw you in the supermarket. I hope you don't mind. I took care of you, brought you here to my house. I didn't know where you lived, and I didn't know how you would feel about the hospital."

He stroked the hair out of my eyes. "You feel a little cooler. You were burning up before, but I managed to get a little medication into you before you were out for the count. I'm sorry about undressing you as well, but your clothes were sodden from the snow."

It sounded like he was rambling. Maybe I had shaken him up, but he'd been good enough to care for me when I needed it, and I was grateful.

"I feel better. Still tired, feel like I could sleep for a week." I cherished his touch on my face. I could have stayed here indefinitely, but I needed to get back home, didn't I? I remembered it was almost Christmas, but I had nowhere else to go.

"In answer to your question, you're at my house in Crosby, so you know where you are. As for how long you've been here... I saw you the day before Christmas Eve, in the evening, and I brought you here straight away." I saw him frown and wondered why. What could be so difficult about telling me the rest of the story?

"You've been here just over a day. It's Christmas Day, about three in the afternoon." I looked at him with wide eyes, waiting for his words to sink in. I'd been here for almost two days, asleep for most of them, it appeared.

"Christmas Day?" Seriously? How could I have been here so long? As if to answer my question, my stomach decided now was the time to make itself known. I was embarrassed by the sound, but Damian laughed and his eyes lit up.

"Sounds like someone might be hungry. How about I get us food and bring it up? We can eat it right here on the bed. A Christmas treat for you."

Mmm, it sounded so good. I was starving and feeling more like myself. I wondered why he was here with me and not with his family. I remembered him saying there was no significant other, but not whether or not he had family. The last time we'd been together had been a bit of a strange evening with us talking and eating.

I snuggled back down under the covers after Damian left, trying to get my head around the fact it was Christmas Day. I had no one to celebrate with, so for me, it wasn't a big deal, hadn't been for four years, but I was still puzzled as to why Damian was here alone.

I decided to ask him over lunch but must have dozed off again. A gentle shake to my shoulder and the bed dipped as Damian sat back on the edge.

"No turkey, I'm afraid, but I do have some chicken, potatoes and some vegetables. Hope this is OK."

At this point, I'd have eaten a horse. I was so hungry, and remembering how I'd been last time we ate, remembering his disapproval, I managed to eat normally.

The food was amazing. It was a simple meal, but that might have been the hunger talking, and as I cleared my plate, Damian took it from me. I remembered about him being alone and plucked up the courage to ask why.

"Where are your family, and why are *you* alone this Christmas?" I could see the muscles in his jaw tense, but he schooled his expression into a smile and turned to face me. His words made me fall for the man even more.

CHAPTER SIX

"I have no one." The pained expression on his face was too much for me to bear, and I reached out and gently touched his cheek.

"I'm sorry. I didn't mean to pry. You don't have to tell me." I felt bad for blurting it out, but that was me. Speak now, think later. It was something Suzie always scolded me for. I dropped my hand to the bed, and Damian placed his hand on mine.

"No, it's OK. I can talk about it now." He gave me a brief smile, then a deep breath. "My parents died when I was fourteen, and Georgie, my wife, left about six years ago. She walked out with our two-year-old daughter, and I haven't seen either of them since."

"Oh my God. I'm so sorry, Damian. I shouldn't have asked." Now I felt terrible. Why couldn't I keep my fucking mouth shut? This had to have dredged up old, painful memories for him if his sad expression was anything to go by.

"Honestly, it doesn't hurt so much these days. I'm used to it, I suppose. But not having any contact with Daisy has been hard for me, especially this time of year."

"Well, if you want to talk about it, I'm a good listener." I wasn't really and was often just full of myself, but I'd never had the need to be any other way. It had always been about me since I'd left home. Other than Suzie, I hadn't had to worry about anyone else, and she was pretty self-sufficient herself. You had to be in our profession. Well, my profession now.

"Maybe another time. Let's enjoy the rest of Christmas Day, and we'll see where tomorrow takes us." He leaned over me and grabbed the remote for the TV, turning it on. *Indiana Jones and The Last Crusade*, my favourite. I scooted over on the bed and patted the space next to me. "Come sit next to me. We'll watch it together."

He raised his eyebrows, asking if I was sure. I nodded, yes I was sure. Surer than I'd been of anything lately.

I considered his words too.

Us.

I liked that there could be an us. I was starting to like him more with each passing moment. The way he'd taken care of me, I could almost forgive him for giving me an expensive gift.

We sat watching the movie, although I'd seen it so many times, I was word-perfect. This was nice, though. I'd never done this with anyone other than my brother and sister when we were younger. Suzie and I hadn't owned a TV, usually more content to listen to music, stream movies on our phones or just collapse, but as the movie continued, my eyes grew heavy.

He woke me as the credits played, and I found myself lying on Damian's chest, snuggled in deep. Fuck, I hoped I hadn't drooled on his shirt.

"Hey. Do you want a drink? I'm about to get one for myself. I've got soft drinks, alcohol, tea, coffee, whatever you want."

"Could I have some more water, please? I could do with taking some more painkillers." I wasn't a big tea or coffee drinker. I just wanted to quench my raging thirst. I also needed the toilet again and suddenly realised I was still naked under the covers.

"I need the toilet too, but…I'm, er, naked. Would you mind?" I know, I was a sex worker and shouldn't be embarrassed, but it didn't seem right to dangle my goods in front of him.

"Of course, sorry." He glanced around the room and handed me the sweats I'd laid on the bed earlier. "I'll go and get your drink."

He left the room, and I threw them on quickly, making my way to the bathroom. I made it back to the bed as he started up the stairs.

I took more tablets and ate the nibbles he'd brought up with him. Nothing much, just peanuts and crisps, but I was careful not to drop them in the bed. And that reminded me, where should I sleep tonight? I knew now this was his bed, and I was an interloper.

"So, I'll sleep in the other bed I found earlier when I was looking for the bathroom. I know this one is yours." I looked over at him to see his reaction.

"It's fine. I'll sleep there. You've made yourself comfortable, and I'd need to change the sheets anyway before I got in, so you might as well stay."

Well, I knew I'd been sleeping here and had a temperature, but the comment was a little off. I suppose some people weren't OK with someone sleeping in their bed, so I let it slide and nodded in thanks.

"I'll leave you to it. Will you be OK? Do you need anything else?" he asked as he stood.

I said I was fine, and he bent down to kiss me on my head.

"Goodnight, Ziggy. I'll see you in the morning."

I had no idea what time it was, but I was so sleepy. I made myself comfortable before falling into a deep sleep.

A weak light woke me the next morning, and I felt so much better than I had the day before. I needed to go back to the flat today. I couldn't keep relying on Damian's hospitality and said as much when he came in a little later.

"If you're sure," he said, a disappointed look on his face. I think he must have been thinking the same as me, how this had been the nicest Christmas for a while. At least I'd had someone to spend time with instead of being on my own. It must have been the same for him.

"I'll get out of your hair. I should go home and see if the flat's warmed up for a start. Any chance we could stop at a shop if there's any open? I could do with some bread and milk."

"No need. I've got stuff you can take with you. It'll only go to waste. Take it, please."

I reluctantly agreed and dressed in the clothes I'd been wearing when he last saw me, realising how impractical they'd been. Going out in those clothes, it was a wonder I hadn't died of hypothermia, but Damian had washed and dried them, so at least they were clean.

Half an hour later, and we pulled up outside the block where the flat was. I'd been hesitant to give Damian the address, but he wouldn't take no for an answer and refused to drop me where he normally picked me up.

We stepped out of the car, me struggling against the torrential rain that had started up and him carrying another bag full of food. He must have cleaned out his fridge!

The lift was out of order again, so we walked up the five flights of stairs, the stench of stale piss making me gag. It wasn't the best place to live, but it had been all we could afford. We finally arrived at my door, seeing a pile of what looked like rubbish against the wall.

What the fuck?

As I neared, I saw all of my meagre belongings piled up, a note pinned to them.

A fucking eviction notice? I wasn't even late with the rent. Well, not by much. I suppose Greg had had enough and decided to kick me out.

What the hell was I going to do now? I had nowhere to go. I

couldn't go back to my family home, nor would I anyway. I was now homeless! I slumped on the dirty floor, my back to the wall, my head in my hands. Could this get week get any fucking worse?

I felt a hand stroke up and down my back, and I started to cry. I was so exhausted from the flu. I had no money and no home. How the hell was I going to survive?

Damian's tender words finally broke through my tears.

"It'll be OK. We can sort something out, don't worry."

He started picking up the bags and balanced a box on his arm, leaving a couple more bags for me to collect. I don't know what he had planned, but sitting on my arse crying wasn't going to get me anywhere. I slowly descended the five flights of stairs, and as I arrived at the car, he was placing all of my stuff into the boot. I walked over to him, placing my hand on his arm.

"What are you doing?" It was pretty obvious what he was doing, but I think I must have been in shock. The past few days had been a rollercoaster of emotions, and the enormity of me now being homeless was hitting hard.

"You can come stay with me for a while. Just until you're back on your feet and have somewhere else to stay, and I'll be coming back to have a word with your landlord. What did he think he was doing? Kicking you out at Christmas. I'm sorry, but that's all kinds of fucked up."

I'd never heard him swear, so to say I was shocked was an understatement, and as much as I hated taking handouts, I was out of ideas. I nodded absently. I would have agreed to anything right now. Plus, I needed to check to see if all my stuff was there, including the small amount of cash I'd managed to squirrel away.

If Greg had nicked my money, I'd be back to have a word myself that might or might not involve a kick to the bollocks. I might be skinny, but I was a mean motherfucker if I wanted to be.

CHAPTER SEVEN

We arrived back at his place an hour after leaving. The journey had been quiet with me trying to take it all in and Damian no doubt wondering what the hell he'd done by inviting me to stay with him.

But what could I do? I had nowhere else to go, but I'd make sure I didn't outstay my welcome. I vowed to be out of there as soon as I could. I'd need to move into the smaller of the two bedrooms, though, and let Damian have his back. I'd wash his bedsheets when we got back to his place. At least that way, I wouldn't feel so guilty about staying.

It would mean talking, figuring out how we were going to do this. I hardly knew the man. Christ, I knew more about his dick than anything else. I'd had it in my mouth twice, so to say this could be awkward was putting it mildly. We moved silently, carrying my mixed assortment of carrier bags, holdalls and boxes into the house and leaving them inside the door.

"I don't know how to thank you, Damian," I started as we stood looking at the pile. "I'll start looking for somewhere to go as soon as I can. I promise I won't be here long." I could feel tears pricking my eyes again. I seriously needed to get a handle on my emotions.

I wasn't normally like this, but I felt an overwhelming sense of hopelessness. I was always a glass half-full type of guy. Don't get me wrong, I had bouts of anxiety that came and went, making me feel utterly useless, as if I wasn't worth the bother and no one would notice if I just disappeared. Those feelings were ordinarily tucked away in the recesses of my mind, but today they surfaced with a vengeance, and my mood dipped, chasing away the good mood of the previous day.

"OK, OK. Let's get this upstairs. We can sit and talk about what we're going to do. I'll give you the tour too as you'll be living here. I suppose you'll need to know where everything is."

Was it my imagination? Did he seem a little perturbed, a bit put out by this situation? It had been out of my control, and if he hadn't insisted on coming upstairs with me, he would have never known my current predicament. I didn't ask for his help. He'd offered, for fuck's sake. I made a vow to myself that I'd be gone within the week. It didn't matter where I went. I couldn't take advantage of his generosity; he'd already done so much. After taking my belongings upstairs and a brief tour, I ventured into his bedroom and began stripping the bed. He came into the bedroom, helping me as I struggled with the huge duvet.

"You don't have to do this, you know. I could have done it," he said, irritation in his voice.

"I know, but you've been kind enough to let me stay. This is the least I can do, and if you get me some clean sheets, I'll make it up for you again, so you don't have to do it." I knew I was flagging. Between being ill and the emotional drain of today, I was exhausted but determined to do this for him before I crashed.

"I said I'll do it, Ziggy. I can see how tired you are." I almost snatched the sheets off of him. I wasn't a fucking invalid. I could do this. I would do this.

"I'll manage, then get out of your hair for the rest of the day." I was sulking like a child, but he was making me feel like one and I didn't like it.

At my words, he moved around to my side of the bed, gripping my arms and forcing me to look at him.

"Listen to me, you've been ill, off your feet for days. I can make the bed. Now, go put the bedclothes in the washing machine downstairs. I'll take care of this, and then we can eat and sit down to rest. It is Christmas, after all."

He thrust the dirty bedclothes at me, and I did as he said. I put away the food he'd given me and decided to make something to eat for us both. We'd had nothing since breakfast time. There wasn't much to make a meal out of, but I managed to put together a couple of omelettes, setting them down on the table as he came into the kitchen.

"You didn't have to do this, Ziggy, but I'm grateful, really. Once we've eaten, you can sit while I tidy up."

I didn't speak as we ate. I'd said all I needed to say on the matter of living here, and I'd meant what I'd said. I'd be out of here in a week, two at the most. I wasn't a scrounger and had managed on my own for four years, pretty sure I could do it again. I needed to get to one hundred per cent first. But, as I lay in bed that first night, I realised Damian had never asked me about Suzie.

———

The first week passed with us dancing around each other, giving each other space. We ate together most of the time. I tried to stay out of the way as much as possible, and Damian never forced me to sit with him in the evening. I still didn't feel right and would tire quickly, so when we weren't eating, I was often sleeping.

One evening, over our meal, Damian announced he'd be returning to work.

"You can still stay here, though. I don't mind,"

"I couldn't. You don't know me, Damian. I could rob you blind while you're at work, and you'd never know where to find me. It wouldn't be right. If you drop me back in Liverpool tomorrow, I'll find a hostel to stay in. I need to start earning some money anyway." I picked at the food on my plate. My appetite had disappeared completely.

"No, I don't think it's a good idea, Ziggy." He stared at me across the table, and I again felt like a naughty child. "You're still not well from the flu you had a week ago, and I don't like the idea of you standing on a cold street corner again, selling yourself."

"I have no other way of earning money, Damian, and I can't stay here indefinitely, rent-free. I'll need to pay my way somehow or move out," I retorted, becoming a little more annoyed with each exchange.

His jaw clenched, but he softened his expression before continuing again.

"I like you in my house, Ziggy. Like hearing you move around. It's been so long, living on my own. I would like you to stay. As for selling yourself…" he said the last comment as if it were a dirty thing, which I supposed it was. "I think you should find yourself a different job. You don't need to do *that* anymore. I can take care of you."

"I get that, but as I said before, you don't know me or owe me. If anything, I owe you for taking care of me and letting me stay here. Why would *you* want to take care of me?"

"Because I like you," he said with a sigh. "Probably more than I should."

"Really?" I was surprised by his admission. "You hardly know me. In fact, you know nothing about me." I'd not told him any more about my personal life than I had in our chat before Christmas.

"And that's where I'd like things to change. I want to get to know you. I want you to know me too. If you know what I mean."

I knew, but I wasn't sure until he reached across the table, taking my hand in his and tracing my upturned palm with his finger. Only then did I fully understand what he meant.

If I was honest with myself, I did want to know him more. He was sexy as all fuck. Kind, considerate and I loved his dick. Since I'd been living here, I'd seen glimpses of him moving around the house, sometimes dressed, other times wearing little more than a pair of tight-fitting boxer shorts. He'd occasionally glanced my way, and I'd hidden, hoping he hadn't seen me, but the sight of his semi-erect cock had done things to me. The amount of times I'd taken a shower, jerking myself off. Well, I didn't want to count.

"I've been wanting more from you, Ziggy, much more. I've been afraid to ask you. I know you're still not feeling well, and I don't want to rush you."

Maybe this was my chance, the chance to get out of the deep, angst-ridden hole I'd been in since leaving home four years ago. I'd had good times, but it had become harder and more soul-destroying the longer I'd worked the streets, and after Suzie left, my world got a whole lot lonelier. Perhaps Damian could be my saviour, my Good Samaritan, my knight in shining armour.

CHAPTER EIGHT

Suddenly hit with the idea that this could be my chance to make something of myself, to have someone to care for and look after me, I closed my hand around his, looking into the dark of his eyes.

"I think I'd like that," I replied, needing him to know I felt the same. I wanted more too. I'd been alone for so long, and I knew I could do worse than Damian.

He wrapped his other hand around mine, and we sat looking at each other, our quickened breaths sounding loud in the quiet room. Was it my imagination, or had it suddenly become hot in here?

I stood up, knowing I needed to take the next step. He was waiting for me to make the first move. I'd always been the reluctant one, so this only seemed fair.

Unsure of how far to go, I sat down on his lap, straddling his thighs, my cock demanding attention as it tented my sweats.

"I'm all in with this turn of events," Damian said with a smirk, and as I looked down, I could see he was as aroused as I was. Throwing caution to the wind, I placed a tentative kiss to his lips, melting further into it as his soft mouth opened for me, allowing my probing tongue access.

I couldn't remember the last time I'd kissed like this. Tongues tangling and panting for breath. Damian tilted his head and deepened the kiss further as his hands wandered beneath my T-shirt.

I stroked the hair at the nape of his neck, threading my fingers through the soft strands. He moaned and moved his hands down my body to grip my arse, pulling me closer so our cocks rubbed together. I wasn't as well-endowed, and I ached to touch him. He rocked me back and forth on his lap, building the tension between us until I was moving of my own accord.

I didn't want to come like this, though, and Damian must have had the same idea as he stood, hefting my almost six-foot frame easily in his arms. He set me down on my feet and continued to kiss me, his lips moving frantically against mine, nipping and biting until I knew my lips would be sore.

Fuck! I'd forgotten just how sensual a kiss could be, and I lowered my hands to his sides, feeling the taut muscles as they quivered beneath my touch.

He broke away, gasping for air. "Shit, you taste so fucking sweet, Ziggy. I'll never get enough."

He dove in again, this time pulling me in close, wrapping his arms around my back as he clung to my body. I did the same, and as we stood there, lips fused, bodies as one, I pondered how my life had changed in such a few short weeks.

After what seemed like hours but was merely minutes, we parted, and Damian took hold of my hand, leading me to the stairs. He continued to grasp it in his as we climbed them, on our way to his room to do who knew what. I knew I wanted this, craved this. The feel of a man moving inside me, not just for their pleasure but for mine too.

An act I knew would change our relationship, for better or worse, I didn't know, and at this point, I didn't care.

As I took the decisive step, Damian held my other hand and walked backwards into his bedroom, dragging me along; the quirky smile on his face no doubt mirrored my own.

I was all in, and as we stepped through the door, I dropped his hands and slowly removed my clothes, watching as he did the same until we stood, naked, both of us undeniably aroused.

His erection curved upwards, and I knew it would hit me in all the right spots. My hole twitched. I couldn't wait any longer and stepped towards him, his smile morphing into a grin.

Our lips met again, and Damian folded me in his arms, pulling me until we both fell onto the bed, laughing.

I'd never been this carefree about sex before, never been comfortable enough with anyone, and even though we hadn't known each other long, the connection I felt towards him was intensifying.

Sex for me in the past had been lacklustre at best. I was a virgin when I left home, and after moving to Liverpool for a better life, I'd realised things didn't always work out the way you wanted them to. I put the notion from my head, I needed to be present, in the moment, as this was by far the best one I'd had.

Damian had stopped laughing now, looking at me with dark eyes and a predatory gaze. I should have felt scared, another time I would have, but here in this lust-filled daze, I wanted so much from him. I just needed to take it.

I leaned up on my elbows and dropped my thighs, giving him full access. Instead of diving in, he lifted my right foot to his mouth and kissed each toe in turn before kissing the sole of my foot. He scattered light kisses along my calf, slowly licking the back of my knee. I giggled and tried to pull away, but he held on tighter, gradually moving up my inner thigh towards my pulsating dick.

He dropped my leg and lifted the other one, doing the exact same thing. When he got to my knee, I was prepared and sank into the feeling, hoping this time he would finally touch me and relieve the tension I felt.

As he lowered my leg to the bed, he knelt between my thighs and rubbed his hands over my torso, pinching my nipples and eliciting a sharp gasp, the sting almost taking my breath. I'd never experienced anything like this before. All my other sexual encounters had been performed hastily in the back of a car or on the bonnet.

Never like this. This was something different. This was as it always should be. I'd never felt so cherished, never had a man worship my body the way Damian was, and the emotions crashed over me, overwhelming me. I closed my eyes and felt tears begin to form. I willed them not to fall, but they did anyway, and a gentle brush of a hand against my cheek wiped them dry.

"Don't cry, my beautiful, please don't cry. Let me make it good for you."

I nodded, my eyes still closed. I wanted him to make it good, make me feel like I was worthy of someone's attention, not just a hole to fuck in the dark of the night, not something dirty to be cast aside.

"Please, I want that. Make me feel, Damian." I could hardly get the words out, but I know he understood as he bent and captured my lips with his, a gentle, sensual kiss, my swollen lips fitting perfectly with his.

His soft hand finally gripped my shaft, squeezing rhythmically, gliding his hand up and down. It was so much better than anything I'd experienced before. All my earlier experiences were limited to a quick wank in a bathroom stall or were by my own hand. This was so fucking good, making my eyes roll to the back of my head. I could feel my release barrelling forward, and I knew it would hit me hard when it arrived.

Damian released me and reached over to his side table to take out the supplies, lube and condoms.

I couldn't believe how desperate and eager I was to get his dick inside me, almost to the point of begging.

"Do you want this, my beautiful boy? Do you think you can take this?" I glanced at his hand as it circled his own cock, tapping it against mine. "Tell me how much you want it, Ziggy."

"Oh my God, Damian. I need it, please." It was almost painful how my dick was aching. My balls were full; one more touch would have my orgasm spilling over my stomach.

"Good boy. Lift your legs for me. I need to see you, get you ready for me. I'm going to make this so good for you, beautiful."

I did as he asked, and he lubed his fingers, circling my hole before plunging his finger in, setting a brutal pace. I knew I could take him. I'd fingered myself as I'd jerked in the shower. I was limber despite my height and could easily suck the head of my own dick. Yeah, I'd tried it!

He worked my hole, stretching and scissoring until I was panting and begging for his cock.

"I think you're ready, baby. It'll feel so good for both of us." I heard the crinkle of the wrapper as he opened the condom and the sound as he rolled it on his dick before lubing it.

I knew I needed to relax. The thought of his delicious dick entering me had me squeezing in anticipation.

"Let me in, Ziggy. I need to be inside of you now." He spoke softly, as if knowing I needed those kind words, needed him to be good to me.

He pushed gently, easing himself into me, and I groaned at the sensation.

"Fuuuck!"

"I know, I know. Relax, baby. Take it all!" He filled me completely and utterly, and I couldn't stop the shouts leaving my mouth as he drilled into me.

This was unlike any sex I'd had before. It was pain and excruciating pleasure, uncomfortable but so fucking addictive. I never wanted it to stop. Damian gripped my hips and rammed into me, over and over again. I reached down to my own dick as it leaked onto my stomach, knowing I was so close to coming.

"Oh, God, Ziggy," Damian shouted, his movements becoming more erratic. He quickly pulled out, removed the condom, and then released a huge stream of cum onto my cock and balls. This brought on my own orgasm, and I grunted as I came over my fist, both of us panting, catching our breath.

Damian collapsed on top of me, smearing cum on both our bodies, the sweat dripping from his forehead on mine. He seized my lips again in a punishing kiss before rolling off to the side and onto his back, his breaths still ragged.

As for me, I was lost for words. Ziggy Coleman had nothing to say.

CHAPTER NINE

The next few days passed in a whirl of sex, food and sleep. Damian didn't seem bothered by the state of his bed like he had before, but after two days of sleeping in crusty sheets, I decided we needed to change them.

We crawled out of bed, and while I jumped in the shower, Damian went to make dinner. He was due back to work tomorrow, so we'd made the best of our last full day together. One thing I needed to do was contact Suzie. We'd exchanged texts over Christmas, but no more than that. Before I stepped in the shower, I found my phone and called her.

"Ziggy, my bestie! How you doing?"

"I'm good. How are things with you?"

"I'm great, actually." Without waiting, she launched into a tale about a guy she'd met at a New Year's Eve party. They'd met up a couple of times since, and she told me he was the one.

"Aw, babe, you know I'm happy for you, but remember what happened last time."

We'd been here before, and I hoped it wouldn't end the way it usually did. At least she wasn't a sex worker anymore. That had been the sticking point.

"How's the flat? Has Greg fixed the heating yet?"

I hesitated about telling her my recent turn of events but knew she needed to know.

"I was evicted." I waited for the shout and wasn't disappointed.

"What the fuck, Ziggy! Where are you staying? Are you in a hostel?"

I'd lowered my voice, not wanting Damian to hear what I was saying.

"I'm staying with Damian, Mr Velvety-Smooth. Been here for almost two weeks now." I went on to tell her about my collapse and how I'd spent Christmas. She had many choice words for Greg but was glad I'd managed to find somewhere to stay.

"So, have you shagged him yet? Has he nailed you with that cock yet? You couldn't stop talking about it before."

"We might have had sex. I might have taken his fine cock a time or two now. I honestly didn't know sex could be so good, Suzie. He's spoiled me, and when I eventually have to go back to work, nothing will ever be good enough again."

"Aw, babe. Maybe he's your prince, come to save you from the depths of despair?"

I snorted. "Yeah, fat chance of that happening. I'll take this for the time being until he gets fed up with me and kicks me out."

"You'll see. You'll find someone who loves you. You're such a good person, Ziggy. How could anyone not love you?"

I was quiet for a moment, letting her words sink in. I'd never found anyone to love me and was under no illusion that at some point, this thing with Damian would end. I needed to earn money. I couldn't continue to live on his charity forever, and when I eventually did go back to the only thing I knew, he'd see I wasn't what he imagined or what he wanted me to be.

Emotions threatened yet again. I needed to end the call and get in the shower. Damian got annoyed if I wasn't sitting at the table when he served up the food. Not often, but I didn't want to ruin what we had going.

With that running through my head, I ended the call with her, promising to call again soon and to look after myself.

I showered quickly and stepped into the bedroom to change. Where had I put my phone? I wanted to text Suzie to tell her I was OK. She could read me like a book, and I knew she'd worry about how we'd left the call.

Had I taken it into the bathroom? I didn't think I would have. Perhaps it had slid off the bed. I was about to get on my hands and knees to look when Damian shouted to say our meal was ready.

I'd have to look for my phone later. I quickly slipped on my shorts and rushed downstairs as he was dishing up.

"So, what are you going to do while I'm at work tomorrow?" Damian asked, slowly eating his food. I'd noticed this was a thing he did, and he often told me not to eat so quickly. It was a bad habit for me. I was always rushing somewhere, and sitting down to eat took time.

"I don't know. I could do some housework, a bit of washing. Do we need any shopping? I could get some groceries."

"No, I'll get those. You don't have the money, and you wouldn't be able to carry it anyway. We can go together when I get home."

I nodded. Definitely a better idea, I hadn't considered that. Suzie and I never bought a great deal, so it was never too much hassle, but perhaps he had a list of things he needed to get.

"OK, sounds good. I'll make sure the house is tidy." He winked at me and carried on eating.

"Make sure you make yourself pretty for me as well for when I get home. It'd be nice to have someone waiting for me for a change."

I preened at his words. I'd never had someone to dress up for before, and I was lost in thought, wondering what I could wear to please him when he spoke again.

"I'd love to see you in a cropped top and shorts, like you wore the first time, but I think it'll be a little cold. How about you wear your skinny jeans?" He leaned in close, and his breath ghosted my lips. "And no underwear. It'll please me no end, my boy."

He placed a gentle kiss on my mouth, and I felt myself blush. What this guy did to me, not just with his words but his actions too. I was falling hard for him and now knew how Suzie had felt.

Remembering Suzie reminded me of my missing phone.

"Did you see my phone anywhere? I had it before I went into the bathroom, but I couldn't find it when I came out."

"What do you need your phone for? Aren't I enough for you? Maybe I should give you something to take your mind off it." Damian gripped the back of my neck and pulled my face to his, placing a bruising kiss to my lips. My teeth pressed against the inside of my mouth, and I tasted blood. He released me, swiping his thumb across my lips, licking the blood from it, his eyes dark.

He stood and collected the dishes from the table. "I don't know where your phone is, beautiful. Probably fallen on the floor. You need to take better care of your stuff." His tone was brusque, and I looked at his back, shocked by the change in his mood.

I put it down to him not being happy about going to work tomorrow, but I couldn't have that. I wanted him to be happy, and I wanted him to remember me when he was at work tomorrow.

I stepped up behind him and slipped my hands around his waist, resting my cheek on his back as he stood at the sink.

"I'm sorry. Nothing is as important as you right now. I need you to know that, not my phone nor my friends. Let me take your mind off everything, make it alright."

Damian turned in my arms, and I dropped to my knees. The cold, hard tiled floor hurt my knees, but I ignored the pain. I pulled down the lounge pants he was wearing and mouthed his now hardening cock through his cotton shorts, breathing hot breaths along his length.

He threw his head back and moaned, grabbing my hair.

"Yes, Ziggy. You have such a beautiful mouth, my boy. Open up and take me, take it all."

As Damian removed his shorts, he thrust forward, and as his cock entered my mouth, he continued to move, the head of his cock hitting the back of my throat every time. He was relentless as he moved in and out, his engorged head cutting off my airway.

I gagged and panicked as I struggled to breathe. Shit! Damian wasn't letting up and set up a frantic pace, barely giving me time to take a much-needed breath. Putting my hand on his thighs, I tried to push him away, but he was too strong, holding my head in place as he fucked my mouth.

A short moment later, and he pulled out. I heaved in a breath, my throat sore, and was shocked when Damian shot all over my face and hair. I hadn't realised he was so close, but at least he hadn't come down my throat.

He moaned as he came down from his orgasm and reached down to gently stroke my hair.

"Oh, baby. I'm sorry. Your mouth is too fucking good."

I felt like crying. He'd used me, and the shame I felt had me dropping my head to my chest.

"Oh my God, Ziggy. What have I done to you? My poor boy."

He fell to his knees and carefully stroked my hair from my face, kissing my eyes and cheeks.

"I got so carried away with it all." He lifted my chin, forcing me to look into his eyes. They were full of remorse, and I started to feel bad. How could I think he would hurt me on purpose?

"Can you ever forgive me? I promise I'll never do it again. And look at you. I'll admit to loving my spunk covering your face. I should take a picture so I can remind myself this is what I have to look forward to when I come home. But Ziggy, I won't hurt you again.

"Let's go shower and get cleaned up. We'll change the bed, then we can sleep. I have a busy day ahead of me and you, my boy, need to rest tomorrow. We have shopping to do, and I want to buy you some nice things. You need new clothes, and we need to get more of those sparkly trainers you love so much."

As much as he'd hurt me earlier, how could I stay mad at this man? This man who'd taken me in when he didn't need to, who'd looked after me when I was sick and who was making a play for my affections.

That night, we did all he'd said and more. He held me as we drifted off to sleep, and when I awoke the next morning, a single white rose lay on the pillow beside my head. We were an us, me and Damian, together as one.

CHAPTER TEN

So, this is where we ended up, two weeks later. Damian was true to his word and had been attentive and considerate ever since. The 'not so nice' Damian that abused me had been nowhere in sight.

He'd taken me out, bought me clothes and gifts and was as perfect as any boyfriend could be. While he worked, I tidied around the house and had even started to plant flowers in pots we'd picked up one weekend at the garden centre.

17 East Street was slowly becoming home, and I was loving every minute of it.

I was planting the last of the winter pansies in a pot when my phone started ringing. With dirty fingers, I answered the call, excited to see Damian's name.

"Hi. Is everything OK?" He didn't usually call me, so I was wondering what he wanted.

"Ziggy, baby. I know you were going to cook tonight, but a friend of mine is popping around, so I thought we could order food instead. I want you to enjoy the evening. I've already placed an order from the Indian restaurant you like, and they'll deliver it at seven. We should be home in time, but just in case we aren't, it's all paid for, so there's no need for you to worry your beautiful head, my boy."

"OK, I'll keep it warm if you're not back in time. I'll see you later, Damian."

"Oh, before you go. Wear something good for me. You know what I like you to wear. I'd prefer you in nothing, but it might be a little much for our visitor. Good boy."

I said I would and ended the call. I'd been unsure of his continued use of 'boy', but the more he said it, the more I began to love it. It made me feel wanted.

I looked at my phone, seeing I still had hours before the food and Damian would arrive, but he said he wanted me looking pretty, so I decided a long, luxurious bath was in order.

I ran the water, putting in the bubble bath we'd bought when we last shopped, and I relaxed in the warm water. I felt my eyes growing heavy and slowly drifted off to sleep.

I awoke a little later, noting how dark it was outside.

Fuck. How long had I been here?

I jumped out of the bath, grabbed a towel from the rail and ran to the bedroom, glancing at the alarm clock on the side.

Shit. It was almost six, and I still needed to dress. I hoped Damian was late coming home.

I dressed hurriedly, throwing on my shortest shorts and my mesh crop top I knew Damian liked me to wear. I hoped his friend wasn't a stuffy banker. What if I got him into trouble dressing like this?

I decided I wasn't going to worry about it. He'd told me to dress like this. I hadn't bothered with underwear as Damian hated it, preferring instant access to my cock at all times. Not that I was complaining. There'd been a couple of times when he'd almost been caught with his hands down my shorts or jeans, squeezing my dick, trying to make me come. Our last visit to the supermarket had been interesting, and I'd had to go to the in-store bathrooms. Talk about clean-up in aisle three!

I made it downstairs in time to hear a car pull up outside. I didn't know whether it was Damian or the food, but as I opened the door, Damian's form filled the doorway. He was laughing at something his friend must have said, but his eyes darkened as he looked me up and down.

Without missing a beat, he pulled me forward and kissed me, a toe-curling kiss that had my dick hardening in my shorts. Guess he didn't mind his friend seeing this. He reached down and gripped me, squeezing me.

"Good boy. Just how I like you," he said, breaking away from the kiss, rubbing me harder, making me groan.

I stepped back into the front room, trying desperately to adjust my erection. His friend came in behind him, looking down at my shorts, a wicked smile on his face. He was a little shorter than Damian and just as good-looking. Did they only employ Adonises at the bank?

"Stuart, I'd like you to meet Ziggy. Ziggy, this is Stuart, a *very* good friend of mine."

I held my hand out and shook his, my other hand covering my groin. His hand was as soft as Damian's, and I was sure it lingered a little longer than necessary before it fell away.

"The pleasure's all mine, Ziggy. Damian's description didn't do you justice. You truly are gorgeous." His eyes flitted to my still rock-hard dick, but there was nothing I could do about it.

I frowned a little at his words and looked at Damian, expecting to see displeasure on his face, but all I saw was pride, and he pulled me to his side, placing a kiss on my head.

"Let's get a drink before the food arrives. It hasn't arrived yet, has it?" I shook my head, unsure where my words had gone. "Don't be shy, baby. Stuart doesn't always bite."

Both he and Stuart laughed, and I must admit, I felt a little uncomfortable for the first time in a while. My Spidey senses tingling, not at Damian, but at Stuart. I wasn't sure what it was about him, but I felt like I couldn't trust him. But, he was Damian's friend, and if he was good with him, I should make the effort to be too.

A while later, after we'd eaten, Damian and Stuart drank a fair few bottles of beer. I stuck to water and soft drinks; I wasn't a huge fan of alcohol.

"Come 'ere, beautiful." We were sitting in the front room where we'd had our first encounter, and Damian pulled me over to sit on his lap, facing him.

I straddled his thighs as he leaned in to kiss me, the smell of alcohol filling my nose. He thrust his hands down the back of my shorts, squeezing my arse. I tried to pull away. Stuart was sitting mere feet away and would have a good eyeful if we weren't careful.

"Don't worry about him, Ziggy," Damian said as if reading my mind. "He really won't mind, will you, Stu?" Damian spoke over my shoulder, and I heard his friend grunt.

"Not at all, feel free. Just pretend I'm not here." Stu's voice was raspy, but I didn't dare turn around, worried at what I might see. I'd heard that tone of voice too many times not to know what was running through his head.

"Ziggy, baby. Rub yourself against me. You know I love it when you do that. Can you feel me, boy? Feel how hard I am for you?" He grabbed my hand and pressed it on his cock. My dick pulsed with need, but the discomfort I felt with Stuart watching, threatened to ruin the moment. The thought that Stuart was getting off too was creepy but I wanted to please Damian.

Ignoring the smell of booze, I kissed him again, and Damian moved his hands to the front, pulling my shorts down, releasing my stiff cock. My breath caught as he stroked me. I could hear my heart thumping in my ears, and I tried to pull away, aware Stuart was seeing my impending orgasm.

"It's OK, baby. He won't mind." Damian sensed my discomfort, soothing me with his words, but continuing to work my shaft. "Lie back, my boy."

He manoeuvred us both so I was on my back with him between my knees. He unzipped his trousers, pulling his own impressive cock out, rubbing against mine, both of us panting. I turned to the side to see Stuart working his own dick. I couldn't believe what was happening. I'd never once in my life been into anything like this, but someone watching, someone wanking whilst Damian was getting us both off, was too much.

I arched into Damian's hand and shot my load. He followed shortly after, and as I came down from my lust-driven high, I heard the man to the side of me sigh loudly at his release.

"Fuck, that was all kinds of hot, Damian. I bet his cock felt good in your hands. It looks good enough to eat, but maybe next time, eh?"

"Hey, no one gets Ziggy's dick except me, but I must admit since he moved in, he's saved me a fortune." They both laughed at this, but his comment stung.

Was that all this was? Had he moved me in so he didn't have to pay for my services any longer? Well, we'd see about that. This was still prostitution, but a different kind, and it wasn't one I was comfortable with. Here I was, thinking we had something good, but I'd clearly been wrong.

I pushed at Damian, struggling to get from beneath him. I could feel my cheeks flush as anger took hold, and I ground my teeth. The fucker, I was still Ziggy the sex worker to him. A cheap shag he didn't have to pay for. Well, no more.

"Hey, boy, stop struggling." A sharp slap to my cheek stopped me in my tracks, and tears stung my eyes.

"Get the fuck off me," I said through gritted teeth, my fists beating his chest. He didn't budge, just gripped my hands in his. "I said, get off me."

"Ziggy. It was a joke." He sneered at me, and I saw red, my heart pounding.

"Don't you fucking slap me again, ever." I wrestled with him, trying to get free, but he was so much stronger than me. But I wasn't a pushover, and no way was anyone getting physical with me. I managed to free one of my hands and pushed at his chest, hard. He fell back and sneered at me, tucking himself into his shorts.

There was no way I was staying here to be slapped around. I was out of there. It was too late for me to go anywhere tonight, but tomorrow, I'd be out the door.

I dragged my shorts on, ignoring the drying cum on my stomach. I was not going to give him the satisfaction of seeing me cry. I'd save that for the shower, and if he thought I'd be sharing his bed again? Well, he could fuck right off.

As I stormed up the stairs, I heard Stuart telling Damian he'd see him tomorrow at work, but their voices became muffled as I closed the door of the bathroom, locking it behind me.

I cried as I showered, the salty tears stinging my cheek where I knew I'd have a red mark. I knew what I needed to do. My time here was over.

For the first time in almost two weeks, I stepped into the cold spare room and crawled into the unmade bed. I could hear Damian moving around downstairs, and if there'd been a lock on this door, I'd have locked that fucker too.

I fell asleep, but during the night, I felt the dip of the bed as he sat next to me. I tensed, expecting him to slide in behind me, but instead I heard him speak in a soft voice.

"I'm so sorry. I don't know what came over me. I know you're sleeping right now, and I can't tell you how bad I feel." His fingers brushed over my cheek, but I kept myself still, not wanting to give away that I was awake.

"I promise I won't do it again, ever. I hope you'll believe me when I tell you and that you'll forgive me. I want to blame it on the alcohol, but we both know it's me being overprotective. Stuart's words riled me, and I made light of what we had together. You have to know this means so much more to me than I let on to him. You are my whole world, beautiful."

A heavy silence filled the room, and I was conscious of my breathing, trying to keep it as natural as I could. My chest heaved. Did I believe him? Would he do this shit again? I supposed the main question was, could I trust him?

That was the million-dollar question.

CHAPTER ELEVEN

I woke the following morning, my eyes gritty and sore. Had I slept? Fuck, today was the day I'd leave this little haven I'd been staying in since before Christmas. I rolled onto my back, looking up at the ceiling. Fuck! This was going to be harder than I'd thought, but I needed to do it, make the break.

I crawled out of the bed, threw on clothes and left the bedroom. I crept slowly to the bathroom, listening for any sounds *he* might be around, but the house was silent, not a creak or squeak.

As I peed, I looked around the small room, and my stomach dropped, realising what I was leaving behind and what I was going back to. I knew I couldn't stay here, not now. Damian still saw me as a prostitute, but I'd built a life for us in my stupid little head. A life where we lived together with a cute dog, taking walks along the beach, hand in hand as Honey would run in and out the breaking surf, her tail wagging with joy.

I shook my head, bringing me back to the here and now. I'd made my decision, and with shaking hands, I collected my toiletries from the cabinet and shower cubicle, ramming them into my bag.

I did the same in the bedroom we'd shared, staring with a heavy heart at the bed, now neatly made, remembering the nights we'd spent together. Tears pricked my eyes, and I turned away. This was no time for them. I nibbled on my lip. I'd have to leave most of my things behind. I couldn't carry it all. Packing the essentials and sentimental belongings, I closed the door behind me and made my way downstairs.

It was silent. The kitchen was clean and tidy. Damian hated mess, so I wasn't shocked, but I was surprised to see a note lying on the worktop, my name scrawled across the front in Damian's messy handwriting.

I huffed out a laugh. This was about the only untidy thing about him. Everything else in his life was kept in regimented order right down to the alphabetised tins of food in the cupboard. And who in their right mind ate fucking Skittles in colour order? Weirdos, that's who.

To me, these were the things that made him what he was or what I'd imagined him to be. Until last night, he'd been the perfect man for me, the one who was going to bring me up from the ruins of my life, the one who was going to make me a better person.

Instead, he'd disappointed me, like every other fucker that had crossed my path, and now it needed to end. I picked up the note, shoving it in my pocket. I didn't want to know what he had to say. We were done.

Could I go back to living on the streets, selling myself so I could afford my next meal? Wasn't like I had a choice, now was it? It was either that or stay here—with a man who considered it OK to slap me around and insult me. Yeah, it was a no-brainer as far as I was concerned. I was no one's punching bag. I'd lived out there for four years. I could do it again.

The walk to the bus station took me a good half an hour. For a start, I didn't know where it was, but after a few wrong turns and garbled directions, I found myself waiting for the next bus into Liverpool. The weather was freezing. It was still January after all, and I was glad I'd remembered the gloves Damian had bought for me.

By the time the bus arrived, I was shivering and my nose was running from the cold. What the fuck I was going to do when I got to the city, I didn't know. The journey took an hour, and I arrived in Liverpool around lunchtime. I needed to find somewhere to stay before nightfall.

It proved easier said than done, and every hostel I visited had no vacancies. At this rate, I'd be sleeping in a doorway. By four in the afternoon, I was no nearer finding somewhere to stay, and it was getting dark, the temperature dropping to below zero.

I was knocked and jostled as I walked. Shoppers and commuters alike breezed past me as if I wasn't there. I was invisible again. No one saw Ziggy.

I made my way to the flat Suzie and I had shared, wondering if Greg had managed to let it out. I could make the rent, I'd have to work my arse off, but I knew I could do it, but as I arrived, I could see lights in our former flat and knew it was a lost cause. Fuck, what was I going to do now?

I trudged back to the street where I'd first met Damian to be greeted by a few people I knew. Maybe I could crash with one of them until I could find a place of my own.

A guy I only knew as Sprout shouted at me from across the road.

"Hey, Ziggy. Where've you been, man? We thought you'd finally got out of this shit. But here you are, large as life. Looks like you've been living it up. You've put some weight on."

Had I? I hadn't noticed, but I supposed weeks of eating properly and sleeping in a warm house had spoiled me.

I walked across the street to speak to him. He gave me a half-hearted hug, and I felt how skinny he was beneath his clothes. Had I been that way?

"Sprout, how's it hanging? You doing OK?"

"Can't complain. Fucking freezing standing around, but I'm good. Where've you been?"

"Around. I was ill but stayed with a friend until I was well again. Back to it now, though. How's business been?"

"Off and on, quiet some days, other days, it's one trick after another. My arse has never been so sore." Sprout laughed but winced, and I cursed myself for wanting to come back to this fucking business.

"I don't suppose I could bunk down with you for a few, could I? I got kicked out of the place me and Suzie were renting."

"Ah, man. I don't have any room. There's already six of us in the flat, and I can't squeeze another in. Try asking Duke over there. There's only a couple of them in his digs. Anyway, are you back with us now? Haven't seen the guy in the BM around here for a while. He'll be back now you are; seems like he had a soft spot for you."

I waved him off. If only he knew, but I wasn't going to tell him where I'd been for the past few weeks.

"Cheers, anyway. I'll see you around."

We fist-bumped, and I hurried across the road to speak to Duke before he disappeared. I had the same conversation with him, but this time, I managed to grab a space in his house for a couple of nights at least.

"Let's go now. I'm fucking freezing standing here, and I've already had a couple of guys today." Everyone wanted Duke. He was gorgeous, dark-skinned and fit as fuck. He often wore leather trousers, looking more like a rock star than a hooker.

"Thanks. Can't tell you how grateful I am. You know how the hostels can be."

We arrived back at his place, and as I took off my coat, Damian's letter fell out of my pocket. I stooped to pick it up, running my fingers over the letters of my name, regret starting to make me rethink my decision.

"You OK there?" I looked over at Duke and the puzzled expression he wore.

"Mm, sorry? Oh, yeah. I'm good. Just a letter I need to read." I was debating whether or not to talk to Duke about Damian. I knew him a little from being on the streets, but my only close friend was Suzie. I'd already tried her number, and it had gone straight to voicemail.

Duke handed me a beer. "Want to talk about it?"

Did I? Getting a guy's opinion on it might help, I supposed, and I could do with some advice.

I took the beer from him and drank, grimacing at the bitter taste.

"Yeah, I think I do." As we sat on the sofa, I relayed my brief relationship with Damian, watching Duke's reaction.

"So, you think he still sees you as a cheap prossie, and you hoped it was something more. Am I right?"

"Yeah. But what about the slap and choking me with his dick?"

"Par for the course in our profession," Duke said matter-of-factly. He pointed to the envelope in my hand. "Open the letter. Let's see what it says."

Reluctantly, I opened it, trying not to tear the envelope too much. Damian wouldn't like that. I took a deep breath, scanning the written words.

"Read it out. Let's see what the prick has to say." Annoyed at the way he spoke about Damian, I started to read to myself, not willing to share the words he'd written for me just yet. He reached to snatch it from my hands, so I stood, walking to the window to read.

My dearest Ziggy

I won't blame you if you decide to leave. My words and actions last night were unforgivable, and you have every reason to hate me. I know you were awake when I came to you, and all I wanted to do was bring you into my arms and hold you close, whisper words to make you stay, words to prove to you how much I care.

I'd watched you for a while on the streets before approaching you. I knew I had to have you from the start. You were so beautiful, with your long legs, your gorgeous smile, and I knew I was falling for you.

I took a chance, and, oh Ziggy, it was everything and more. Having you with me these past few weeks has been heaven. I've found myself wanting you more, but I'm scared, Ziggy, so fucking scared my actions might have driven you away.

I never deserved you. You were always too sweet, too innocent, too good for me.

My darling boy, my darling Ziggy. I hope you can find it in your heart to forgive me. I want you to stay but if you decide to go, just know I am sorry, so very sorry.

Yours always, Damian

"So what's the dickhead got to say?" I spun around to see Duke behind me, trying to read over my shoulder.

"Oh, he says he's sorry. He didn't mean it." I handed him the letter. I could do with another opinion. His words had touched something inside me, a part of me that wanted to be loved. "See what you think."

I chewed on my nails as I looked out of the window, my reflection staring back at me in the darkened windows. I touched my hair. Was I really beautiful? I didn't think so, I'd always seen myself as average-looking, but the longer I looked, the surer I was I wouldn't find anyone to take care of me like he'd done.

Perhaps I'd been too hasty to walk out. Maybe I should give him another chance? Tell him it couldn't happen again. I deserved to have love, didn't I?

"Wow, this guy has it bad for you." Startled, I turned to see Duke looking at me. I'd forgotten he was there.

"Do you think so? Why would he slap me around? I just don't get it."

"Some people do crazy things when they're in love. I remember a guy used to go mental if he saw someone else even talking to his girl, but he'd have pulled the moon out the sky for her if she'd asked."

"What happened to them? Did she put up with him?" I was curious, was this normal?

"Yeah, they live over the water now. Got a place in Moreton, a couple of kids and couldn't be happier."

I jumped as Duke put his hand on my shoulder. "Things don't always have to end in disaster, you know? Aren't we always looking for the one? Someone to look after us? Maybe this Damian guy is the one for you, but you won't know if you don't give it a chance. Up to you, though, babe. Do what your heart is telling you to do. Our heads don't always make the right decisions."

He looked sad as he talked, and I wondered if he'd had something similar happen to him.

He carried on talking, sounding as sad as he looked. "What do I know? I'm just a broken boy from a broken home, shagging my way through all the closeted guys in Liverpool. Not gonna find Mr Right there, am I? Take the chance, Ziggy. Don't let this pass you by. You'll regret it eventually."

He turned away from me, grabbing another beer and taking a long pull.

"Regrets are for losers, Ziggy. Believe me, I should know."

I nodded, thinking about his words. Did I have enough time to get back there? It was already after five.

"Stay here tonight and think about it. Make your decision in the morning, and if you're gone when I get up in the morning, I'll know where you've gone. Tonight will be pizza and a few more beers, I reckon."

CHAPTER TWELVE

The following morning, I woke with gritty eyes…again, but this time it was from too many beers. At least I didn't feel sick. I wasn't a big drinker, but we'd had sufficient for me to sing with Duke far too loudly to the queen of break up songs, Whitney Houston. We'd belted out "I Have Nothing" at the top of our lungs, and I was surprised the neighbours hadn't complained.

I groaned as I sat up, my mouth felt like cotton wool, and I was as thirsty as hell. I rolled off the sofa and lurched into the kitchen in search of a glass and water.

"Look who's finally up." Duke stood in the kitchen, a smirk on his face. He looked far too fucking awake considering he'd downed two beers to my one every time.

"Fuck off, Duke. How can you look so good? You drank more than I did."

"Used to live in a pub in another life. Drinking was what I did. Not so much these days, but I can still hold my own." He handed me a glass of water, and I drank it down in one.

"Anyway, have you decided what to do?"

Had I? That was the question, but in between songs and

drinks, we'd talked about how tired I was of turning tricks, about Damian and what he could offer, about Duke's life. It was nice to talk to a guy for a change. I loved Suzie, don't get me wrong, but sometimes, guys understood.

"I think I'm going to go back. But before I agree to stay, there'll be ground rules. If he can't stick to them, I'll be out of there. I don't need regrets, and I think that's what I'll have if I don't at least give it a try." Duke nodded, a knowing look on his face. Was I so transparent?

"I get it, I do. Give me your phone and take my number just in case."

I grabbed my phone from my bag, realising as I picked it up that it'd be out of charge.

"Here, plug it in." Duke handed me the cord and waited a minute while it turned on.

The phone lit up like a beacon as message after message came through.

"Seems someone's popular." Duke laughed as it kept beeping and beeping. There were a couple from Damian, but it looked like Suzie had blown up my phone with texts and missed calls. Typical, but I'd need to fill her in. She'd never forgive me if I didn't tell her what was going on.

"Are they from your man?" I shook my head.

"No, a few but most are from Suzie. You remember her? We used to live together, but she's moved back home, for good this time."

"Ah, it happens. This life isn't for everyone. You of all people should know. What did you say last night? Four years on the streets, but only a couple on the game?"

Fuck. I could hardly remember what we'd talked about, but it seemed I'd spilled more of my secrets to him than anyone else.

"Ten years for me, as I said. I left home when I was seventeen, but that's another story for a different day. Feel free to take a shower, but I need to get going. I've another job to get to, and you'll more than likely be gone when I'm back. Don't hesitate to call me, anytime. You hear me?" He picked up a travel mug and hugged me before leaving the house.

I checked my phone again but concentrated on Damian this time. There were no calls, just messages starting from around six p.m. last night. Each one was sadder than the previous one—until I got to the final one.

I miss you, please come home

Those six words and my heart shattered inside. Home, he wanted me to come home.

I rushed to the bathroom, skidding on the floor in my rush to get ready. I felt as giddy as a schoolgirl, the earlier worry about what he'd done gone from my mind. He missed me, and fuck if I didn't miss him too.

After showering, packing up my stuff and leaving a quick thank you note for Duke, I rushed to the bus station and hopped on the first one to take me back to Crosby and Damian. It was then I realised I didn't have a key to get back into the house.

Shit, I hadn't considered that, but I was happy to sit around and wait. There was a coffee shop at the end of the street. I could wait there. It'd be a long time, but he was worth it, I decided.

The bus stopped at every fucking stop and every red light between Liverpool and Crosby, but it eventually arrived. I hopped off, a bounce in my step. I was excited to be back and almost ran from the bus station to East Street.

I'd have to pass the house to get to the coffee shop, so I was surprised to still see Damian's car on the street outside. Had he not gone to work? Only one way to find out.

I rang the doorbell, my bag digging into my shoulder as I waited. I wasn't sure what to say if he answered, but I'd find out soon enough.

The door swung open, and a grumpy-faced Damian stood

there. As he looked up and saw me, his face broke into a grin, and he swept me into his arms.

"Fuck, Ziggy. I didn't think I'd see you again. I'm so fucking sorry, for everything." He pulled back and took my face in his hands, peppering every inch of it with his kisses.

He walked backwards, dragging me with him, and pushed the door shut with his foot. I laughed at his antics. How could I have doubted him? This right here was proof I'd made the right decision.

"God, I missed you so much. I love you. God, how I love you. Can you forgive me? Please say you forgive me." His words came out in a rush, so I silenced him with a press of my lips to his.

"I forgive you, but we have to have ground rules. No more, Damian, no more of the comments, no more of the abuse." But oh my God, he'd said he loved me, and I squealed inside at his words.

"I know, I know. It was wrong of me." The remorse I saw in his eyes made me think he really did mean it this time and that coming back had been the right thing to do.

I dropped my bag to the floor, and we kissed again, walking back until we bumped into the sofa, Damian falling backwards with me on top of him.

"Don't leave me again, ever. Stay with me." He stared into my eyes, never breaking contact, and I noticed how tired he looked.

I threw my arms around his neck, kissing him like my life depended on it. Of course I'd stay with him; he was my one. I hadn't said the words back to him. They'd stuck in my throat, but I couldn't understand what was holding me back.

To my surprise, we didn't take it any further. We lay snuggled on the sofa, him telling me how sad he'd been when he'd got home last night to find me gone. How he'd barely managed to get out of bed this morning, not able to face the day without me.

"If I didn't hear from you, I was going to drive into the city to try and find you. I'd have tried the street where I originally saw you. It would have killed me to see you back there, but at least I could have found you."

I rested my head on his chest, speaking from the heart. "I have to admit I wasn't looking forward to going back there, but I don't know anything else. I spent yesterday trying to find somewhere to stay." The admission hurt, but it was all I knew, and I realised if I was going to make anything of us, I'd need to change. I'd need to find something else to do. Damian hated my line of work. I wasn't too keen on it either, but what else could I do? What else did I know?

"Please say you didn't sleep on the streets last night. I couldn't ever forgive myself if you did." He held my hand tight in his and stroked the hair from my face with his other. "Tell me, Ziggy. You found somewhere safe and warm to stay."

"I did, but it was close for a time. I tried the hostels, but they were all full. I even tried our old flat to see if Greg had let it out, but there was someone there." I sighed, remembering the despair I'd felt at not being able to find somewhere.

"In the end, I managed to grab the sofa at my friend Duke's place." I felt Damian stiffen beneath me and not in a good way. "I slept on his sofa, not his bed, Damian," I said, my voice terse.

"I'm sorry, I know I can totally trust you, but not others when they're around you. You're my beautiful boy. No one else's."

"I know, Damian, but Duke's the same as me, a hooker. We don't sleep together, so don't go thinking anything happened between us. He's a good guy. He let me stay at his home last night."

We lay for a while longer, him stroking my hair, lulling me to sleep, but my stomach took the opportunity to grumble. I realised I hadn't eaten anything all day, so eager to get back to Damian.

"Come on, let's go out for something to eat. How about we

take a walk along the beach and we get fish and chips or something? You'd like that, wouldn't you?"

I nodded. This was so close to the story I'd imagined in my mind I didn't hesitate to say yes. It had been a good day. I was glad I'd come to my senses, and now, everything was turning out perfectly.

CHAPTER THIRTEEN

The rest of the month, we lived an idyllic life. I stayed at home and tended the house, and Damian went out to work. We were the perfect couple, perfect boyfriends.

I felt myself falling for him more, and the 'L'-word was on the tip of my tongue. Damian said it constantly, but not once did he ask me to return the sentiment. I loved what we had, loved the way he was with me. I adored living with him and tried to please him as much as I could. I didn't want to experience angry Damian again, so I did what I needed to make him happy.

February arrived, and with it came another meal with Stuart. I was dreading it after the last time, but Damian assured me things would be different. He'd found himself a little, a boy, and he'd be bringing him with him this time.

I'd heard the words 'little' and 'boy'. Hell, Damian called me his boy all the time, but I knew what Stuart and his boy, Liam, had was different, and I was intrigued to see how it worked.

It was a Tuesday again, and I'd cooked this time. Damian instructed me to make up only three plates of food and to leave a smaller portion to one side and mash it up in a bowl. I thought it was strange, but who was I to argue?

They arrived at seven as planned. We needed to finish by nine as Liam needed to be in bed early, and I was wondering how old he was. I presumed he was of age; I wouldn't have anything to do with Stuart if he wasn't.

I opened the door to them, Stuart looking the same, and he again lingered as he shook my hand, a searching look in his eyes. I squirmed under his gaze, but he soon let go when Damian came up behind me.

"This is Liam." From behind him stepped a small boy. I had to look twice as he looked so young, but when he spoke it was clear he was definitely older than he looked.

"Hi, I know. I look like I'm about twelve, but I am eighteen. I'm just small for my age." He sighed as he spoke as if explaining this was something he did often.

And he was. I was just shy of six feet, and Liam must have been five feet one at most.

"I'm tired, Daddy. I've been on my feet all day at work."

"OK, baby. Hop up, and we'll go take a seat and wait for our food, shall we? You've been such a good boy today."

I looked on in amazement. I'd never seen anything like it as Stuart lifted Liam onto his hip and carried him into the front room. He sat on the sofa, and Liam snuggled into his chest, sucking on his thumb.

I couldn't take my eyes off them, and if it hadn't been for Damian touching my shoulder, startling me out of my head, I'd have been standing there all night, watching them.

"I'll go get the food ready. Do you want drinks or anything?"

"I'll have a beer, and Liam will have some juice. Do you have a straw or anything?"

"Erm, yeah. I think we do." I turned away and walked into the kitchen, Damian following behind me.

"He looks so young. Are you sure he's eighteen?" I asked him as I cooked.

Damian laughed. "I'm sure. Boys like him are checked out

when they go to the club to make sure we, sorry they, aren't breaking any rules. They both enjoy it. Stuart likes someone to look after, and Liam likes to be looked after. It's the same as us a little; only you're far more independent than he is."

I looked at him in shock. I was nothing like Liam. I didn't need looking after, but the more I thought about me and Damian, the more I realised we *were* like them, just not so extreme. He went out to work, and I stayed home. He did and bought everything for me. I wasn't sure how to process that.

I pondered his words as I dished up the meal, Damian sorting the drinks out. I stood open-mouthed as he prepared a drink in a cute pink sippy cup. He looked over and saw me watching him.

"What? It used to be Daisy's. I never threw it away, but it'll come in handy for Liam. He uses them when he's at home."

This was another new thing for me, and when Damian called them through to tell them the meal was ready, I wasn't surprised to see Stuart pull Liam's chair close to him and put a bib around his neck. I felt a kick under the table and looked across to Damian, and he shook his head. I must have been staring, but this whole thing was so new and odd to me.

As the night wore on, I tried not to stare even more as Stuart fed Liam the food I'd cooked. At least there were no airplanes or trains when he fed him. I'm not sure I could have kept a straight face if that had happened.

The conversation was mostly between Damian and Stuart as they discussed work and new contracts they'd been working on, so it left me with Liam to talk to. I didn't know what to say.

"How long have you been Damian's boy?" I furrowed my brow as I looked at him.

"Boy? I'm nobody's boy, Liam. What gave you that idea?"

"Oh, it's just Stuart mentioned something about Damian having a new boy living with him, so I assumed it was you. Is there someone else living here?"

"No, only me and Damian. I think you might have heard

wrong. We're..." And that's when I stopped. I didn't know what we were. I assumed we were boyfriends, but my brain refused to function, then I heard Damian reply.

"Ziggy's my boyfriend, not my boy. Right, beautiful?"

I nodded and smiled absently at him. I stood to clear the plates from the table, not sure I liked the direction the conversation had taken. I wasn't anybody's boy. I wasn't.

I walked into the kitchen to load the dishwasher. Even though I'd cooked, it was still my responsibility to keep the kitchen tidy.

I felt rather than heard Damian step up behind me, and he slid his arms around my waist.

"He didn't mean anything with his comment, and I could see you were struggling to put a label on us, but I think boyfriend fits, don't you?"

I turned in his arms and placed my soapy hands behind his head.

"I think that fits us perfectly." I kissed his lips, tasting the beer and food we'd eaten. He deepened it, as he always did, and we almost got carried away.

"Are we having dessert, Daddy? Because I need the toilet before we do."

I peeked over Damian's shoulder to see Stuart lifting Liam from his chair and making his way to the downstairs bathroom.

"Is he going to take him?" I looked incredulously at Damian, not believing what I was seeing.

"Yes, he does everything for him, I told you. I don't think he's wearing a nappy tonight, so he'll stand with him while he goes. Help him out, you know?"

I didn't know and wasn't sure I wanted to. This was all so new to me. I'd heard the guys talking about it but seeing it? Yeah, not sure.

They came back to the table, Stuart praising him for being such a good boy and kissing his fingers. I served up dessert. It wasn't anything special, just cheesecake, and again, I was mesmerised by how Stuart looked after Liam.

The rest of the evening passed fairly uneventfully, and Liam didn't speak to me again. A little later, he crawled into Stuart's lap and proceeded to suck on his thumb and go to sleep.

"We'll not stay much longer. I need to get him home for his bath and story before he goes to bed. I must say, though, Ziggy, you've taken this extremely well. People can be judgemental when they see the relationship we have, but you? You've taken it all in your stride."

"I was a little shocked if I'm honest, but who am I to judge anyone? I'm a sex worker, selling myself for money on the streets. I could hardly comment on someone else's lifestyle, now could I?"

Stuart smiled tightly and looked over at Damian. I looked over too and saw the tension in his face. I know he hated what I'd done before, but it was part of me, who I was. It had made me the Ziggy I was today, and I refused to be ashamed of my past.

"Yes, well. You don't have to do it anymore. I'm here to look after you now." He reached across and took my hand, kissing it before letting it go. He was upset, I could tell, but he knew where I'd come from, what I'd done. It was how we'd got together after all.

As Damian continued to chat with Stuart about football and how well Liverpool were doing in the league, I cleared up. Damian liked it all done before we went up to bed, and I didn't want to disappoint him.

About ten minutes later, I heard the chairs scraping back from the table, and Stuart carried Liam over to me.

"Thank you for a lovely meal. I'm sure Liam would thank you himself, but as you can see, he's out for the count. The poor little lamb."

"It was nice to meet him too and to see you again, Stuart. I'm pleased you've found someone to share your life with."

"Well, all the good ones were taken, you know?" He winked at me, and my Spidey senses tingled again. I was getting a bad feeling from this guy, but at least with Liam in the picture, he might turn his attention away from me.

"So, what did you think of Stuart and Liam's relationship?" Damian asked me as we lay in bed.

I turned onto my side to look at him.

"Like I said, who am I to judge and if it's what they want, up to them." I shrugged. "I'm not sure it's something I'd be comfortable with. I'm past the stage of someone taking me to piss and feeding me."

"I know, but we have a milder sort of relationship, don't you think? You are my beautiful boy, and I do take care of you." He placed a quick kiss to the end of my nose, leaning over to turn off the light.

I lay on my back, looking up at the ceiling. He had a point. A good point, but there was no way I was going to be like Liam, and I hoped Damian realised that.

CHAPTER FOURTEEN

We met a few more times with Stuart and Liam, and I got used to their dynamic. Sometimes Liam was independent, feeding himself, going to the toilet, but other times, he regressed to being a baby, well, more like a toddler.

As for Damian and me, our relationship went from strength to strength. I didn't suffer at his hands the way I had in the past, and he was able to control his temper for the most part. There was the odd occasion I'd see a flash of anger, but it disappeared as quickly as it appeared. He continued to tell me he loved me, but something held me back. I knew he was starting to get frustrated with me, but the words wouldn't come.

One day in early March, I'd been working in the garden, planting pots with primulas and pansies. The domesticated life was suiting me, and although the Daddy/boy thing had initially played on my mind, I hadn't given it any more thought.

We had guests again for dinner, a regular occurrence now, and my cooking skills had improved sufficiently to rival Suzie. I'd spoken to her a few times, and we'd laughed about it, but our contact had become less and less. She was busy, and when I was with Damian, he hated me being on my phone, repeating the conversation we'd had months ago about him not being enough.

Time had run away with me, and when I checked my phone, I was running late. I still needed to prepare the meal, tidy up the garden *and* have a shower.

Shit. If I left a mess anywhere, Damian would not be happy. I was sure he had OCD. I tidied up as quickly as I could and dashed into the kitchen, hastily putting the meal together and throwing it in the oven.

I decided to quickly go for a shower and tidy the kitchen when I came down. I calculated I'd have enough time before Damian came home.

How wrong could I be? As I stepped into the bedroom after showering and preparing myself for later, I saw Damian standing there, his jaw clenched and his fists pumping by his sides.

Fuck. This wasn't good. He stalked towards me, bending to my ear as he spoke.

"What have we said about keeping things tidy, Ziggy? I came home and went to the kitchen for a drink. Imagine my surprise when I see dishes in the sink, food still needing to be put away and the table not even laid for tonight."

As he spoke, he gripped my upper arm, his fingers digging in so much I knew he would leave a mark. I winced with the pain, and even though we'd talked about this before, I knew I'd done wrong. I should have cleaned up before I even stepped in the shower. He would have preferred me to be dirty than the house untidy.

"I, I, I'm sorry, Damian. I thought I'd have enough time before you came home."

"Really, Ziggy? You know what happens to boys who don't do as they're told."

I did and had a pretty good idea where he was going. He'd told me before naughty boys were spanked, but I hadn't thought he was serious. Guess I'd been wrong.

"Boys who misbehave get punished…spanked. I've been very patient with you of late, and you have been so very good, but I can't let this go unpunished. Don't you agree?"

Did I agree? I'm not sure I did and him putting me over his knee was not my idea of fun at all. It was humiliating, and I backed away from him, clutching my towel close to me.

"I'm sorry, Damian. I won't do it again. Please don't do this." My heart pounded, and my hands shook at the thought of what he was about to do. I did not want this.

Damian chuckled, a dark sound, not remotely light-hearted, and for a second, I wondered who he was. Where was the Damian I lived with day after day?

He sat on the bed and patted his lap, encouraging me to lie across it.

"Come now, Ziggy, you *will* obey me." I shook my head, continuing to back up, hitting the wall. I had nowhere else to go. I couldn't do this, but if I didn't, he'd be displeased with me.

"I think at least ten will be sufficient for tonight, but then you'll dress and go downstairs to clean up the mess you made. Agreed?"

I was torn. I felt humiliated, degraded and all because I hadn't tidied the kitchen. But the urge to move towards him and take my punishment was overriding my usual good sense. I wanted to please him. I didn't want to disappoint him.

"You deserve it. Now come here and take it like the good boy you are."

I edged towards him with my hands on my arse, protecting it. I lay across his thighs, my body tense.

"Move your hands, Ziggy. Don't make me have to do it for you."

Tears coursed down my face, frustrated at the ease with which I'd surrendered, and I reluctantly moved them, not knowing what to do with them.

"Hands to the floor and no sound else this could last longer than it needs to."

I glanced to the side and could see his cock straining against the fabric of his suit trousers, and I squeezed my eyes shut. How was this such a turn on for him, doling out punishment?

But I complied and tensed, waiting…

The first one stung like a bitch, and I fought back a shout, pressing my lips together to stifle any sound. Fuck, I had at least another nine of these, but I could take it. I needed to take it. I gritted my teeth and held my breath.

"That's it, my boy, you're being very good." He stroked my cheek gently before swatting it again, over and over, and as much as I hated to admit it, the feeling of pain soon morphed into a weird kind of pleasure.

I lost count of the amount of times he spanked me, but the sensations the hits brought, sent my blood south, and my cock swelled against Damian's thigh.

"Are you hard for me now, Ziggy? Do you want me to make you come?" I bit back a groan. It was all getting too much.

I'd lost the sensation in my arse at this point, but my dick was ready to blow.

I moaned involuntarily, and Damian tutted. "Ah, Ziggy, my boy. That deserves at least another two. I said no sound."

I nodded reluctantly, feeling light-headed, and I hoped to God he could see it. As much as my dick loved it, my arse didn't. It was going to hurt when I sat down on it later.

Two more hard slaps, and I felt like I was on fire. I could feel tears wetting my face.

I heard the snick of a bottle lid opening and jumped as a coolness eased my skin. Damian gently rubbed in a soothing lotion. I hadn't even seen him get any out, so far into my head by the pain he'd inflicted.

"Just look at those rosy cheeks. I love to see them marked by my hand, and you were such a good boy, but I did have to give you a couple more. I said no sound, and for your first time, you did well. Now let's have a look and see how you liked it."

He helped me to stand, and my cock jutted out in front, begging for his touch and a hand to relieve me. He didn't disappoint and ran his finger along my shaft, fingering the slit.

"Mm, do you know what sounding is?"

I shook my head; I didn't, but at this point, I just wanted to get off.

"Maybe another time, but I think you'd like it. Here, let me give you your reward."

He stroked my cock up and down, and I again couldn't stop the moan leaving my lips. He suckled on the head while frantically working me, and I felt my orgasm building. I clenched my fists and thrust my hips forward as I erupted, my cum splattering his face and hands. Shit, that was fast.

"That tasted so good, Ziggy, and to think at first you wouldn't let me get you off. Now you crave my touch, don't you, boy?"

I nodded. His touch was everything. "Oh, God, Damian. That was so good. It hurt, but I haven't come so hard or so quickly for a long time."

"I know, baby, and maybe we can try again. Would you like that, Ziggy? Would you like to feel my palm again?"

I hesitated. Did I want to feel it again? My head was saying a definite no, but other parts of my body were all for it. I nodded reluctantly but lowered my eyes, ashamed by my response. How could I have enjoyed that? Why did I enjoy that?

"Good boy. Now, you need to get dressed and tidy that mess away, else you'll be getting another spanking a lot sooner than you think."

My arse didn't think that was such a good idea, and as he leaned in to kiss me, I noticed him palm his own dick, pressing his erection down.

"I can help with that if you'd like." Maybe if I offered to do that for him, he'd be less disappointed in me. It dawned on me that's what I'd despised, the fact that I'd let us both down.

"It's OK, my beautiful boy. You can help me out later when our company is gone, make up for today. Now get ready."

I turned to leave, and he patted my backside gently. I still felt it. He hadn't exactly gone easy on me even though it was my first time. I dressed gingerly, opting for looser fitting bottoms so the fabric wouldn't rub my tender skin.

A little later at the table, I tried not to show how it hurt as I sat, but I could see Stuart lifting his eyebrows at Damian, a silent question passing between them. I knew what he was asking in his own way, and I saw the sly smile Damian gave him in return. I couldn't help but feel uncomfortable with Stuart knowing what had happened between us and even more so at Damian's response. It wasn't fucking funny, and I'd make sure to tell him later when we were alone.

Liam, as usual, seemed oblivious to the whole thing. He'd come around in one of his regressive states, and toddler Liam was happily colouring in his book while the 'grown-ups' talked.

As the night wore on, the pain receded, and I was able to move around more freely, scrubbing the kitchen down. There was no way I was leaving it a mess tonight. Damian came in a little later to tell me that Stuart was leaving.

I almost told him I didn't care either way, but he always liked me to say good night to our guests. He stood behind me at the door, his arms around me, resting his chin on my shoulder.

"Good night, Stuart. Make sure you get Liam to bed safe and sound. He's been a tired boy tonight."

"I will, and thanks for a lovely meal again. Your skills are improving, Ziggy. I hope you'll be more comfortable soon, though. I know how much being disciplined can hurt." He turned to Damian, and I was surprised at his next words. "I wouldn't mind doing that to him at some point. Perhaps you'd let me."

Damian laughed in my ear.

"Perhaps we could trade? I'm sure Liam would love another Daddy, and I wouldn't mind getting to know him a little better, if you know what I mean. It's been a while."

I froze at his words, thinking we'd got over this, these stupid words that he'd say when Stuart was around, and I tried to pull away.

"Not now, Ziggy. You *will* behave." He whispered the words in my ear and tightened his hold as Stuart walked away, his little boy in his arms. "I like to give him hope, but you are all mine, Ziggy. No one else's. Remember that."

My mind went back to what had happened earlier as I lay on my front in bed that night, and I knew I had to say something, tell him how it'd made me feel, but before I could say anything, Damian spoke.

"Spit it out, Ziggy. Say what you need, then sleep. You've had an emotional day." He sounded irritated, and I debated whether or not I should speak, but if I didn't say it now, I never would.

"I hated it," I spat out. "What you did to me tonight. It was degrading and humiliating."

"Oh, PLEASE, come on, Ziggy. I didn't hear you complaining when you were shooting your load all over me. 'I've never come so hard'." His mimicry of me stung as much as his palm, and I turned onto my side, refusing to answer or look at him. I fought back tears, wondering why I was still here, but Damian did what he usually did and moved in behind me, being careful not to rub against me.

"I'm sorry, baby, but you needed that tonight. You needed me to show you that there are consequences if your behaviour isn't acceptable, especially when I've asked you to do something. Now, be a good boy and do as you're told, and it won't happen again."

He kissed my shoulder and nuzzled into my neck, and I realised that as much as I hated to admit it, I'd fallen for this man when he was Mr V-S to me and he *loved* me. I liked being his and having someone to care for me, and I'd do whatever I needed to do to please him.

CHAPTER FIFTEEN

The following day, Damian was back to normal, no mention of the previous night and the discipline he'd administered. He went to work, and I lounged around the house with nothing to do, still aware of my tender arse. I was getting bored, to be honest, so used to doing something during the day, and even though I'd loved playing house these past few months, this inactivity was starting to bother me.

After Damian left for work, I made sure everywhere was tidy. There was no way I was getting caught out again. I had mixed feelings about last night, and my fears had kept me awake during the night, remembering how tender my arse had been, and still was, but also how my traitorous dick had responded.

The speed and force of my orgasm had taken me by surprise.

Fuck, thinking about it now had my dick twitching.

I needed to speak to someone, run this crazy situation by someone else to see what they thought. I was so conflicted.

I tried Suzie's number, but it went straight to voicemail. The only other person who'd given me advice so far was Duke.

I was about to hang up when he answered.

"Yo, Ziggy. How's tricks?"

I could hear grunting in the background, and Duke's breath was heavy down the phone.

"Please tell me you're not doing what I think you are?" I groaned, hoping it wasn't.

"Hey, I have some class!" he exclaimed. "I'm working at my other job right now, but I can take a break. What do you need, my friend?"

"Oh, thank God. That could have been awkward!" I paused, deciding how much to tell him.

"I'm not sure how to word this, so I'm gonna come right out and say it." I took a deep breath and rushed the words out. "Damian spanked me last night!"

"Woah, I thought you'd said no abuse! Do you need me to come get you?"

"No, no. It wasn't like that. It was…good but bad. He got me off right after, and I've never come so hard in my life. My dick certainly enjoyed it, but I felt ashamed and humiliated, and now I don't know what to do."

"Why did he do it? Was it some sex game you were playing? 'Cos I'm telling you now, a bit of arse slapping during sex can be a fucking turn-on."

"No, unfortunately, it was nothing like that." Again with the pause, I felt degraded by the whole situation but knew Duke would understand. He was a man of the world, had been around. "I didn't tidy the kitchen and lay the table before he got home. He wasn't happy. I stepped out of the bathroom, and he was there, waiting for me, and that's when he did it."

"So he disciplined you then. I've known a few people that like that, turns them on. Was he turned on?"

"Oh yeah, he had a massive hard-on. So did I after the first couple of slaps, but I don't know. I liked it but didn't, you know? Like it was humiliating or something. I don't know how to feel about it."

"I can understand that. It happened to me when a punter got rough. You'll have to tell him how you feel else he'll do it again. Do you want him to do it again?"

"Honestly? Maybe? Maybe not? Fuck, Duke. It's messed up in my head."

"Do you want to meet up and talk about it? I don't mind."

"Not yet, no. I wanted your advice on what it might mean for us, me and Damian."

"It means what you want it to. Has it put you off him? Do you want to move out?"

"No, nothing like that. It's put me off a little, but I suppose I wanted to know if it was normal."

"Only you can make that decision, but if you want my thoughts, see how it goes. If it becomes uncomfortable, leave him, but if you're enjoying it, stay. Experiment with it. You might like it."

"You're right. I should see how it goes. Living here with him has been so good for me and for us. I was so tired being out there, and now? I feel like I've got a new lease on life, that I can do and be whatever I want and Damian will support me every step of the way."

"Well, that's great, man. I only hope I can find that in time. If you need me, just call, OK? Have to go anyway, got another client waiting."

"Thanks, Duke. You've given me something to think about."

I ended the call and sat looking at my phone. I couldn't sit here doing this every day; I'd be bored out of my skull. I needed to find a job but doing what, I didn't know.

Damian's laptop was set up on the table. He wouldn't mind, would he? It felt a little like snooping, but if there was no password on it, well, he mustn't be that bothered about what was on there.

I jiggled the mouse and watched as the lock screen came to life. Fuck it. It was asking for a passcode, and I had no idea what it could be. Perhaps if I spoke to him later and explained why I wanted to use it.

What seemed like fucking hours later, Damian arrived home. I was prepared tonight. Our meal was ready and in the fridge to be cooked and the kitchen was spotless. No way was I falling for that again.

I knew he always loved a beer when he came home, and I'd had one chilling in the fridge all afternoon. I knocked the top of it and turned to give it to him as he stepped into the room.

I almost dropped the bottle as there he stood, the most beautiful bouquet of flowers in his hand and a red gift bag, covered in pink hearts.

"Hi, baby," he said bashfully. He stood with his hands outstretched, giving me the gifts.

"Oh, Damian, these are beautiful." I exchanged the beer for the flowers and brought them to my nose, smelling the fragrant blooms. "I love them. I adore flowers."

"I know you do, silly boy. I've seen what you've done in the garden. I got you this too." And he handed me the bag. "If you don't like it, I can always take it back, but I hope you will."

I peered into the bag, not knowing what to expect and almost laughed when I saw what he'd bought me. A beautiful pink glass dildo. Much better quality than the ones me and Suzie had wasted our money on.

His eyes lit up as I pulled it out of the bag and massaged the end of it.

"I mean, we don't have to use it if you don't want to, but I thought maybe we could bring a bit of spice to our relationship. If you want to, of course, you can say no."

The hope I saw in his face and the way my dick was hardening in my sweats at the thought of using it on him or me had me wanting to put our meal on hold and go try it out right now.

"How hungry are you?" I asked, a teasing tone to my voice.

"It depends on what you mean by hungry? If you mean hungry for food, I can wait, but if you're asking me if I'm hungry for that gorgeous arse of yours…" He gave me a wicked grin, and those eyes of his darkened with lust. "Let's go."

CHAPTER SIXTEEN

That night in bed, Damian was attentive and took such good care of me. He caressed my body and played it like a fine-tuned instrument. We never got around to eating the meal I'd prepared but contented ourselves with snacks we found in the cupboards, feeding each other morsels of food, laughing and joking with each other.

The night was perfect, and we reaffirmed our relationship. He told me he loved me over and over as we made love, and I couldn't believe I'd ever doubted his intentions towards me.

We showered together. It took twice as long as usual as we still couldn't keep our hands off each other, and kiss after kiss, he showed me how deeply he cared. I melted under his touch, and as the water ran cool, we dried off, finally making our way back to the bed.

"What did you do today, my love?" he asked as I lay with my head on his chest, stroking up and down my arm with his gentle touch.

"Not much. I tidied up, pottered around in the garden." I hesitated, not sure if I should mention the job to him. I had no income of my own and wanted to start paying my way, contribute to the house I was living in.

"I was thinking of looking for a job. Would you mind if I looked for one on your laptop? I tried to get on it today, but you have a passcode on it. I didn't mean to pry, sorry." I hastened to add the apology, realising he could take it the wrong way.

"It has a passcode for a reason, Ziggy." He stopped stroking my arm, and the tone of his voice changed. I didn't think it was that much of a deal, but clearly he did.

"OK, and I'm sorry for looking, but I don't have a lot of credit on my phone now with me not working."

"Again with the phone. I don't know why you need one! You're obsessed, Ziggy." He sounded exasperated as he moved away from me.

I turned to look at him.

"I have friends, you know. Suzie, Duke." I stopped when I realised I didn't have any more friends. They were the sum of the last four years of my life, two fucking friends. I was a sad bastard.

"You have *me*, Ziggy. You don't *need* anyone else. We'll look for a job for you tomorrow when I come home from work, but I don't see why you need one. *I* look after you, *I* feed you, clothe you. Why would you want to work?"

"Oh, I don't know. Maybe because I'm bored staying at home every day." My voice rose as I spoke. He really didn't get it.

I'd been fine at home to start with, I'd been ill and couldn't work, but as the weeks had passed, there were only so many chores to do around the house, only so much daytime TV I could stomach.

Fuck this. I wasn't going to argue over it tonight, but I'd stand my ground, and we *would* look for a job for me. Even if it was in the coffee shop. Suzie would have laughed her tits off after our conversation at Christmas, but it was looking more appealing the longer I thought about it.

I went to turn away from him, but he pulled me back into his side and continued stroking my arm.

"I don't see why you won't let me take care of you, look after you. I like doing it, Ziggy. It gives me immense pleasure."

I thought about arguing back, but I was tired. Tired of the day and tired of this conversation.

I sighed deeply. "I know it does, but I'm not used to it. I need to be doing something. We'll talk about it tomorrow. I'm tired, and you have work. It's already after midnight. You should get some sleep."

"Ah, my darling boy, always thinking about me. And yes, we'll discuss this more tomorrow when you're in a better frame of mind."

What the fuck did that mean? Better frame of mind, my arse. It was on the tip of my tongue to say something more on the matter, but I thought more on it and decided to sleep. I had another day of doing fuck all planned for tomorrow. I needed to keep my strength up.

The following evening, I'd already cooked the food I'd planned for yesterday, and we sat to eat as soon as Damian came home.

We ate in silence as we often did but as soon as we finished and I cleared the plates away, I brought him his drink and sat. I was going to have this discussion come hell or high water.

"I need a job, Damian. I know you said you like to look after me, but I need to do something more. I'm bored and want to contribute."

He looked at me, an exasperated look on his face. "Look, Ziggy."

"Don't 'look, Ziggy' me." He raised his eyebrows at me, and I knew I was skating on thin ice here. He was perilously close to losing his temper. "I want a job, and I don't know why you think it's such a bad idea."

"I just don't see why. You have everything you need. Other boys would give their right arm to be in your position, and all I hear you do is moan about it."

"It's OK for you. You go out to work every day, get to speak to other people. All I do is watch stupid daytime TV and slob around the house, doing nothing. I don't know anyone around here, so it's not like I can go out for coffee or anything."

I glared at him, trying to get my point across, but he looked down at his bottle, picking at the label.

"Fine. If that's what you want but with your 'work experience'..." The derision I heard in his voice rubbed me up the wrong way, but I ignored it and let him continue. "What are you going to do? It's not like you have a lot to offer."

"What the fuck is that supposed to mean? I know I've only sold sex, Damian, but I'm pretty sure I have excellent customer service skills."

I was bouncing now, so fucking cross with him and his high and mighty ideas. I stood from my chair, intent on going upstairs and out of his way. If I continued with my thoughts, I'd end up over his knee again. Fuck that! I was humiliated enough without adding that into the mix as well.

"Sit down." He gripped my wrist and forced me back into my chair. "I didn't say you couldn't get a job, just that you had no skills to speak of."

"Yeah, well, it didn't sound like that. Don't belittle me, Damian. I have a brain, and I know how to use it."

"I know, but let's look at this rationally." He stood and grabbed his laptop from the table, opening it up and entering the passcode.

010501.

That was odd. It was my birth date. Surely it was a coincidence, but a niggling thought sprang up at the back of my mind. I tucked it away as he turned the screen to face me.

"Let's see what's about and what you'll actually be able to do, shall we?" Patronising bastard. There was no need to speak to me like a child. I ignored the tone and smiled sweetly at him.

"Yes, let's." The sarcasm in my voice didn't go unnoticed, and he glowered at me. I was really pushing it now, but at this moment in time, I didn't give a fuck.

After an hour of searching, I had to concede that I didn't have the necessary skills to do most of the jobs that were advertised.

I could either work as a shop assistant or learn how to be a barista.

Out of the two, I'd chosen the shop assistant job, and between us, we'd completed the online form. I wasn't hopeful, but it was a start.

Damian closed the lid of the laptop with a thump and moved it back on the table.

"Happy now?" he asked. The mood I was in, I could have gladly wiped that condescending smile from his face, but I kept myself in check.

"Yes, thank you. I didn't realise how unqualified I was to do absolutely anything. How would I ever have managed without you?"

"You're pushing for another spanking at this rate, Ziggy. I suggest you change your tone of voice."

The thought of him doing that again to me had me changing my attitude. I needed to stay on his good side so he'd let me go out and get a job. I needed to apologise and make it sincere.

"I'm sorry, Damian. You're right. I am unqualified. I left school with nothing, no qualifications, and all I've done is live and work on the streets."

He smiled at me, and I knew I'd got away with it, but I needed to cement this in his mind, that he was right.

"How about I show you what I am qualified to do?" I sidled

over to him, falling to my knees in front of him. "How about I show you how good I was at my previous profession."

He grinned at me and stood, undoing his belt and dropping his trousers. I loved blow jobs, especially for Damian. I'd grown to love his cock even more and relished the feel of it in my mouth. I looked up into his dark eyes as I slowly swallowed his length, hardly gagging as it slid down my throat. Thanks to my former job, my gag reflex was non-existent, and I hummed around him, a strangled moan leaving his lips.

I knew he wouldn't last long, knew the telltale signs he had before he'd come. My dislike of spunk was still there, and being together for so long now, he knew I didn't swallow. After mere minutes of me taking his dick in my mouth, he pulled out, his release spurting in my hair and over my face. I could feel it dripping off my eyelashes. Jesus, there was always so much.

"I'd pay you to do that every day, then you wouldn't need to get a job," he panted as he spoke. Oh, the irony of that statement.

CHAPTER SEVENTEEN

The next few evenings, I badgered Damian every night so I could look for jobs on his laptop. All the while he sat next to me, commenting on what I could and couldn't do. What I should and shouldn't apply for. I rolled my eyes so often they were in danger of staying that way.

He was starting to get on my very last nerve. I didn't need my hand held, didn't need him to watch me all the time. It was as if he didn't trust me.

As I sat gazing at the screen, my phone rang. I almost jumped out of my seat, not remembering the last time it had rung.

"Hi, this is Ziggy." I bounced up and down with excitement on my chair while Damian looked on, an amused look on his face, a twinkle in his eye.

"Hi, this is Sandy. I see you've applied for the job here at my shop, Sandy's Small Delights. Are you OK to talk now?"

"Of course, I'd be happy too." I squeezed my eyes shut, hoping and praying that this was the job that would get me out of the house.

Sandy's Small Delights was a small cafe on the seafront. I could walk there, and they were only looking for someone to work in the afternoon. It suited me perfectly. I'd have the morning to clean up the house and have my little job in the afternoon.

I reached for Damian's hand and squeezed. I know it wasn't much, but it was a start. I could get out of the house, and I'd get experience doing something other than selling myself.

She conducted the interview over the phone and, subject to a successful shift at the cafe, told me I'd got the job. I ended the call and turned to face Damian. I was fit to burst.

"I need to go in tomorrow for a shift at 2 p.m. I can't believe it; I'll have a proper job." I leapt into his lap and kissed him. This was a far cry from a few months ago when I'd never properly kissed anyone.

Damian pulled away, though, and almost pushed me from his lap.

"I'm happy for you, but I don't want you taking the job."

"I mean, I haven't got it yet, but why not? Is it because I won't be here in the afternoon? I can still keep the house tidy, make sure it's all done. Please, Damian. I really want this job."

"You know I was never happy with this. You don't need to work. I can take care of you."

"It's not about you taking care of me. It's about me occupying my mind. I'm going to do the shift, Damian. Let me at least do that." I climbed back into his lap and pouted. "I might not even get the job. I might drop all the plates on the floor, spill tea in someone's lap, but I need to at least try."

He looked away from me, and I could see his jaw twitch and the gears turning in his head.

I leaned in and nuzzled into his neck.

"This would make me happy, Damian, and if I'm happy, well, I think it would be good for both of us."

This finally got his attention, and he turned back to look at me, a resigned look on his face.

"OK. You can do it tomorrow, but we'll see what happens

from there. If you don't get it, you give up this stupid idea of getting a job. If you do get it, we'll have to see where we go from there."

I knew he hadn't wanted me to get a job, but this was ridiculous. He didn't control my life, regardless of what he thought. I was my own person, I was Ziggy, but I nodded in agreement. I'd let him think that he'd won this round, but I was not going to give this up.

"I promise. We'll see what happens tomorrow. Now let's go to bed. I have a big day tomorrow." I jumped off his lap, doing a little jig.

"Yes, and you need to make sure the house is tidy before you go." He tried and failed to be strict with me, a small twitch at the side of his face giving away his smile.

"Yep, no problem. I can do that." Nothing he had to say would upset me tonight.

———

The following day, I woke up early. Damian left for work, and I rushed around the house, getting it tidy, ready for my shift at two.

I left the house at 1.30 p.m., determined to be early. She'd said to wear black trousers and a T-shirt. That I could do with the amount of clothes Damian had bought for me.

As I approached the shop, I could see a young guy, similar in age to me, wearing similar clothes and an apron. He was very good-looking, with blond hair, blue eyes and the most gorgeous smile.

"Hi, Ziggy?" he asked tentatively as I walked towards the door.

"Yep, that's me. I know I'm a little early."

"We like early." He shook my hand vigorously. "I'm Beau, by the way. If you get the job, you'll be working with me when you're on shift. It'll be good to have another guy on the team. The girls are great, but they can be a bit much at times."

He opened the door for me and led me over to the counter.

"This is Sandy, our fearless leader." She pinched his cheeks as he smiled that dazzling smile.

"You should watch this one, Ziggy. He's a proper tease."

I'd be watching him alright, I thought as Sandy talked me through the various things I needed to do.

She handed me an apron, a notepad and pen, and suggested I shadow Beau for the rest of the shift.

He showed me the ropes and flirted with the customers, telling me we got better tips that way. He made me laugh, and the afternoon flew by. In no time at all, it was the end of my shift. If I got the job, I knew I was going to really enjoy it here.

"I think you'll fit right in here, Ziggy," Sandy said before I left. "I can see you get on well with Beau, and the girls all love you. When do you think you could start? There might be some weekends thrown in as we can get busy sometimes, but you won't be working every one. Would that be OK?"

"I'd love to work here. Everyone's so friendly. I can start whenever. Let me know when and I'll sort it out with my boyfriend." As soon as the words were out of my mouth, I wished I could take them back. I hated to blurt out I was gay, but I didn't think, so happy with today.

"That's no problem, my dear. We can work around if you have plans with him. You'll have to bring him in sometime."

That had gone better than I'd expected. Not all people were so accepting, but it seemed they were here.

"Did I hear you say boyfriend?" Beau sidled up next to me, a glint in his eye and a flirty smile on his lips.

"Yeah, you did. Why? Is it a problem?" I glanced over at him, waiting for his response.

"Quite the opposite. I think we're going to get on very well." He winked, and I blushed from tip to toe. It had been a while since someone had flirted with me, and I had to say, I liked it. Damian was a great boyfriend but was all serious sometimes, so to have someone my own age flirt a little was nice.

"Come on, I'll walk you out. It's the end of my shift anyway."

We walked out the door, me laughing at something Beau had said, him walking next to me, bumping my arm as we strolled along the front towards the house.

I was so engrossed in our conversation I didn't hear the car pull up next to us.

"Ziggy. Get in the car, now." I turned to see Damian alongside, his face in a scowl and his hands tight on the steering wheel.

I turned to Beau, an apology on my tongue. "I'm sorry. I have to go."

"No worries, man. I'll see you next time. Good to meet you." Again with the dazzling smile and I couldn't help but return it.

"I said, now, Ziggy. In the car." Damian's voice was harsh.

I opened the car door and sat inside, turning to look at him.

His eyes were dark, and the flush to his neck and cheeks showed me just how pissed off he was.

"You're not going back there. I don't care if they did offer you the job." He put the car in gear and pulled away from the curb to the sound of car horns. He screeched around the corner, heading towards home.

"You said I could keep the job if I got it, and I did. You don't own me, Damian. No one owns me."

"That's where you're wrong, Ziggy. I own every single piece of you, and don't you forget."

CHAPTER EIGHTEEN

We pulled up outside the house, and I could see Stuart waiting, no sign of Liam. My hands shook as I opened the car door and stepped out into the cool evening, and a shiver ran down my spine.

I glanced between the two of them, noticing the nod Stuart gave to Damian. He could fuck right off if he thought he was going to be giving me a spanking. Damian unlocked the front door, and the three of us went inside; Damian led and Stuart brought up the rear, his hand in the small of my back.

As we stepped through the door, Damian turned and gripped my arm tight. I winced and cried out at the pain, but there was no way he was letting go.

"Who the fuck was that, and why were you flirting with him?" He twisted my wrist, and I shouted even more. He backhanded me across my face with his free hand, anger flashing in his eyes, my cheek heating with the pain.

"Fuck, Damian. Let me go." I struggled to get free, his grip getting tighter the more I fought him. "It was just a guy that works there, and I wasn't flirting. We were talking, having a laugh."

"I don't know how many times you need reminding, Ziggy. You're mine. This is why I didn't want you taking a job. I knew this would happen. You'd flirt and cheat behind my back." He hit me again, the other cheek this time. "I can't have that. I think I'm going to have to teach you a lesson." He tried to grab for my other arm, but I twisted out of his grasp and ran for the door to find Stuart standing there, a sneer on his face.

"Nuh-uh. You're going nowhere, Ziggy. Damian told me what would happen, and I offered to come along and see if you needed that lesson. Seems you do." I hated the look on his face. He was a creepy arse fucker. I'd known that from day one, but I was properly shitting myself at this point. He'd removed his jacket, rolling up the sleeves on his shirt. Fuck, this guy meant business.

"You see, Damian has been keeping you sweet, for me. He knows that I've wanted and watched you for a while. We were always going to share you. So when he says you're his, you're actually ours." His smile was vicious, and he trailed his finger along my cheek. I should have listened to my gut all those months ago. Here I'd been thinking that this was real, that fairy tales were real when in fact, there was no such thing, not for me anyway.

It'd all been a fucking lie; Damian had said he hated it when Stuart said things. What the fuck? I'd been played. All this time, I'd thought I was his, but he was keeping me warm until he was ready to share me?

No fucking way. That wasn't happening. And what about Liam? Where did he fit into all this?

"What about Liam? I thought he was your boy. You always seemed mighty cosy when you came around here. Why the change?" I couldn't stop the questions, nor could I stop the attitude even though I knew I was pushing my luck with these two.

"Ah, the lovely Liam." He stalked towards me. "Such a good boy until his bratty mouth wouldn't stop talking, wouldn't do as he was told. He deserved everything he got. I don't know what it is with you little boys. You think you have us wrapped around your little fingers, when actually you're playing right into our hands." He pinched my cheeks, moving closer to my face.

"I love my littles, but I like them compliant, and Liam wasn't. You, on the other hand, I think between us we can make you do what we want." He turned to Damian, a cruel look on his face. "What do you think, brother? I wonder what we can do to make him obey."

"Only one way to find out." Damian said as finally, I managed to break from his grip. But Stuart covered the only way out of the house, I had nowhere to run, I was trapped!

As Damian lunged for me, I managed to duck under his arm and ran towards the kitchen. If I could just make it to the back door, I could shout for help. Someone would hear me.

Before I even made it a few steps, I was tackled to the ground. My head bounced off the wall, and I saw stars. Warm liquid ran down my face, and I tasted blood. I struggled, but whoever it was held me tight.

"You little shit. You think you can get away from us?" Foul-smelling breath filled my nostrils, and I gagged.

Hauled to my feet, my world spun. Between the smell and the bang to my head, my stomach lurched. I reached out to grab on to anything to stop the incessant spinning but was pulled against a hard chest I knew wasn't Damian's.

"Keep fucking still, or else you'll regret it." A whispered comment, but a threat nonetheless.

He needn't have worried. Paralysed by fear, my legs refused to work. Half carried, half dragged back into the front room, I was thrown on the sofa, where I was made to sit. Damian stood behind me, his hands tight around my throat.

"One more move and I will end your life. Don't think I'm a stranger to this because I'm not." I hardly recognised Damian's voice. Gone were the sweet words; only violence remained.

By now I was terrified and could hardly breathe, let alone form a coherent sentence.

Stuart moved in front of me, undressing me, pulling my jeans down, removing my shoes at the same time.

I was losing consciousness; Damian hadn't relinquished his hold one bit, and I felt my head starting to droop to my chest.

"Woah, Damian. Don't kill him yet. There are things we need to do to him. Make him realise that he really is nothing. Just a plaything, our little sex toy."

The iron grip on my throat loosened, and I was able to draw a breath, the air flooding my lungs. I breathed deeply and slowly, and the black spots behind my eyes gradually subsided.

My arms were yanked above my head, my T-shirt removed. I was naked now, and I'd never felt so exposed, so utterly degraded. Tears filled my eyes, but I blinked them away. I would not let them see me cry. They didn't deserve my tears.

I heard the sound of a zipper and watched as Stuart released his dick from his shorts. I almost snorted with laughter, despite the situation I was in, clearly hysterical. Whereas his brother, if that's who Damian was, had a long, curved dick, Stuart had the most average dick I'd ever seen. Call it tiny if you will, but I wasn't sure what he intended to do with it.

Another slap and my head pounded. "You think this is funny? You think I won't shove this so far down your throat you'll be puking? Don't push me, you fucking whore. That's all you were and all you'll ever be.

"You think Damian loved you? He's a damn good actor; that's all he is. He used you, got what he wanted for free and now"—he gave his half hard dick a stroke—"now, I get to sample the goods."

I struggled to rise, but Damian's hands on my shoulders held me down as Stuart stood, straddling my thighs, his knees pinning my hands to the sofa. I clamped my mouth shut, fully aware of the assault that was about to happen.

"Open up, Ziggy. This one's for you." Stuart waggled his

flaccid dick in my face. I turned to the side. I was not taking it. I would not take it.

With his free hand, he reached for my face, squeezing my nose, forcing me to open my mouth so I could breathe. I struggled and fought against him, trying desperately to dislodge him from my lap. I shrugged my shoulders, anything to release Damian's hold, but the more I struggled, the more they both held tight.

The tears that had threatened now fell, and I gasped for air, moving my head from side to side. I didn't want this. All I'd ever wanted was a man to love, someone to look after me, care for me. Yet here I was. I felt helpless, and soon my strength began to ebb as these two men held me against my will.

I knew what would happen next. Stuart edged nearer and finally forced his way into my mouth. They laughed as I gagged, and he started to thrust, brutal strokes that hurt my throat. The tears continued to fall as he pushed further and further, setting a relentless pace.

The black spots in my vision reappeared as my breath was cut off. My lungs burned with the effort of trying to get the smallest amount of air into my body. In a way, I welcomed it. I knew they wouldn't leave it at this, knew that more was to come, and I centred my thoughts.

Thoughts of a happier place where Honey and my love, whoever he was, would stroll along the beach. Honey meeting and playing with other dogs and me and my lover, basking in the glow of our love for each other.

The sudden realisation that Stuart's hard dick was pulsing in my mouth as he came had me puking over him, my stomach contents spilling on my chest.

"You dirty whore. Hold him, Damian. Someone needs to learn a lesson."

CHAPTER NINETEEN

I braced myself for the blow I knew was coming; only it was not a slap this time but a full-on punch. My teeth rattled in my jaw. Fuck, but that hurt. He continued with the onslaught, punch after punch landing on my face. I wasn't sure how much more of this I could take, but finally he stopped, swearing as his knuckles bled.

"Shit, Stuart. He'll not be fit for anything if you carry on. Jesus, man." Damian reached across me and pushed Stuart away.

Stuart lunged forward again.

"That little shit deserves everything he's going to get. I'm telling you, Damian, I'll fucking kill him."

"No, you won't." Damian shoved him away again. "What fun would that be if we did that? We want him at least awake, you dozy bastard."

I took the opportunity to try and assess my injuries. The sound I made when I breathed suggested my nose was broken, and it hurt to open my mouth. He'd used my face as a punching bag, and I was no doubt going to have scars. As much as that thought bothered me, I needed to make it out of this alive first.

I'd taken blows to the ribs, and it hurt to breathe. I hoped this would be over sooner rather than later but they were both so cruel and vicious I had no doubt I could be spending my last moments here if I didn't try to do something about it.

Stuart left the room, complaining about the vomit all over him, so that left me with Damian. Was everything he'd said to me a lie, or did he really feel something for me? There was only one way to find out. I needed to ask him.

My jaw hurt like hell, but I had to at least try.

The words sounded garbled even to my ears, and I wasn't sure if he understood me.

"Let me go, please. Didn't I mean anything to you? All these months we've spent together?"

"Fuck you, Ziggy. You mean nothing to me and never did."

"Why are you doing this? Why are you both hurting me like this?" Shit, it hurt more than I thought to talk, but I'd do anything at this point to get out this fucking house.

"It's what we do. Prey on the weak like you, like Liam. It's where we get our fun, Ziggy. I never loved you. It was all part of the game. We've played it for years, me and my brother dearest."

"Now be a good boy, beautiful, and shut your fucking mouth."

This was getting me nowhere fast, but I was running out of ideas. Minutes later, Stuart appeared dressed in nothing but a pair of sweats, his bare, muscled chest wet from the shower.

He walked towards me with a swagger, grabbing my hands.

"Hands and knees, Ziggy. I think it's about time I sampled the goods. Damian told me how good it was." He turned to Damian. "Get the tape. I don't want him making any noise."

He threw me onto my back on the sofa, and a sharp pain shot through my chest. Fuck, something definitely wasn't right; I could only manage shallow breaths.

Damian returned, a roll of tape in his hands. A piece was slapped over my mouth, and my wrists were bound in front of me. There was no escape and the horrible thought I wouldn't get out of this alive ran through my mind.

I couldn't let that happen. I was not going to die here, bound and gagged. I kicked out, connecting with Stuart's balls. He screamed in rage, clutching his groin.

"You stupid fucker. You've asked for it now."

As if nothing had happened, he lunged for me, grabbing my arms. He head-butted me, and this time, I definitely heard my nose crack. Shit, that fucking hurt, but he didn't stop there, raining punch after punch on my face and body.

I could vaguely hear Damian shouting at him to stop, but he didn't. I was going to die here in this godforsaken house in Crosby where I'd built some semblance of a life, albeit a lie.

Blow followed blow, kick followed kick, but all I could think about was Suzie and Duke, my family and how they'd never know what had happened to me, so sure was I that this was the end.

I must have passed out as I remembered nothing more; I just felt the pain spreading through my body.

This was it. This was the end of Ziggy Coleman. A twenty-year-old boy, unloved and with a life unlived.

CHAPTER TWENTY

I lay on the cold, wet pavement and felt my life force ebbing away. I thought of Damian. How he'd said he loved me and how that love had morphed into obsession. How my life hadn't been my own for such a long time, it seemed. And now, it would never be again.

My vision began to blur as the blood slowly seeped from my wounds. I wondered if I'd ever see the sun and blue sky again, smell the scent of fallen rain.

I tried to move, but the pain in my stomach was too intense, and I sucked in a breath. It was all too much, just too much. I had no fight left in me, and I knew with certainty that I'd die here in this dank, dark place, a broken boy.

There was no one to save me now. I was alone, as I'd always been.

I thought Damian had been the one, the one that would make me whole again, feel again, but all he and Stuart had done was drain me, life and soul, until I was nothing.

I slowly closed my eyes, possibly for the last time and wondered if this was it. Would my next breath be my last?

It hurt so much to breathe, to even live, and I wasn't sure I wanted to do either anymore.

My breath stuttered in my chest, becoming shallow as the wounds I'd sustained continued to bleed. I could feel my blood seeping into my clothes as I lay in the ever-increasing puddle, the cold of the night penetrating my bones.

So this was it. Not how I'd envisaged my life, dying at the tender age of twenty, never having lived my life to the full.

Eventually, as time wore on, my pain receded until I could feel no more, and my breathing slowed to almost nothing.

I tried to open my eyes, to take one last look at the world around me, but the effort was too much, and slowly, I felt no more; no pain, just peace, and as the sun rose over the rooftops, my broken body lay there, my life seemingly cut short by those deranged monsters, one of whom had claimed to love me.

In the distance, the sound of sirens cut through the quiet of the early morning. Would they be too late to save me, the boy who'd loved too much?

CHAPTER TWENTY-ONE

MARC

The report came through at five in the morning, a body dump. Not unusual in this part of Liverpool but not common enough for us not to be concerned. It could have been anything. A shooting, stabbing, a gang-related attack. Hell, even a homophobic attack. They'd been increasing over the last few months, and to me, that was a worry.

Being gay, those were the cases that hit home most, and Kyle, my work partner, knew how they affected me.

"How soon until we arrive?" he asked, driving at speed but keeping his eye on the road even though traffic was light.

"Five minutes, max. Good job the roads are clear. Rush hour would have been a nightmare." Kyle and I were paramedics, into the last hour of our shift.

I radioed control with our ETA and sat gazing out of the window as the city sped by.

"Hey, how was your lunch date yesterday? How was Edward?" Kyle smiled as he asked his question. He'd been trying to get me set up with someone for a while now, but it never worked.

"It was OK, but I'm not going to be seeing him again. He was nice and all, just not for me. No spark."

"No one does it for you these days. Not since you split up with what's his face, Henry. He was a prize prick, and you certainly could have done better. I don't know why you spent so much time with him." Kyle shook his head. He knew I'd loved Henry, but it had all fallen apart after several years together.

"Me either, now I think back." Henry was my ex and the man I'd thought I'd be marrying, but after qualifying as a paramedic, the shifts and my mood swings when I came home from work became more than he could take and eventually, we drifted apart. He found someone else, and I found a gym and a tattoo parlour.

I'd run into him about a year ago, and his face as he looked me up and down told me all I needed to know. We'd made the right decision to split up. It would never have worked.

Flashing lights brought me back to the here and now, and after pulling up behind the nearest police car, we grabbed our coats and kit and ran over to the prone figure lying on the floor. It was difficult to tell whether it was a man or a woman or if they were alive or dead.

All I could see was a mound of black clothes, and as the crowd parted to let us through, I could see it was a man. A badly beaten man. He appeared to be young, and it made me wonder how people could do this.

We strode towards the body, and the officers on the scene filled us in on what they knew so far. It wasn't much. He'd been thrown from a blue BMW, but the witness didn't get the plate number, and looking at the surroundings, I could see why. Boarded-up windows and doors, no doubt with squatters sitting behind them, not wanting to get involved.

We needed to work quickly. There was a pulse, albeit a weak one, and the shallow, noisy breathing suggested a punctured lung. We needed to get him off the floor, stabilise him and get him to the hospital as quickly as we could.

I strapped him to the stretcher, and we loaded him into the back of the ambulance, careful not to jostle him.

I climbed into the back and made him comfortable, checking his vitals as Kyle drove quickly and carefully to the Royal Liverpool Hospital. A couple of minutes into the journey, his eyelids fluttered, and a soft moan left his lips.

"Hey, you're OK." At my words, his eyes flew open, a panicked expression on his face. He reached up to claw at the oxygen mask over his face, but the strapping held him down, and he thrashed around, trying to release his arms.

"Calm down. Everything's going to be alright." He was going to do himself more damage at this rate. I needed him to stop and lie still.

"Lie still, please." My voice was firm, but it made him listen. I softened my tone. "You'll hurt yourself more if you don't." He looked over to me with his soft brown eyes, and I melted. There was such sorrow in their depths, and I wondered why he was here. Who'd done this to him and brought him so close to death?

"We'll be at the hospital soon and get you fixed up, good as new, as soon as you like. No one's going to hurt you now."

He finally lay still, and I continued with my assessment of his wounds. His nose was definitely broken, possible fractured jaw, a punctured lung maybe? There was blood coming from a couple of knife wounds on his torso, but he'd been so badly beaten, not one part was his normal colour. He was a mass of purple bruising. His knife wounds weren't deep enough to kill him but deep enough that he'd lost a fair bit of blood. His face was bruised and swollen, and I had no idea if he had any internal injuries. He'd taken a beating, one potentially meant to kill him, but somehow, he'd survived.

I hoped he'd pull through. It was never good to see someone this battered and bruised to find out the next day they hadn't made it.

I continued talking to him the whole time, knowing he couldn't reply, but my words seemed to soothe him, and that was what was important. We'd be arriving at the hospital soon, and I needed him to be as calm as possible.

Minutes later, we arrived, and the rear doors were thrown open; a flurry of doctors and nurses congregated outside waiting for him to be wheeled out. The noise and commotion must have been overwhelming, and before I knew it, he'd gripped my hand, refusing to let go.

I squeezed it, letting him know I wasn't going anywhere and walked by his side, reeling off the injuries I knew of to the doctors surrounding him.

We eventually reached a cubicle, and I went to release his hand, letting the doctors move in, but as I looked across, he gave a subtle shake of his head. Did he not want me to go?

"These doctors need to check you out, and I need to do some paperwork, but I can come back. Is that OK? I will come back." I looked at him and saw a terrified young man, but there was so much pain in those brown eyes, I felt bad for leaving him.

He grimaced as he nodded, and I couldn't imagine the pain he was feeling right now. He had so many injuries. I wanted to know who'd done this to him and why, but without any information, not even a name, it'd be hard.

He slowly released my hand, and I stepped away, glancing back at him as I stepped through the curtain.

I blew out a breath, looking across at Kyle as he did the same.

"Shit, I thought we were gonna lose him at one point. God knows what his insides look like. Did you see the cuts and bruises? He's got a pretty deep gash that'll need stitches. Looks like someone took a blunt knife to him."

I don't know why, but he meant something. I wasn't sure if it was because he was young or frightened or both, but I knew that I'd be following up on this one. I needed to know whether he'd come through it. I wondered about family, next of kin, but again, without a name, we were in the dark.

"Fancy a coffee?"

"Yeah, maybe something a bit stronger?" I looked at my watch. It was almost knocking off time for us, our shift ending in an hour. It'd take that long to complete what we needed to, but I knew I wouldn't be going home. Not yet anyway, not until I'd checked up on him, made sure he was going to make it.

Paperwork done, our shift over, Kyle went home and I went for a shower. I needed to get out of this uniform and wash the smell of blood from my skin. I would normally go home but not today.

I stood for longer than I needed to under the spray, my chin on my chest, watching the water drain away, every thought on him and what he must have endured to be in such a bad state. This wasn't a simple mugging. There had to be more to it than that.

A quick visit to A&E and I found out he'd been moved to ICU, so I made my way upstairs and over to the nurses' station.

"Hey, Marc. We don't usually see you up here. What can we do for you?" Joanne, the nurse in charge, smiled. We'd chatted a little on nights' out, and she was someone I trusted.

"Young guy, brought in a couple of hours ago. They said downstairs he'd gone for surgery. I wondered how he was doing?"

"He's still in surgery. With the x-rays done, they found a ruptured spleen, so that had to go. He'll be back on the ward soon. Do you know him?"

I shook my head. "No, I've never seen him before in my life." I scratched at the scruff on my face. Did I want to wait? I had nothing else to do, and I *had* told him I'd come back.

"Can I hang around for a while, if that's OK?"

"Of course, you can keep me company. It's quiet so far this morning." She poured me a coffee and handed it to me.

"So why the interest?" Her raised eyebrow asked more than her words, and I wasn't sure how to respond.

"It's not what you think." I stared into my coffee cup, finding it hard to put into words why I felt the way I did, but I tried.

"I suppose I just connected with him. When he came around in the back of the ambulance, he was petrified, eyes wide, grabbing for the mask, but we'd strapped him down. I managed to calm him, but when we arrived, he wouldn't let go of my hand."

I was reading far more into this, but Joanne was nodding.

"There's always one that grabs us, one we feel close to. This one's yours. It'll be a while before he comes around after the op. You sure you want to wait?"

"Yeah. I've nowhere else to be today, and I don't think I'd be able to sleep if I went home. Not until I know he's going to pull through anyway."

"I can't say either way," she said, matter-of-factly. "As you know, he had a lot of injuries. Why don't you go grab food from the canteen? He might be done by the time you come back."

I nodded. That sounded like a good idea, and now that I thought of it, I hadn't eaten since mid-shift. Kyle and I often stopped for food at the end of our shift, but today, it'd been the last thing on my mind.

"I'll be back in a while." I took the lift down to the canteen and sat with a plate of bacon and eggs, but I had no appetite. I chewed on a piece of cold toast and drank a lukewarm cup of tea. Canteen food was shit, and I remembered why we never ate here. I idly checked my phone and saw a text from Kyle.

How's the guy? Any news?

No news yet. In surgery, splenectomy. I'll let you know when I do.

There was no response from him, but I didn't expect it. I would normally have been asleep as he was now.

I checked the time. I'd been sitting here for over half an hour, and we'd left him in A&E over two hours ago. He could be out of surgery by now, but it'd be awhile before he came round, if at all.

After another fifteen minutes, I cleared my plate and headed back upstairs to see him wheeled into a room and hooked up to a myriad of machines.

I knew each and every one was necessary, but the sight of him looking so lifeless and pale hurt my heart. I waited while the nurses finished and cleared the room.

I looked over at Joanne, and she nodded.

I walked into the room, and as I got closer, his injuries became clearer. His face was a mess of bruises; black eyes, cuts and grazes, his hair matted with goodness knows what. His eyes were closed, but I couldn't help but remember how they'd looked at me, pleading and terrified.

I reached out to touch his hand; it was cold to the touch. I wanted to wrap it in mine, keep it warm, but I stepped back, the back of my knees bumping against the chair at the side of the bed.

I sat with a thump and leaned back, exhaustion suddenly taking hold. He was OK, for now, and the longer he managed to hold on, the better his chances.

A gentle shake was the next thing I knew, and I looked up into the eyes of Joanne.

"Hey, you should go home. It could be a while before he wakes, and your body won't thank you for sleeping in that chair."

"How long have I been here?"

"An hour or so, but I think it could be a while. Why don't you give me your number and I'll let you know as soon as he wakes?"

It would have to be, but she was right. I couldn't stay here indefinitely, and I desperately needed to sleep, preferably in my own bed. I wasn't at work until the following evening, so I had time to catch up on my missed sleep.

I stood from the chair and rolled my shoulders. That was not the most comfortable chair to sleep in, and my neck cracked.

"Fuck. I need my bed."

"I'll say you do. Phone. Now."

I unlocked it and handed it over, waiting while she sent her details to mine and vice versa.

"Now, go home, get some rest. I'll call you, and if I'm not here, one of the others will. Don't worry. We'll look after him."

I knew they would, and before I left, I looked over at him lying in the bed. There'd been no discernible change that I could see since I'd come in. I took a step closer, watching as his chest rose and fell. At least his breathing seemed a little easier. I could only hope that the trend would continue.

"Go on. Home with you." Joanne ushered me out of the room, and I fought the urge to look back at him. I didn't want it to be the last glimpse I had. I had to believe he'd be OK.

I walked out of the hospital in a daze, the glare of the sun blinding me momentarily. A car horn blared as I stepped into the road. Shit, I needed to get myself together, get some rest and hopefully, when I awoke, there'd be news. The best kind, though, I don't think I could cope with anything else.

CHAPTER TWENTY-TWO

ZIGGY

I woke to the sound of beeping and whirring. My head felt as if it was full of cotton wool, and my face hurt…a lot. I don't know what Damian and Stuart had done to me, but it hurt like hell.

Did I dare open my eyes? I wasn't sure I could, but I needed to see where I was. I groaned as I opened them, but thankfully the lights were dim. It was still an effort, and I could just about see.

"Hey, you're back in the land of the living! Welcome back. I'm Joanne. I'm going to check you over, make sure you're OK."

When she was done, she gently took my hand.

"Well, young man, looks like you were very lucky. It's mostly bruising to your face and body. Your jaw is badly bruised, and how you got away without it being broken or fractured, I don't know. You do have a broken nose, and depending on how we go, you might need someone to look at it.

"As for the rest of you, fractured ribs, a few nasty stab wounds which we've cleaned out and stitched, but the worst thing is we had to operate and remove your spleen."

Fuck! Could I live without a spleen? I must have looked shocked because her next words put my mind at rest.

"Don't worry. You can live without a spleen. A couple of adjustments to your daily routine, and you'll be fine. It's going to take a while to heal, but as long as everything goes to plan, you'll be here for a week or so and then you can go home. Try to sleep. You'll need it to help you recover. You were incredibly lucky."

I gave a small nod, amazed myself that I'd managed to get away with what I had. I'd felt sure that I was dying when I was lying in the street, and if it hadn't been for the paramedics, I knew I would have.

I remembered being naked in the house, beaten until I passed out. I don't remember the stabbings, don't remember being redressed, but they must have done that. I also couldn't be sure whether they'd done anything else to me. My arse wasn't sore, but I was so pumped full of painkillers, I probably wouldn't feel it anyway. As degrading as it might seem, I would have to ask them to do tests.

I knew I'd be getting tested as soon as I could. I wouldn't put it past those fuckers to pass something onto me.

Joanne smiled at me, and I sank further into my pillows, my eyes suddenly becoming heavy again.

"I'll leave you to it, but there's a button here if you need anything." She left it next to me on the bed and patted my hand, finally leaving the room.

I woke several times that evening; the excruciating pain I felt all over made it difficult to sleep. The anaesthetic had worn off, and if it hadn't hurt so much to do so, I'd have cried.

Lying awake, trying to think of what had gone wrong, how I'd ended up in this position, had my head aching. If only I hadn't been so desperate to find that special someone, putting my trust in that shit Damian only for him to have turned out to be the villain of the story.

Fuck my life! Would it ever get any better? Would I ever get a break? As I lay there, contemplating my bad decisions, a gentle knock on the door pulled me from my thoughts. I blinked as the light from the hallway stung my eyes.

"Hey, I bet you're about ready for some more pain relief, aren't you? That anaesthetic will be about wearing off now. It's almost one in the morning." The soft-spoken nurse entered the room, a small tray in her hands. "I'm going to pop this into your IV. Hopefully it'll help you sleep. I'm sure you've been told that rest is the best medicine."

I blinked lazily, feeling exhausted. If I could just rest, I'm sure it'd help, but right now, it eluded me.

"Marc called to make sure you were alright. We told him you were doing fine, but he said he'd come by to visit you tomorrow."

I frowned at her. Who the hell was Marc? I had no recollection of meeting anyone by that name, but the look on my face must have clued her in that I had no idea who she was talking about.

"Silly me. You don't know who I'm talking about, do you? You're a lucky man if you've caught his eye. All the nurses are always all over him. All those muscles and tattoos? But he never bothers with them. We reckon he's got a girl waiting for him at home. She's very lucky, that's all I can say.

"Anyway, Marc," she said, fluffing my pillows. "The paramedic that brought you in. He stopped by earlier, but you were out of it. You'd only just come up from surgery. He'll pop by tomorrow."

I had a vague recollection of a paramedic, but my memory was sketchy at best right now. I could hardly remember yesterday, let alone a ride in an ambulance, but as I lay there, waiting for the pain meds to work, a soothing voice came to mind and piercing blue eyes. I wouldn't forget those in a hurry, and if that was Marc?

Before I could finish my thought, my eyes started to close as the medication took effect. Blue eyes swam in my mind, and a swirl of tattoos filled my thoughts until I fell into a dreamless sleep.

The next time I woke, I was alone, and it was dark. I had no clue what time it was nor where I was. Was I back in Crosby? I didn't think so, but in my drug-induced haze, I couldn't place my surroundings. What if Damian or worse, Stuart, would come back for me? What if they were going to finish the job?

My pulse raced, and I couldn't catch my breath. My fingers and arms were numb, and the panic rose. Shit, I needed to get out of here. I knew they'd kill me this time. I needed to leave.

I struggled with the mask and tubes attached, ripping them out of the back of my hand. Blood spurted everywhere, but the urge to escape was too much. I threw the covers back, the hospital gown I wore tangled around my legs as I got out of the bed. I fell in a heap on the floor as pain shot through my body. Jesus, I could hardly move, but the thought of them coming back spurred me on.

I crawled towards the door but the pain! Fuck! My head spun, my eyes blurring. I felt sick, and bile burned my throat as the urge to throw up became too much. I threw up on the floor, my hands slipping in my own vomit as I tried to get to the door.

They went from beneath me, and I fell forward, my forehead hitting the floor with a resounding thud. I tried to move away as the sound of footsteps came nearer. I couldn't escape through the door. Maybe if I hid under the bed, they wouldn't find me. I could be safe there.

Before I could get any further, hands grabbed my arms, and I turned onto my back, kicking out with my feet. I didn't care about the pain now. I couldn't let them hurt me again. They'd kill me this time, I was sure of it. I tried to scream, but the sound wouldn't come, my throat dry and hoarse.

"Hey," I heard someone call, but it made me panic even more. "Come on, calm down. You're safe." I put my hands over my ears as I tried to block out the sound, but it wouldn't stop. I thrashed around, flinging my arms in hopes of getting them away from me. I felt a sharp scratch. It all went black.

CHAPTER TWENTY-THREE

MARC

I didn't know why I was doing this, going to visit someone I didn't know. I had no name, just a slim connection to someone who might not even want to know me. I was a big guy, could be intimidating at the best of times, and I wouldn't be surprised if I terrified him.

"Marc. We didn't expect you back so early. Couldn't keep away, I see." Joanne smiled, a smug expression on her face.

I shook my head and laughed. "I want to see how he is, that's all. Nothing more."

She nodded, clearly not believing a word I'd said.

"Well, we thought we'd lost him again last night. I don't know what happened, but we found him out of bed, bleeding from his wounds and where he'd ripped his drip out."

"Jesus, Joanne. Is he OK? Will he be alright?"

"He'll be fine, but we sedated him for his own good. We can't have that happening again. If we hadn't got to him last night when we did, he could have seriously hurt himself again."

"Can I go in? I want to see if he's OK."

"You can, but like I said, he might still be out of it."

Out of it or not, I needed to see for myself that he was alright.

I stepped into the dimly lit room and heard the machines quietly doing their work. I thought he was asleep, but he slowly opened his eyes, glancing over at me. His eyes widened momentarily, but as I got nearer, he seemed to relax a little.

"Hey, it's me. The paramedic that treated you earlier. Remember?" I spoke as quietly as I could, not wanting to scare him, and I stepped closer. "I'm Marc."

Was that a nod? I couldn't be sure, but he appeared calm enough as I moved to stand at the bottom of the bed, checking his chart. I was no expert, but things did seem to be improving. His oxygen levels and vitals were looking much better than when we'd brought him in.

The bruising was still bad, but I knew it'd be a couple of weeks before that faded.

"Well, you're doing better than the last time I saw you. You were in a bit of a mess. Can you talk? Can you tell me your name?"

He slowly moved his hand to his face, and I realised he wanted the mask off. I moved his hand away and removed it as gently as I could, aware of his broken nose.

God, he looked awful. His face was swollen, and his bruises were dark purple, making the skin I could see deathly pale.

He tried to speak, but I couldn't hear what he said. I moved closer, placing my ear on his lips. His warm breath feathered across my skin as I strained to hear. I heard something, but his voice was so raspy, it was hard to understand.

"I'm sorry. I didn't get that. What was it again?"

A small sigh escaped his mouth, and he tried again.

"Ziggy. I'm Ziggy," he croaked.

Ziggy, an unusual name for an unusual man.

I placed the mask over his face and turned to look into his eyes. He looked exhausted, but a hint of gold circled the soft brown of his iris, and I lost myself in their depths. I stuttered before speaking again, unsure why he had such an effect on me.

Ziggy. We had a name, something to go on at least. I'd need to let Joanne know, but that could wait for a moment.

"We'll find who did this to you, you know. The police won't let this go." His eyes widened at this, and I heard his breath quicken. Did he think it'd just be ignored? That the police wouldn't get involved? "You were almost killed, Ziggy, and that won't be taken lightly."

He closed his eyes and turned his head. I guessed the conversation was over for the moment. Choosing this time to go speak to Joanne, I started to leave but was surprised when he gripped my wrist.

"I'll be back. I promise. I said I would last time, didn't I? I won't be long."

I made my way to the nurse's station and leaned there, looking for Joanne.

"His name's Ziggy," I told her as she approached.

"Well, it's more than we knew before, but I'll need to let the police know. They've been here asking if he's come round yet. They wanted to question him, but I told them not yet. You know he'd been restrained, don't you?"

"Yeah, I heard." I turned back towards the door, the draw of this man pulling me back into his room. "I might stay a bit longer, if that's OK. I'll get out of the way if you need me to."

"Stay as long as you want, but we will be in to check on him."

Ziggy was sleeping when I walked back into his room, but I'd promised to stay and I had hours to kill before visiting Ma, so I sat back in the chair I'd occupied before and waited to see if he woke again.

I stayed with him for the next few hours, dozing myself or reading on my phone, but he didn't wake again. I needed to go, though. Ma was expecting me.

Rising quietly from the chair, I approached the bed, taking

care not to make a sound. He needed his rest to heal, and as I gazed down on his damaged body, I realised I needed to know his story.

I carefully swept the hair from his face, avoiding the cuts and bruises. What I wouldn't give to see his face without them, but I knew that as soon as he left here, I'd never see him again.

Leaving the ward, I said goodbye to Joanne, telling her I wouldn't be back for a couple of days but to let me know how Ziggy got on.

"No problem, Marc. I don't know why but he seems important to you. You look exhausted. You'd best get some rest if you're on shift tomorrow."

As I left the hospital, Ziggy refused to leave my mind. There was something there, something not right about the whole thing. He didn't seem like a typical gang member, but that meant nothing in the grand scheme of things.

Battling my way through the rush hour traffic, I made it to Ma's house around six thirty, just as she was dishing up the dinner.

"Where've you been, son? You're never normally this late when it comes to shepherd's pie. Come give me a kiss."

I leaned down and kissed her cheek. She was a small lady, barely five feet tall. My dad hadn't been much taller at five feet nine, so where my six feet three height had come from, I didn't know. Ryan and Cheryl, my younger brother and older sister, were smaller than me. Ma used to joke that I was the milkman's. Dad always laughed it off because I was the image of him, just a taller version. But we'd lost Dad over a year ago, so I spent time here, keeping her company.

The local news was on the TV as I stepped into the front room. A reporter standing where we'd been the previous day, telling everyone about Ziggy and how he'd been thrown from a car, presumed dead.

"Marc, stop watching the feckin' TV and come get your dinner before it gets cold," Ma shouted from the kitchen.

I waved my hand at her, shushing her. I needed to watch this, see if there was any more news, but I knew all the reporter had to say. The police were asking for witnesses to the crime, the victim's identity was unknown and he was currently in a serious condition in the Royal.

His identity was known now, and no doubt someone would come forward to say they knew him, but until then, I'd visit, make sure he was OK.

As we sat around the table, the four of us, Ma dished up the food and we waited until she sat before tucking in.

"Great scran, Ma. Love it when our Marc comes round; you always serve up the good stuff."

"Ah, you get a bloody good meal every night, Ryan, and don't you forget it." She batted him around the ear as he tucked into his food.

Ryan and Ma's banter at the table continued throughout the meal, but I heard none of it, my thoughts still on Ziggy and where'd he come from.

"Marc, Marc. Are you listening to me?"

I looked over at Ma, not realising she'd been talking.

"Sorry, I was miles away."

"I could see that. What's got you all maudlin? You're usually arguing with your brother but tonight, nothing."

As I looked around the table, I saw that Ryan and Cheryl were doing the dishes in the kitchen. I really hadn't been paying attention.

"Just someone at work. I don't know why I can't stop thinking about him."

"Who's got my boy so wound up he can't even finish his favourite dinner?"

I looked down at my plate, my food half-eaten and I

continued to push it around as I contemplated how to explain it to her.

"Did you see the local news? The body dump yesterday." She nodded and I continued. "Kyle and I picked him up, a young man, can't be more than twenty-one, maybe even younger." I paused again. Every time I tried to talk about it, the hold he had over me was difficult to put into words.

"He'd been badly beaten, and when we dropped him off at the hospital, he refused to let go of my hand. Had me walk in with him until the docs took over. I went to see him earlier. The nurses have been keeping me up to date with his condition.

"He has a story, one that involves a horrific beating, and I don't get how anyone can do that to another person. It got to me, and now I want to know why."

"That's not your job to do, son." She reached across the table and held my hand.

"I know that, but…I don't know; I feel like I need to know."

"You've such a big heart, just like your Dad, Marc, but don't let this tear you apart. He's likely got a family, boyfriend, girlfriend, and I know what you're like. You'll get too involved. Look what happened with that Henry." She spat his name out as she spoke. Ma had never liked him, always thought he was taking advantage and looking back, he probably was.

"It's not like that. I'd like to follow this one up, that's all. Nothing more." She nodded, a knowing look on her face. She knew exactly what I was like, I wouldn't let this go until I knew the full story.

"I know, son, I know. Just don't get too involved with this one. OK?" I patted her hand and stood, taking my plate to the kitchen to clean up. I needed to go soon. I had a shift the following evening and seriously needed to sleep.

I laughed and joked with Ryan and Cheryl as we cleaned up the kitchen, but as I pulled on my coat, ready to leave, Ma came over for her customary hug.

"Take care, son. Remember what I said, and don't forget I love you."

I kissed the top of her head and turned to leave, her words sounding in my head, but it was too late. I was already too involved.

CHAPTER TWENTY-FOUR

ZIGGY

For the next few days, I did nothing but sleep, the pain and exhaustion gradually getting better the longer I stayed in the hospital. I had no more visitors. Marc obviously thought I wasn't worth a visit, and I could understand that. He didn't know me, but it irked me a little. He'd said he'd come back, and he hadn't.

I remembered giving him my name, and now all the nurses had started to use it, making me feel a little less worthless. Being nameless was a horrible feeling, not being seen for who I really was. It made me feel a little better anyway. Joanne said if I continued to improve, I could go home. What a fucking joke that was. I had nowhere to go. I could hardly go back to stay with Damian, and there was no one else. I didn't think Suzie or Duke would be happy having me hang around.

And that reminded me. I should try and contact them, let them know where I was or at least that I was still alive. I had nothing, though, just the clothes I'd been wearing, and they'd no doubt been thrown away. What the hell was I going to do when it was time for me to leave? No phone, no money and no clothes.

At least I had a TV to watch in my room, but days of mindless

TV programmes were starting to get on my nerves. It wasn't like they had a streaming service or cable, so the main five channels were all they had to watch. Australian soap operas were becoming my best friend, and even a locally set soap was beginning to look interesting.

I was about to settle down to my early evening fix when the door opened and in stepped Marc. Well, this was a surprise and not an unwelcome one. He was out of his paramedic uniform, wearing blue jeans, that hugged muscular thighs, and a soft grey T-shirt. He had an impressive set of muscles. He definitely hit the gym, and the colourful tattoos covering both arms, images of flowers, dragons and wolves, were a work of art. I swear if my jaw hadn't been so sore, it'd have dropped open.

"Hi, Ziggy. Remember me?" he asked in that soft voice of his.

How could I forget him? As his blue eyes found mine, his long lashes swept his cheeks as he blinked. Having eyelashes like that on a man was absolutely criminal. I envied him and remembered Suzie trying to put false ones on me after a few glasses of wine. The result had looked like a caterpillar crawling over my face. Not our best work, that was for sure.

I nodded, momentarily lost for words. He was hot, ridiculously good-looking. Dirty blond hair, shorn at the sides, longer on top, an eyebrow piercing with a small hoop, yesterday's scruff still on his chiseled face. He was tall too, easily topping six feet.

I'd got better at talking the last few days. My voice was still croaky, no doubt from when Damian had tried to strangle me. One of the nurses had commented on the bruising on my neck, telling me I should speak to the police, but I'd shaken my head. I wasn't ready to do that, not yet anyway. I was terrified if I was honest. I knew they could still come for me, but I wasn't ready to report it.

"I'm sorry I've not been around for a couple of days, but I had a few shifts to work. The girls have been keeping me updated.

You're doing well, or better anyway, and your face looks a hundred times better than it did."

I knew it didn't. I'd seen myself in the bathroom mirror when I'd taken a piss and it told no lies. I looked a fucking mess, black and blue all over, especially my face. I hoped the cuts wouldn't scar too much when they eventually healed. After Damian told me he loved my beautiful face, he'd had no problem beating it to a pulp. Bastard!

"I can leave if you want me to. I don't want to be an imposition." Jesus, this guy could never be that.

"No," I squeaked, then coughed, my throat hurting, but I tried to at least sound a little more manly. "Please sit, stay for a while."

He did as I asked, leaning forward with his elbows on his knees, looking anywhere but at me. He seemed a little nervous, so I tried to put his mind at ease.

"I never did say thank you, you know, for saving my life and all. You and your colleague."

"It's what we do." He looked embarrassed, but he shouldn't be. They'd both done an amazing job.

"I know but thank you anyway. I remember thinking I was going to die out there, in the street. So yeah, saving me was a pretty big deal for me."

Marc blushed, the tips of his ears turning pink. Had no one ever thanked him before? I couldn't thank him enough, but I didn't want to embarrass him any further.

The TV played quietly in the background, but we sat in silence. I guess neither of us knew what to say.

"So..."

"Have you..."

We both laughed, his a deep rumble in his chest, mine not so much, more like a squeak.

"No, you go first." We both spoke together again, eliciting another chuckle from him.

He gestured to me. "Please, Ziggy. You go first."

I was only going to make idle talk, but I spoke anyway.

"Have you been busy? On shift? Just haven't seen you around." My voice faded at the end, not having been used for some time, and I coughed again. Pain wracked my body, and I inhaled sharply. Fuck, that hurt.

"Here, let me get you some water." He poured water into a glass, leaning me forward so I could drink from the straw easier.

His heavenly smell surrounded me, and I wasn't sure if it was the cologne he wore or just the scent of him, but it was intoxicating. A heady mix of musk and him. I groaned, but Marc took that as a sign I was still hurting.

"Shall I get a nurse? Doctor? Shall I check you over, make sure you're OK?"

God, no. Him checking me over was the worst thing that could happen, and I shook my head as he moved the cup away.

"I'm good. Honestly, the water was just delicious."

"Really?" He took a sip from the cup and made an appreciative noise. "Not bad. Not bad at all." Was he teasing? He looked down at me, a twinkle in those startling eyes, and I knew that he was.

He was about to sit when there was a knock on the door.

"Ziggy, you have a visitor." In walked Joanne with my worst nightmare behind her. Damian!

Oh, my fucking God! How had he found me, and what the fuck was he doing here? My heart started to pound, and the terror I'd felt nights before threatened to resurface. I swallowed hard and was sure everyone in the room had heard me.

"Ziggy, baby. We thought you were dead." He rushed to my side and grabbed my hand. Too right he did. Him and his fucking crazy brother had beaten me to within an inch of my life, then in he waltzes, bold as brass as if nothing had happened.

I saw Marc bristle out of the corner of my eye, and if I could have run from the room again, I would have done. He moved closer to the bed and took a defensive stance with his hand on the bed next to mine.

Damian looked over at him, a sneer on his face.

"Who are you, and why are you standing next to my boyfriend?" Jesus, he was going with that line.

Marc drew himself up to his full height and answered him in that sexy voice of his.

"I'm Marc Hutton, the paramedic that brought him in." He stuck his hand out to Damian, but he ignored it.

"Well, I don't appreciate you standing that close to him. I suggest you move. Better still, why don't you leave? Don't bother coming back. I'll take care of him now."

"Gentlemen," interrupted Joanne, "if you could take this outside. I don't want Ziggy distressed in any way. It's not good for him."

"*He* was just leaving." Damian pointed at Marc as he spoke. I hoped he didn't, but Marc moved towards the door.

"I'll go, Joanne, don't worry, but I'll be outside if you need me."

She nodded at him and turned to me.

"Are you OK with your boyfriend staying, or do you want him to leave too?"

What did I want? I know I didn't want Damian here; that was a given.

Damian reached over and took off my oxygen mask. "Tell them you want me to stay, beautiful. We've so much to talk about, you and me."

The meaning behind his words was clear, and my eyes widened as he turned his onyx eyes on me.

I managed to croak out a 'yes'.

"Good boy, you always did know what was good for you." Damian turned to Joanne, "Could you leave us alone, please? I promise I'll behave."

She nodded and walked out of the door, closing it gently behind her.

Instead of replacing the mask, he moved it down so it was over my chin and squeezed my cheeks hard. The pain was excruciating, compounding the damage he and Stuart had already done. I winced, tears springing to my eyes.

"One fucking word from you, one word to anyone. I'm warning you. God knows Stuart's annoyed enough that we didn't finish the fucking job when we had the chance. You send the police our way, and you won't even live to regret it. Do you understand, *beautiful*?"

The emphasis he put on the last word left me in no doubt both he and Stuart would carry through on that threat. I nodded, certain I was about to piss myself. If I'd been scared for my life before, I was terrified now.

"And as for lover boy, you couldn't wait to move on. What's it been? Four days and you already have a big cock to suck. You're a whore, Ziggy, a dirty fucking whore."

The door opening made him jump back but not before Marc saw Damian move his hand from my face.

"What's going on? Are you OK, Ziggy?" He turned to Damian, a fierce look on his face. "I suggest you leave before I call security. Oh, and don't think you'll be allowed in here again. You lay one more finger on him, and so help me, God." He didn't need to finish that sentence to get his point across.

"And you'll do what? You've no proof of anything, and as for this little cocksucker?" He flipped the mask back over my mouth, took my hand and brought it to his mouth, noisily kissing the palm. "He's got a good arse for fucking, but that's about it."

He dropped my hand back to the bed and turned to leave the room.

"Don't forget what I said now, beautiful. You wouldn't want to get that pretty face damaged again, would you?"

He left the room and I swear, we both breathed a sigh of relief. Why had Marc come back into the room, though?

He reached down the side of the bed and pulled out his phone.

"I left it in here, but I'm thinking now I came back at the right time. It was him, wasn't it? He was the one that did this to you. You have to tell the police, Ziggy."

I shook my head, Damian's threat still at the forefront of my mind. I couldn't now even if I'd wanted to. They wouldn't make the same mistake next time. Next time, they'd kill me.

CHAPTER TWENTY-FIVE

ZIGGY

I turned my face away from Marc, not wanting to see the disgust I knew would be there. My tears slowly fell, and I hadn't realised how Damian's words had hurt me nor how I hated that Marc had heard them too.

I genuinely feared for my life, and there was no way now I could go to the police, no matter what Marc said to me.

"Ziggy, look at me." I shook my head. I wanted him to leave. "I'm not going anywhere. I want you to look at me."

Reluctantly, I turned my head but kept my eyes closed.

"Damn it, Ziggy. I need to talk with you, and I can't do that if you won't even look at me."

I knew as soon as I opened my eyes he'd see the shame in them. I wasn't ashamed of being a whore or a cocksucker, as Damian had so eloquently put it, but to have it broadcast for all to hear… Yeah, I didn't like that.

"I don't care what you did before, Ziggy. What your so-called boyfriend said has no bearing on how I see you. I still want to get to know you, want to help you, and the first thing we need to do is report that bastard for what he did to you."

No, no, no. I wouldn't do that, couldn't do that if I valued my life. I had no doubt they would come after me.

"I heard part of what he said to you, and I can help you. I want to help you."

As much as this was going to hurt, I had to speak, had to tell him no.

I removed the mask from my face. Damn thing, I don't even think I needed it anymore.

"No police. They'll kill me next time."

"There won't be a next time if you go to the police or better still, let me look after you. I can keep you safe from them."

That wasn't what this was about, though. This was about my survival, me living to the ripe old age of twenty-one, which was looking less and less likely.

"What if they do this to someone else, Ziggy? What if they've already done it? Don't they deserve justice too, the same as you do? You can't let this go."

My thoughts went to Liam and what Stuart had said about him. He was such a small, young boy. I know he was eighteen, but he'd never looked his age and what if they'd done the same to him? He wasn't big like me, and it was then it hit me. He could be dead. They might have killed him. From what they'd said to me, they were no strangers to this type of violence, and they had hinted at having killed before. There was no doubt in my mind I shouldn't have survived that beating, I should have died that night.

Maybe Marc was right. Perhaps I should talk to the police.

"Think. I need to think," I croaked. "Give me a day, please."

"OK. That's something at least, but this has to be reported, Ziggy. I know deep down you know this."

He was right. I knew it was the right thing to do but not today. I was too shaken up by Damian's visit.

"Not today. Tomorrow." I slumped back into my pillows, stressed to fuck, and all I wanted to do was sleep, but what if he came back? I know Marc had said he couldn't, but there was nothing to stop him creeping right back in and finishing the job he'd started.

Before I could say anything, Marc spoke.

"Would you like me to stay a while? You look a little shaken."

Shaken was an understatement, but I nodded. I would like him to stay.

He sat back in the chair, but the silence was deafening and my mind continued to work overtime, overthinking every little word Damian had said.

"Tell me about you." I'm not sure why I said it, but I figured his speaking would help.

"What do you want to know? There's not much to tell."

"Anything? Everything? Just talk to me, please." I pleaded.

He leaned forward and patted my hand. I almost flinched away but remembered at the last moment that this wasn't Damian, this was Marc and he wouldn't hurt me. Well, I hoped he wouldn't, that wasn't the impression I got from him.

I know my record with men had been pretty shitty of late, but there was just something about him I couldn't put my finger on but not in a bad way. With Damian, there'd been that period of uncertainty when I hadn't known if I could trust him. Stuart I'd despised from the start and with fucking good reason it seemed, but this man… I had to follow my gut, and it said I should at least give him a chance.

"Where to start." He finally sat back in the chair, his hands on his stomach, his legs stretched out, ankles crossed.

"I'm twenty-nine, a paramedic and live at home with a skinny ginger cat called Smeagol." He held his hands up to me, palms out. "Before we go any further, I should let you know I'm a huge nerd. I love anything *Lord of the Rings*. I know I don't look like I should but hey, stereotypes. I'm not a muscle head, regardless of how I look."

I hadn't thought that for a minute, drawn in by his voice. It wrapped around me like a warm hug, and I realised how I'd relaxed as he'd started talking, the previous half an hour almost forgotten.

"Me too, Suzie and I used to watch them all the time, although I do prefer *The Hobbit*."

"We can debate that at a later date." He winked, and this time it was my turn to blush, heat rising to my cheeks.

"I've been a paramedic for about six or seven years now, I think? I love my job, but sometimes it's tough. Cases like yours hit home, and unlike you, some of them don't make it."

A faraway look on his face made me think he'd seen his fair share of death, and I knew there and then that he was nothing like Damian. *He* relished the thought of hurting people, killing them even, but I didn't think Marc was anything like that. His startling blue eyes portrayed far too much emotion.

He seemed to shake himself out of it and carried on.

"I have a younger brother, Ryan, who's a complete pain in the arse most of the time, but I wouldn't have him any other way, and an older sister, Cheryl. She lives with her boyfriend, and Ryan lives at home with Ma. Keeps her company after my dad died last year.

"I don't think there's much to tell other than that. I'm a simple guy with simple needs. I'm either working or sleeping. Not much time for anything else."

I was desperate to ask if he had a girlfriend, but I got the distinct impression that they weren't his type. After years of being with men, I knew the signs, and something told me I was in with more of a chance than the nurses that fawned over him. I secretly hoped that was the case.

I'd heard them talk about the hot paramedic with the bright blue eyes and knew now it was him they had been talking about.

"What about a girlfriend? You don't have time for one of those?"

"You've been listening to the gossip," he said with a smirk. "I know they talk about me up here. They had a sweep going at one point as to who I'd bring on the Christmas night out. But no. No girlfriend but more to the point, no boyfriend."

Ah, my question was answered and as I'd thought. A little part of me was happy about that, but where usually I'd be all over a good-looking gay man, recent events had put me off them. I hoped not for life, but the way I was feeling at the moment, it'd be awhile before I would put enough trust in any man, regardless of who they were.

I didn't want him to go home but knew that time was getting on. It was dark outside now, and visiting time would be over soon.

"I suppose you have to go now, as much as I'd like to hear more about you."

He looked at his watch and stood. "Yes, I have to go. Work tomorrow evening, but I would like to come back before I start my shift. We do need to talk about the police, Ziggy. I know you don't want to."

He was dead right I didn't want to. I didn't care about me. I'd survived, barely, and knew that if I said nothing, they wouldn't bother me again. Then I thought about Liam and what they'd done to him.

Was he OK? Was he lying in a hospital bed somewhere? Had they killed him? The insinuation had been there for sure.

"I want to help you, Ziggy, and if you want me to, I'll be here when you talk to the police."

"Thank you, I think I'd like that, but let me sleep on it. OK?"

"OK, your decision. I'll see you tomorrow." He turned to leave, and I watched him as he walked out of the door.

Old Ziggy would have appreciated his tight arse in his well-fitting jeans, but new Ziggy wondered what his motive was. Why was he being so nice?

I supposed only time would tell, and it was up to me if I gave him that time.

CHAPTER TWENTY-SIX

MARC

I'd calmed down by the time I left Ziggy's room that evening but earlier on? I'd been prepared to commit murder. I wasn't normally a violent person but walking in on Damian hurting Ziggy, I'd been close to losing it.

What was it they said? Not on my watch? I was more determined than ever now to help him. Help him put that bastard behind bars where he belonged. He'd almost killed him and to walk back in to see him, as brazen as you like, that either took balls or you were stupid as fuck. I was going with the latter. Only a dumb fuck would revisit his victim.

I needed to make Ziggy see that speaking to the police was the best thing to do. When I'd mentioned to him about them having done it before, I'd seen something in his eyes. If I was going to persuade him to report him, I had to push that angle.

My next shift was tomorrow evening, so feeding the cat and sleeping were my main priority now.

As I walked through my front door, Smeagol ran towards me, meowing like crazy. Guess someone was hungry. I stooped to pick him up, nuzzling into his neck as his purrs rumbled in his chest.

"I know, I'm late. Sorry, Precious. I'll get your food for you now." I set him down in the kitchen and refilled his food and water, watching as he greedily scoffed it down.

"Daddy neglected poor Smeagol today, but I'll try not to let it happen again." He was usually pretty good when I was out, and for a cat, he was very affectionate, showing me that he'd missed me when I came home from work.

Spending the afternoon with Ziggy, I'd not had time to eat and was undecided what to have. I looked in the fridge, picking up a soft pepper and limp spring onions. Not much to do with that. Guess it was a takeaway again for me. Sometimes I missed living at home, missed Ma's cooking, but then there were nights like this when I just wanted to be on my own to think.

Ziggy was doing well, considering. His wounds were healing nicely. Most would scar, but before long, he'd be discharged. It got me thinking as to where he'd stay when he was released. It was a question I needed to ask him tomorrow. He could always come and stay here, but I wasn't sure if he was mentally ready to do that.

When I'd touched his hand today, he'd thought he'd masked the flinch well, but I'd seen it. If everything that had happened to him was because of that dickhead, it'd take a while to gain his trust.

I supposed he could stay with Ma if he had nowhere else. She had a spare room, my old room actually. There was only her and Ryan at home now, so it was definitely a possibility.

After ordering and eating grilled chicken from a local restaurant, I decided to call it a night. It was getting on for 10 p.m., and I needed to sleep if I was going to be up most of the day tomorrow.

I thought sleep would be hard to come by, but I succumbed as soon as my head hit the pillow. I dreamt, though. Nightmares where Damian killed Ziggy over and over, but I was always too late to stop it. Every damn time, Damian would turn to me, a cruel look on his face, a bloody knife in his hands.

I woke up with a start in a cold sweat. It wasn't often I dreamed of my patients, but it'd happened in the past. I'd never felt so connected to one before as I did with Ziggy.

It was still early, but there'd be no going back to sleep now and the only thing that settled me when I was like this was a visit to the gym. A good workout and a swim were just what I needed.

I arrived at six, as the doors opened. I waved at Paul, the resident PT, and saw his eyes light up. I'd been out on a couple of dates with him, but again, there'd been no spark. Letting him down gently had proved to be difficult, to say the least. His insistence we were a perfect match every time I visited had made me consider changing gyms at least once.

I put my earbuds in, cranking the volume up as loud as I dared and got to working out. I hit the weights and the treadmill and was changing for my customary swim when he walked in.

"Hey, Marc. Haven't seen you for a while. Anyone would think you'd been avoiding me." He bit his lip in what I suspected he thought was a seductive move, but honestly, I just wanted to get out of here alive. He had a reputation, I'd since found out after our few dates, and I was glad I hadn't taken it further.

"Busy, Paul. You know how it is."

I picked up my towel and tried to squeeze past him to get to the pool entrance. As an avid swimmer, I preferred to wear swim trunks not shorts, so I wasn't surprised when Paul glanced down, clearly eyeing up the goods. I wasn't a small man at six feet three, and my dick was definitely in proportion. I wasn't huge, but no one had complained before.

I swear to God he was about to touch me when the door clattered open and a couple of men walked into the changing area, oblivious to what was going on.

"See you around." I made a quick getaway, thanking all and

sundry that the guys had made an appearance. I wasn't in the mood for Paul's advances now or any day.

By the time I'd finished my after-swim shower and had changed, it was almost eight thirty. Too early to visit Ziggy but not too early for a good breakfast and tea. I knew where to go for it and made my way to my old family home. If I could talk to Ma before going to see him, I could have options for him if he didn't have anywhere to go.

"How's my Marc today? You look tired. Have you been sleeping?"

"Hi, Ma. I'm fine. I was up early to go to the gym."

Her look told me she didn't believe me. I should have known better. She always knew when something wasn't right. Like when Henry and I split up, she'd known by the look on my face that it'd all gone wrong.

"Breakfast and tea? I've got some of those sausages you like, and you need to keep your strength up."

"I'll get the tea while you cook." I busied myself making a pot and sat at the table with a steaming hot cup, putting Ma's opposite me. I knew Ryan would already be at work, so it was just the two of us.

"Now you can tell me what's wrong. Is it that boy again? The one you picked up?"

I nodded. "Yep, there's more to his story, Ma, and I want to help him."

She served up breakfast and joined me at the table.

"Tell me."

Just two words and I knew she was as invested as I was. I went on to tell her all about Ziggy. Well, what I knew anyway and all about Damian and the way he'd treated him, Ziggy's admission that it'd been him that had beaten him up.

"The problem is, when he leaves the hospital, I'm not sure he has anywhere to go. What if he'd been living with him? I could be wrong. He might not have been there with him, but if he was and doesn't have anywhere to go…"

"You want him to come stay here." She finished my sentence for me, and I was grateful she could see where I was going with this.

"Only if it wouldn't be too much trouble. I don't want to put you out. He could have my old room; he wouldn't need to bunk in with Ryan."

She reached across the table to stroke my face. "Of course he can stay. If he needs a home, he has one here."

"Thanks. What would I do without you? He might be OK and have somewhere to go, but at least I have an alternative for him when I see him later."

We finished breakfast, chatting about this and that, what she'd been getting up to at her choir meetings and about a cruise she'd been thinking about taking. It was good to see her getting out. She'd spent so much time wallowing in grief after Dad died. Getting back out there and socialising was bringing her back to us.

I knew that bringing Ziggy here would be good for them both. I just needed him to agree to it.

After helping clear up and saying goodbye, I reckoned I'd be allowed in to see Ziggy, especially if I mentioned talking to him about getting the police involved.

I wasn't wrong, and after arriving, I went straight in. He'd had his breakfast and had been napping on and off.

I knocked gently and walked in but couldn't see Ziggy anywhere. The door to the bathroom was open, and I heard the toilet flush. He must be feeling better to be up and on his feet. I walked further into the room, glancing through the door as I went, intending to help him back to his bed.

What I saw, though, through the gap in his gown, was his beautiful back, marred by bruises, and the curve of his arse as he bent over the sink to wash his hands. My cock took notice of course, and grey sweats weren't the best things to be wearing when that happened. I should have looked away, but the sight of that perfectly formed body had me in a trance.

At the last moment, I turned away, willing my dick to soften before I had to face him, but the image of him writhing beneath me, his arse being pounded, was not helping at all.

"Oh, hi. You're here early. I didn't hear you come in."

Fuck! What was I going to do? I couldn't let him see me like this. I had a raging hard-on for the guy.

"Could you help me into bed? I usually call for a nurse, but since you're here."

"Yep, coming now." I would be too now, knowing I had to get up close and personal with him to help him into his bed, but then another unbidden picture appeared in my mind. The one where Damian held him by the face, and instantly, I was ready to face him.

I turned and was once again faced with Ziggy's bruised face.

"Let's get you into bed, and then we'll talk about speaking to the police."

CHAPTER TWENTY-SEVEN

ZIGGY

I'd spent the majority of last night going over what Marc had said to me about speaking to the police and also what Damian had said to me.

I was torn. On the one hand, I valued my life. I was under no illusion that both Damian and Stuart would have no qualms in finishing me off, but on the other hand… My thoughts went to Liam and what they'd said to me about him. I hoped he was OK.

I was also desperate to be out of here, but therein lay the question of where I'd go. All I saw right now were problems and no solutions, and I had an overwhelming urge to curl up in a ball and try to forget it all.

After Marc had come in and helped me into bed, he sat in his usual chair.

"How's the patient today? Feeling better?" His wink sent all kinds of feelings coursing through my body. You'd think after everything I'd been through no man could ever do that to me again, but this guy, with his caring nature and easy-going smiles was slowly breaking my resolve to never get involved again.

I smiled, lowering my gaze so he didn't see the blush colouring my cheeks. "I'm feeling better, thank you. The doctor said something about me getting out of here soon. Just need to make sure I'm healing OK."

"That's great news, Ziggy, and actually, something I wanted to talk to you about." He leaned forward, his face turning serious, and I knew what he was about to say.

"But first..."

"I don't know." I cut him off before he could ask. "I just don't know." I finished with a sigh.

"If I go to the police, he told me I wouldn't live to regret it. I'm fucking twenty, Marc. I want a life, I want to live, and I don't know if I can take the risk."

Marc's jaw tightened, and I knew he wasn't happy with my response. He stood, walking over to the window, his back to me, his back muscles tensing beneath his shirt.

"I can help you, in more ways than one. Let me tell you my idea, and then you can think about it some more." He turned to face me, and the sunlight filtered through his blond hair, giving him an almost ethereal glow.

"Do you have somewhere to go when you leave here?" I shook my head, unsure where he was going with this. I wasn't sure I was up to moving in with another guy. That was going to be a hard pass.

"Don't worry, I'm not asking you to move in with me, but I may have a solution for you." He moved closer to the bed and perched on the end of it, and I wondered if he'd read my mind. "My ma has a spare room and would be happy for you to move there until you can find something permanent. Only if you want to. There's no obligation at all.

"If you did decide to go to the police and report the assault, you'd be safe there. Ma's a little lonely these days, now Dad's gone. She has Ryan, but he's out a lot of the time, so it'd be company for her too. You don't have to decide now. Give it some thought."

I mulled over what he'd said. That could work. I didn't have anywhere else to go, and the thought of living rough or in a hostel was not appealing in the slightest. Maybe this was the answer I'd been looking for, but I knew if I did this, he'd want me to talk to the police. Images of Liam lying dead on the street swirled through my head, of him beaten and bleeding. Limbs contorted, his eyes staring blankly at the sky. I shuddered at the thought as I realised that could have been me. I, too, could have died.

"OK, I'll talk to them," I said with conviction in my voice, but not necessarily in my heart.

He nodded then. "It's the right thing to do, and I will keep you safe. I promise you that."

Staring at me with those intense blue eyes, I didn't doubt that's exactly what he'd do. I believed his words, every damn one. A glimmer of hope blossomed in my chest. Could this really work?

"Would you stay with me, you know, when I talk to them? I can't guarantee you'll like what I have to say, but if I'm going to be moving into your Ma's house, you'd best know the kind of person I was. The kind of person I am."

"Let me make a few calls, and we'll try and get it over and done with as soon as we can. As for the kind of person you are, you seem like a good person. I know there's a reason you're talking to the police, and I don't think it's about you."

How did he know that? Know that I was concerned about Liam? He was right, though. I'd had my share of bad decisions, but I'd always tried to be a good person, and doing this, reporting this incident, it might help save someone else's life. I just hoped I wasn't too late.

———

Marc managed to set up a meeting with the police for the following day. He'd had to work last night, and I was nervous as hell. Not about talking to the police, but about what he might think of me. I'd often had a 'take me or leave me' attitude. You didn't like me? Well, that was your issue not mine, but with Marc, I wanted him to think the best of me. I cared what he thought. Was it too soon to hope he could see me differently?

A little after midday, two detectives arrived, one sitting, the other standing by the window. The one by the window had an intimidating look about him, and I worried what he'd make of my story, but the guy in the chair almost looked at me the way a caring father would look at his son.

Pfft. Like I would know, my father had left the family home as soon as he could, leaving us to fend for ourselves. That was a story for another day. Today was the story of the last few months and how I'd fallen for the wrong man again.

The detective in the chair spoke first, introducing them both as Detective Woods and Palmer, asking mine and Marc's name. Marc confirmed he was the paramedic that had treated me at the scene and also that he intended to help me once I was discharged from the hospital.

"So, Ziggy." Woods looked down at his notebook, no doubt to make sure he had that right. "Why don't you tell us from the beginning what happened? It'll help us get a picture of how you ended up where you did."

I took a deep breath and began my story. I knew parts of it would seem unbelievable and make me look like a gullible twat, but that's what I'd been. Gullible, looking for a prince when I was looking at a devil. A devil with teeth and the worst of intentions.

CHAPTER TWENTY-EIGHT

MARC

I could see how it hurt Ziggy to tell his story. He stopped a few times, taking a drink when his throat went dry. I sat and listened. Listened to how he'd been taken for a fool and had suffered the consequences.

It wasn't his fault, not one bit, and when he relayed the final assault and I realised that there'd been not one but two assailants, I was ready to go on a rampage and find the bastards that had treated him that way.

When he told them about Liam and what Damian and his brother had said, it was clear that this was the reason Ziggy talked to the police. Not for himself. He feared for his life, but helping Liam had made him do it. He gave them a description and a name. It was all he had.

When we came to the part where Damian had visited him in the hospital, Detective Palmer, the one by the window, turned to me.

"Would you like to tell us what you think you saw, Mr Hutton?" Thought I saw? I knew damn well what I saw.

"I don't 'think' I saw anything. I did see that man holding

Ziggy by the face. I know if I hadn't come in when I did, he would have hurt him again."

Dickhead Palmer obviously liked playing devil's advocate. "Perhaps it was a kindly lover's touch." The contempt dripped from his words, and I saw Ziggy's face fall. He needed these two on his side if they were going to do anything about those bastards.

"If you were my lover and you touched me like that, you'd be on your back and not for anything fun, I can guarantee. That man was out to hurt him, pure and simple. Believe me or not, but if you speak to Joanne, the other nurse that was around, I'm sure she'll be able to give you some insight on how he was acting when he was here."

Ziggy mouthed a thank you, but the detective wasn't finished.

"Are we saying that even after he and his brother beat you up, he then came to the hospital to visit you? Am I getting this right? Seems a little ridiculous, don't you think?"

He turned to look at Ziggy, a challenge in his eyes, and I thought Ziggy was going to cave, but a determined look crossed his face and he spoke up, loud and clear.

"That's exactly what he did. He came here to threaten me, to tell me not to report it to the police, that I wouldn't live to regret it. Sounds like a threat to me, don't you think? He's cocky enough to think he can get away with it, and until I spoke to Marc, I was going to let this go.

"I can't do that now, not when I think they could have done something to Liam. I'm prepared to prosecute if you ever find them. I've given you the address of where I was taken to. If they're still there, take them in, question them. All my stuff was there, and I would imagine there's my blood too. I know I smacked my head on the wall, and from my stab wounds I would imagine there's even more blood in the house. I. Was. Attacked. Sexually assaulted and almost killed."

Ziggy had become progressively more vocal as he spoke, but

the last words were almost a whisper. I walked over to the table and poured more water for him, helping him up so he could drink.

The detectives glanced at each other, and Woods rose from the chair.

"We'll visit the property you mentioned and see if we can find them. They may have left, they may still be there. Once we have something more, we'll come back again and let you know where the case stands. When you get out of here, we'd like you to come down to the station so we can formalise this and get you to sign a written statement.

"Where will you be staying when you're released from here? We'll need to get in touch with you again, obviously."

I'd already pre-empted this question and handed over a piece of paper with the address and my telephone number on it.

"Ziggy doesn't have his phone, so if you need to speak to him, you can contact me. I'll be helping him out, as I said."

After thanking Ziggy for talking to them and exchanging numbers with me, they left with promises of looking into it as soon as they could. Out of the two detectives, only Woods seemed like he cared about what had happened. Palmer? I wasn't so sure.

"You probably hate me now that you know my story. Know who I am. I'm surprised you still want me to move in with your Ma." Ziggy seemed disheartened now I knew his story, but honestly, it made no difference to me. If anything, it made me want to help him more. The guy couldn't catch a break.

"What happened wasn't your fault; you need to remember that. You didn't ask for them to hurt you. They are the ones in the wrong, not you. As for staying with Ma? I know that she won't care about your past, only what happened to you. I can't guarantee she won't kill you with kindness, though. You'll be very welcome."

He looked relieved. "OK. That sounds good then. I just

wonder how much longer I'll have to be here. I've been here a week already, and I'm a bit stir crazy. I've never stayed in bed for this long before."

I didn't think it'd be much longer, and a few days later, I was proved right. I took clean clothes for him to dress in and wheeled him to the hospital doors where my car was waiting for him.

He grimaced as he climbed into my car, his barely healed wounds and cracked ribs clearly bothering him. There was nothing for him to do but rest, and at Ma's house, he'd be able to do that.

Twenty minutes later we arrived. As expected, Ma was waiting on the doorstep with a beaming smile on her face.

"There you are! I thought you'd got lost along the way." She bustled down the drive and helped Ziggy from the car. "Come on, now. Let's get you inside and settled." She turned to me, a stern look on her face. "I hope you drove carefully. Poor lad looks terrified!"

"You do know I drive an ambulance. I'm always careful." She tutted and continued on her way, her arm around Ziggy's waist. "Bring his bags in," she shouted over her shoulder. Like I was going to leave them in the car.

He didn't have much, just toiletries so he could take a shower. When he'd stepped out of the bathroom, dressed in normal clothes, his lithe figure and beauty had become more apparent. He was gorgeous. Brown hair, warm brown eyes with a hint of gold, stunning bone structure and when he smiled, he could light up the room.

I stood and stared after them, Ziggy leaning into her for support and Ma chattering away, telling him God knows what. Maybe this hadn't been such a good idea, after all. She'd spill all my secrets before long!

By the time I made it into the house, he was already on the sofa, his feet propped up on the footstool and a blanket over his legs. Ziggy had the look of a startled rabbit, and I laughed at the expression on his face.

"Wow, she really got you then. Where is she now? Making tea?"

"Mm, I think so. I tried to keep up, but she wouldn't stop talking!"

"I'll take your bag up and put your things away. I got you some more clothes until we can find yours or maybe go shopping."

The frown on his face surprised me.

"I'm not a fucking charity case, Marc."

"Hey, I never said you were, but unless you were going to arrive here with your arse hanging out of the hospital gown… what else were you going to wear? What were you intending to sleep in or wear tomorrow?"

I knew he wasn't being ungrateful. When talking to the police, he'd mentioned how he'd wanted his independence, which is how the assault came about. Damian especially couldn't stand the thought of him not being reliant on him, so Ziggy's outburst wasn't that much of a surprise. Even so, he needed to see not everything was meant as charity; sometimes it was just about helping out a friend in need.

I could tell by the embarrassed look on his face that he hadn't thought about his comment before saying it. In some ways, he was such a worldly-wise person, but other times, he acted like the naive twenty-year-old he was.

"I'm sorry. You're right, of course. I shouldn't have been so ungrateful."

"I know you're not ungrateful. I know why you said it, but I will never take away your independence, Ziggy. I was trying to help you. Hell, pay me back if you want to, if it makes you feel better."

"Maybe this was a bad idea. Perhaps I should go." He threw

the covers from his legs and went to stand, but at that moment, Ma returned to the room with a tray full of teacups and biscuits.

"Jesus, Marc. I can't leave you with him for five minutes and you're chasing him away. What did you say this time? Ziggy, get back on that sofa. You're going nowhere, young man." Her tone brooked no argument, and he sat back, placing the crocheted blanket over his legs again.

"Now which one of you is going to tell me what's going on?" She glared at us both, hands on hips, lips pursed.

Ziggy spoke up first. "It was my fault. I was acting like a spoiled child."

"No, it was me. I should have handled it better."

"Well, sounds like you two need to have a talk, see what you expect from each other. And you"—she pointed at me—"you'll treat Ziggy like the guest he is. When you've both finished your tea, you can take him upstairs and show him the room. I would imagine he's tired after today."

I nodded, and she sat down next to Ziggy, patting him on the leg.

"So, tell me all about you."

"Leave him alone, Ma. He's only just arrived. You'll have plenty of time to interrogate him when I'm gone. Let him finish his tea."

We spent the next half an hour with Ma telling us about the scandal at the choir group and what songs they were practising. I looked across to Ziggy to see he'd fallen asleep. Poor guy must be knackered.

I stood and shook him gently. He slowly opened his eyes and looked up at me, and I was hit with a vision of him doing that every morning.

"Let's get you up to bed so you can rest. I'll be here for a while yet, so hopefully I'll see you before I go home."

He murmured sleepily, and his eyes closed again. Guess I was carrying him then.

I scooped him up into my arms, leaving the blanket behind. He weighed nothing, a slip of a thing, and I carried him with ease up the stairs and into my old bedroom. After laying him on the bed, I pulled the covers over him and turned to leave, glancing back at his peaceful face before closing the door behind me.

It'd take a while, but I'd no doubt he'd get through this. I hoped he'd stick around. I wanted nothing more than to get to know the man better. He seemed to be a feisty thing, and I loved nothing more than a challenge.

CHAPTER TWENTY-NINE

ZIGGY

I knew I'd made a mistake the moment the words left my lips. Of course he wasn't Damian. He wanted to help, and I had to go and open my big mouth and put my size nines right in there.

I'd upset him. I'd known that, but his Ma coming in with the tea and biscuits had helped to diffuse the situation. But then, I couldn't keep my eyes open. The stress and strain of leaving the hospital had taken its toll, and I'd fallen asleep.

The next thing I remembered was being carried upstairs and laid gently onto a bed, the scent of freshly laundered sheets reaching my nose. The covers were pulled over me, and I sank into a dreamless sleep.

I awoke what seemed like hours later, but in actual fact was only about two hours according to the digital clock on the nightstand. The pale-blue glow it emitted casting the room in semi-brightness.

I was in a double bed with soft blue sheets on it. The same colour curtains hung at the window, and I could see it was almost dark outside. I was so comfortable; I didn't want to get up, but the urge to pee was hurting my bladder.

I cautiously got out of bed, trying not to jostle my ribs or pull at the wounds on my stomach. The pain was easing, but one wrong movement and I was wracked with pain. I quietly opened the door, unsure which one was the bathroom, but it wasn't hard to find, just next door to the bedroom I was in, a sign on the door announcing the Throne Room.

I groaned as I peed, the relief palpable. God, had I needed that. I washed my hands afterwards, glancing in the mirror above the sink as I did so. My bruises were fading, and I would have a few small scars on my face, but I could easily hide them with concealer. My nose was fine now, if a little bent. It gave my face character, no longer the baby-faced boy, more a ruggedly handsome man. Yeah, that was pushing it, but I didn't feel quite so youthful-looking anymore, although I still couldn't grow facial hair. Two weeks in the hospital and very little to show for it.

I straightened out my clothes, trying for some semblance of normality and stepped out of the bathroom, straight into Marc's hard chest.

"Ooof. Jesus, it's like walking into a wall!" I prodded at his pecs, impressed with the feel of solid muscle beneath my fingers. I wondered if he was like this all over. He'd mentioned going to the gym, and I imagined him in tight shorts and fitted T-shirt, sweat beading on his brow, his musky smell of sweat, and for the first time in a while, my cock took notice, twitching in my boxers.

This was a new development, and one I was both happy and sad about. Happy because I'd genuinely thought I'd never get turned on by another man again and sad because it was too soon and I couldn't get involved with him. I wasn't good enough for him. The prostitute and the paramedic? Sounded like a bad joke.

"Are you OK? I didn't hurt you, did I? Did you bump your nose again?"

He gripped my upper arm with one hand, turning my face from side to side with his other hand.

"I'm fine, honestly. You didn't break me. Still in one piece, see?"

I stepped back from him, poking and prodding myself to prove to him I was fine.

"No damage done. One thing, though."

"Anything, name it."

"I'm fucking starving. Is there anything to eat? Two custard creams and a cup of tea, and I could murder a burger right now."

"Your wish is my command. There's a chippy down the road, serves a great burger and chips. You want?"

"I want. Cheeseburger if possible, onions, ketchup, hold the mustard, and if there's pickles, I'll have those too."

Before I could say anything more, he'd hoisted me up into his arms and carried me downstairs, placing me on the sofa. God, but he was strong. I'd been asleep when he carried me up, but on the way down, I felt every muscle ripple beneath me and another thrill shot through my body. I quickly covered myself up with the blanket, hoping he hadn't seen the semi-boner I now had.

"I'll be right back, don't move." He turned towards the kitchen and shouted, "Ma, I'm going out to get Ziggy some food. Do you want anything?"

She poked her head around the door, wiping her hands on a cloth.

"Just get me some chicken, and I'll share some of your chips. You know I can't eat a full portion."

Marc rolled his eyes and shook his head, making me think they'd had this conversation before.

As he opened the door to leave, a younger version of Marc walked through it. This must be Ryan, his younger brother.

"Who's this then? New boyfriend, Marc? How come he gets the good blanket? I'm not allowed to even sit next to it."

"Hey, less of it. You know who it is, and don't go upsetting him." Marc gave him a quick smack around the back of the head, and Ryan dodged away from him, laughing as he did so. This was what it should be like, having siblings. Instead, all I'd had was sullen words and sly digs, bullying in a mild form, but bullying all the same. That, plus the situation with my dad's friend, had been my reason for leaving.

I laughed then, a proper laugh, and Marc looked at me in shock. I don't think I'd laughed like that in front of him before, and maybe I'd surprised him but, I felt like I could do that here, that maybe this was a house full of love and laughter and this was what I needed, a place to heal my damaged body and mind.

CHAPTER THIRTY

ZIGGY

The next few days passed in relative quiet. Marc's Ma, or Pat as she insisted I call her, kept me well fed, well looked after and full of tea. I loved every minute. She cared for me more than my mother had ever done. Marc called around when he could, when he wasn't on shift, and I found myself looking forward to his visits. Dare I hope that we could be something or was he just being nice? Ryan was in and out. His job as a baker meant he was up and out of the house before the crack of dawn. The upside of this was he brought home the most delicious bread, and if I ate anymore, I'd end up not fitting into the few clothes Marc had bought for me.

Almost a week after our first meeting, the police turned up again. Marc stayed with me, and I could hear Pat hovering in the kitchen. I'd hoped they had news, but from the grim looks on their faces, I knew they'd found nothing.

The only bright side was they had my phone. A visit to the house in Crosby had turned up nothing but an empty house. None of my belongings were there. The police had conducted forensic tests and found traces of blood and my phone tucked behind one of the chairs. They must have missed it in their rush to leave.

"Can he have it back?" Marc asked after they'd finished their rundown. "There's nothing you need it for now, is there?"

The detectives exchanged a look. "There's no reason why not. We had to check it, but there's been no contact from Damian or his brother. Although you might want to call Suzie back, she's been a little vocal about you not contacting her." Detective Woods laughed, handing the phone to me.

I checked it, and he wasn't wrong. Message after message from her, some from Duke and a couple from a number I didn't recognise. I'd check them later, but we needed to get this meeting over and done with. Marc had promised to take me out to buy new clothes.

"Right now," the detective continued, "we have both their descriptions out there, and are trying to trace them by other means. We have a name on the rental agreement for the house, but it's neither Damian nor Stuart. We have the name of Georgina Miller. Does that mean anything to you?"

"Damian said his wife's name was Georgie, but that she left him about six years ago. They have a daughter called Daisy. Maybe it's her?"

Detective Palmer scribbled in his notebook. "Thank you. We'll look into that. You mentioned someone called Liam too. Without a surname, we don't have much to go on, I'm afraid. If he contacts you, let us know, and we can follow up on that."

He stood to leave and shook both mine and Marc's hand. "As soon as we get anything, we'll let you know."

Marc led them out, and Pat came into the lounge and sat next to me.

"How are you feeling, sweetie? I can't believe those bastards have up and left like that. Although I can't say I'm surprised. That Damian must have known you wouldn't keep quiet. Sounds like you stuck up for yourself with him, and so you should."

If only she knew what had happened when I didn't do as he thought was right. I know he'd only put me over his knee that one time, but looking back on my time living with him, I understood he'd tried to control me with fear. Whenever I did something wrong, he'd be furious. I'd learned fairly early on what he liked and didn't like, what would make him lose his temper.

I'd not been myself, bitten my tongue when I could have answered back. If I'd upset him, I'd be the one to make it right, doing things I knew pleased him. Living with him when he was in one of his moods had been miserable. Everything I'd done was to please him, keep him happy so I didn't have to live with the silent treatment or the fear that he'd have enough of me and throw me out of the house.

I didn't want Pat to think any less of me, so I lied.

"I don't let anyone walk all over me. I've been living here for a few days now. Can you see me letting someone do that to me?" I spoke with a confidence I didn't feel, and I had a suspicion she saw right through my bravado.

Before she could say anything else, Marc walked back into the room and flopped on the sofa next to me.

"I'm so sorry they didn't find anything else, Ziggy. They still need you to go to the station to make your statement, and now they need a sample of your DNA so they can compare it to the blood they found in the house. Do you think it's yours?" He turned to look at me, concern showing in his eyes.

"I know it's mine. I cleaned that house top to bottom when I was there, so any stains will be recent."

"At least you have your phone back. You can get in touch with your family, let them know you're safe." I wouldn't be doing that, friends maybe, but not my family. They hadn't cared about me for the past four years. I couldn't see them bothering now.

"I'm going to give Suzie a call, then we can go out." Maybe he didn't want to go now. I didn't want to put him to any trouble. I felt like I was already imposing too much on him and Pat. "Only if that's alright with you." I smiled weakly. I was being too much again, wasn't I?

"Of course it's OK. It'll do you good to get out of the house. Go do what you need to do, and I'll wait here. Take your time."

Thank God. The last thing I needed to do was upset him.

I rose from the chair, feeling better than I had in a long time. My ribs still twinged a little and the stitches pulled, but it had been almost three weeks since the assault and even I was surprised I'd got away with so few injuries.

Stairs still tired me out, so I took them steadily, one step at a time. No more running up them like I used to. I was annoyed that all of my belongings had gone. Everything I'd had with me, the few sentimental items I'd brought with me when I left home, the little bit of cash I'd managed to save up and every single piece of clothing I owned. I couldn't keep relying on Marc to get stuff for me. He'd soon get tired of that, get tired of me, and then I'd be out again. I was more than aware that good things never lasted for me.

I pulled the phone out of my pocket and dialled Suzie's number. She answered on the second ring.

"Where the fuck have you been? Why was I seeing your name all over the news? Why haven't you called? Oh my God, Ziggy. I could kill you." She burst into tears, and I waited for her to calm down.

"Hey, hey. I'm fine, a little beaten up, but I'm good. I promise."

"What in fuck's name happened? One minute you were playing happy families, and the next thing I know, I hear you've been dumped in a street and in a serious condition in hospital. I'll kill that fucking Damian!"

"I know and the police are out looking for him. I wanted you to know I was still alive." This wasn't a conversation I wanted to have over the phone. I wanted to tell her in person.

"Where are you now? Please tell me you're not in that house."

"No, I'm staying at a friend's mum's house. I've been here

since I was released, and before you say anything, I didn't want to bother you. I know you're busy."

"You're my friend, Ziggy. You could have come and stayed with me. Mum wouldn't have minded."

"I know, but this was easier, and he's a paramedic, so he keeps an eye on my wounds." And he had been. He'd been checking them, making sure they were healing well and there was no infection. Fortunately, the splenectomy had been done via a small incision, so although there would be scarring, it'd be minimal.

"Paramedic? Where'd you find one of those? Don't tell me. I don't want to know."

"Marc and his partner were the ones that took me to hospital." I wasn't sure how to explain the next part. Ever since the moment in the back of the ambulance, where he'd talked to me, calmed me down, I'd felt a connection with him. Not sexual, it wasn't like that, although I couldn't deny that he was fucking hot, but he'd cared, been there with me when the police visited. I was starting to see him as a friend, one that I could rely on to be there, but the more time I spent with him, the more I wanted.

"He's been helping me out with the police interviews and offered me a room at his Ma's house. They've both been very good to me."

She was quiet for a while, no doubt wondering what I was doing getting involved again with someone I hardly knew, and I was feeling the exact same way. I had a habit of falling too fast and too hard, but this time, I *was* trying to guard my heart.

"Well, I'll let you get on. Sounds like you're busy." She sounded pissed off, and I couldn't blame her. When I'd been with Damian, I'd ignored her, messaged her less and less, wanting to please him more than keeping in touch. I should apologise.

"I'm sorry I didn't keep in touch these past few months, and if you'll let me, I can explain everything to you. Can we meet up? Soon?"

"I suppose, if you can tear yourself away from this one." Ouch, that one hurt, but I did deserve it.

"It's not like that with me and Marc. He's helping me out until I'm well enough to get back on my own two feet. What was I going to do, Suzie? Stay at a hostel? Sleep on the street? I had nowhere else to go."

She sniffled, and her voice was croaky when she spoke. "OK, text me when and where. I have to go now."

"I'm sorry, and bye." She ended the call without another word. I'd well and truly pissed her off, and I had to admit, she had every right to be.

I checked the rest of my messages, sending a quick one-off to Duke, telling him I was good and that we'd speak soon. The unknown number, I didn't know what to do about that. Who was it? Was it Stuart? Liam maybe? Only one way to find out.

The message read, *"Hey, heard you were in a bit of an accident. Wondering how you are. Let me know."*

Weird that no name was left.

Hi, who is this?

I went to the bathroom with a change of clothes and took a quick shower, taking care to dry off my wounds. The stitches were almost dissolved, and as I looked at myself in the mirror, I couldn't help but pick fault at my pale, marred skin. I was tall, I was lanky and I needed a haircut.

A flashing light on my phone told me I had a message. Curious as to who it would be, I unlocked it, surprised to see the name.

Sorry, my bad! It's Beau, worried after seeing that guy with you and then you on the news. Thank God ur ok tho.

I couldn't help the relief that coursed through my body. I could relax. They hadn't found me…yet!

CHAPTER THIRTY-ONE

MARC

Ziggy came down the stairs as Ma and I finished talking. She'd told me she thought there was more to what he'd gone through, not just the assault, and I had to agree. The way he'd tensed every time I touched him, even though it was always in a professional capacity, told more than his words ever would.

I jumped to my feet, keys and phone in hand, hoping he hadn't heard us talking. I knew he'd hate it if he knew we were doing that.

"Ready? We won't be out too long, don't want to overtire you." Even over a week after being released, he was still tired, but his stamina was improving.

"Yep, and don't forget to save the receipts. I will pay you back."

"I know you will. See you later, Ma. I'll let you know about tonight."

I'd mentioned that we might go out for food, save her cooking, and it'd be a change of scenery for Ziggy.

Shopping with Ziggy was a nightmare. He kept picking up the cheap clothes, refusing to look at anything in the more expensive shops we went into. No matter how many times I told him it was better to buy quality. We eventually decided on jeans, a few more tops and more underwear. At his request, I kept every receipt, and we got back to the car several hours later.

"Where would you like to eat? I thought you might like to eat somewhere different today."

"Honestly, Marc? We never ate out that often, so I don't know many places to go. Surprise me."

I decided on Indian food. There was a local street food restaurant that served the most delicious food. Ziggy had never eaten there before, and I knew he'd enjoy it.

Thankfully there was no queue, and when Ziggy walked in, he had the reaction I was looking for. The interior was lit with hundreds of fairy lights. Rows and rows of huge jars filled with strings of lights and artificial trees draped with them. The effect was magical, and as I looked over at Ziggy, his face was a picture.

"Wow, so many lights? And are those swings in the window?" He turned to look at me, an excited look on his face. "Can we have a swing? I really want a swing now."

"I'm sure we can get a swing, Ziggy." Sure enough, we were led to a table for two in the window and Ziggy sat on the swing, a little unsteady, but they were chained down, so he couldn't go far.

We ordered food, a selection of dishes we could share and the waiter brought our drinks over. We were finally alone. Since coming out of the hospital, there had always been someone with us, either Ma or Ryan and whilst I didn't mind, there were things I wanted to know. Things about his past. I wanted to get to know him, know the real Ziggy, not the one he showed to everyone else.

"So, how are you feeling now you're out of the hospital? Everything OK? I bet you're glad to have your phone back finally."

"Oh God, yes. I've missed having it. Not that I have many friends to call and my family wants nothing to do with me, so that's no great shakes." His sad smile hit me right in my chest.

Why didn't he speak to his family? I wanted to know but would wait until he felt comfortable enough to tell me.

"Suzie was fucking annoyed with me. Had every good reason to be. When I moved in with Damian—" He stopped then and played with his hair, fidgeting on the swing, making it sway to and fro. "When I moved in with Damian, through necessity I might add, to start with I called her often, but as time wore on and he became more controlling, I stopped calling. Stopped texting. He didn't see why I needed other people when I had him. I'm ashamed to say I listened to him and almost lost my friends in the process.

"I was such a fucking idiot where he was concerned. I'd never ever let a good-looking guy get to me the way he did. He had this way, you know, of making me feel special, making me feel like I mattered when all along, he didn't give a fuck! Just wanted to groom me so him and Stuart could have their way. If I hadn't fought back, kicked out when I did—" He paused then, his eyes misty.

I knew what he was saying and moved my finger on the table so that it touched the end of his ring finger. I thought he'd pull away, the touch too much for him, but he let it stay, looking into my eyes, captivating me with his gaze.

"I feel such a fool, Marc. I knew it was wrong, had this feeling in my gut that how he was treating me wasn't normal. I lived for his praise, wanting him to tell me I'd done good, that the house was tidy, the bed was made. I hated myself when I disappointed him and tried to do better every time."

I didn't want tonight to be spoiled by Damian and tried to change the subject.

"I know, but you're away from him now and that's the main thing. If the police can find them, we *can* get them put behind bars. If we could find Liam as well, that'd help too."

"I did get a message from Beau on my phone. He was with me when Damian picked me up, right before, you know."

"Would he talk to the police?"

"I can ask. It might help if they ever get picked up, I suppose."

Our food and drinks were brought over, and conversation moved to other topics. Ziggy, telling me how well he was getting on with Ryan and Ma and how much he appreciated the offer to stay with them. I'd seen them chatting together, and as I'd thought, it'd been the right decision to move him in there. Add in the fact that I could see him when I wanted to. I was using my house to sleep in, that was all, and poor Smeagol wasn't getting any attention these days.

"So, tell me about Henry." His question startled me. I frowned, wondering how the hell he knew about him, but then I remembered he'd been living with Ma for the last week or so.

"She told you then." I shook my head. Jesus, that woman couldn't keep anything to herself. "How much has she told you?"

He looked a little sheepish then, and I eyed him suspiciously. "She didn't say anything, did she?"

"Maybe? Maybe not? She might have mentioned his name in passing. I just guessed there was a story behind it."

"There isn't too much of a story. No cheating boyfriend, no blazing rows. Well, not many anyway. We just drifted apart, I suppose. He hated my job, hated what it did to me sometimes. Cases like yours would shake me up, and sometimes I'd need to chill when I got home, but Henry had parties he'd want to go to. Climbing the corporate ladder he'd say, and he'd expect me to go along." I took a drink of my beer, Ziggy watching me intently, listening to my every word.

"When I wouldn't talk to people, mingle, we'd have the most terrible rows when we got home. I suppose he'd had enough, and one morning, after I came home from a shift, he was packing. Told me he'd had enough of my moods, that I was hurting his career as a marketing executive. I looked good but was lacking in social skills."

"What a complete twat!"

I barked out a laugh at Ziggy's comment.

"You couldn't be more right. I saw him again about a year ago. He had this pretty boy on his arm, called him Daddy. Can you believe it? He never pulled that shit with me thankfully, it's not my scene, but he looked me up and down, took in my tats, muscles and piercing and shook his head. I guess he didn't like what he saw, and by this point, I didn't care. I had my cat and my job, and I was happy."

"I think he's the one missing out. I mean, look at you." He played with his hair again, and I realised this was a nervous habit of his, but it made him look cute.

"Come on, eat before this all goes cold and then we'll get you home to bed."

"It'll take a bit more than a meal and a cold drink to get me into bed, Marc. The going rate used to be £50. You got that kind of money on you?" He tilted his head, a challenge in his eyes.

I hated that. Hated that he thought he could shock me with the fact that he'd been a prostitute. It didn't bother me. I didn't care what he'd done before.

"You know that doesn't bother me, Ziggy. You can't shock me. Now eat your food. You need to keep your strength up."

I placed a piece of chicken in my mouth, chewed and swallowed, noticing how Ziggy watched my every action, his eyes widening. Well now, that was an interesting turn of events and one I might be wanting to exploit.

CHAPTER THIRTY-TWO

MARC

After we'd gone out shopping and for the meal, Ziggy started to relax a little more around me. He didn't move away if I sat next to him on the sofa and the last time I'd checked his wounds and declared him fit, the tension in his body hadn't been there.

It was a step forward, and I know Ma had noticed it too. Whereas before, when we'd sat down to eat, she'd made sure that he was next to no one, placing him at the end of the table, the sneak that she was, had started setting her place there, leaving him facing me. She was meddling.

I also happened to know from reading his hospital chart that it was almost his twenty-first birthday, just a couple of weeks away, on the first of May.

I wanted to do something special for him, and I'd already had a chat with Ma about it. She agreed we should have a nice meal at home or even a small party. I know he had friends. He'd mentioned Beau, Suzie and Duke, and I knew that he'd fallen out with his family, so I wouldn't be inviting them.

I needed to get his phone, though, find the numbers so I could call them and arrange the get-together, but it'd be tricky to do that without him finding out.

One night, over a meal of Chinese food, I broached the subject, letting him know we knew his birthday was coming up.

"We thought we could have a quiet meal here, just the family, you know?"

"Not my family. You're not inviting them, are you?" He looked horrified at the thought.

"No, just us and Cheryl's boyfriend. That'd be OK, wouldn't it?" I hoped he'd say yes.

"I don't want a fuss. You don't have to do anything."

Ma chimed in then. I could see she'd been watching the exchange, dying to jump in.

"Oh yes, we do, young man. All my children had a party for their twenty-first, and you will be no exception."

Poor Ziggy. He'd been railroaded by Ma, but when I glanced at him across the table, tears coursed down his face. I got up straight away and rushed to his side. Fear of touch be damned, I knelt beside him and took his hand in mine, wiping the tears from his cheeks.

"Hey, don't cry." I turned to Ma. "For God's sake, now look what you've done."

"I-I-I didn't mean to upset you, Ziggy. What did I say? I'm so sorry."

He clutched my hand, the same as he'd done before.

"I'm good," he hiccupped, "no one has ever done that for me before." He carried on wiping the tears with his other hand, holding tightly onto mine with his other one.

"Did your mother never throw you a party?" Ma's mouth was open, not believing him.

"Never, and even after I left home. Suzie and I would just have a burger or fried chicken. This is too much, though; you don't have to do anything for me."

"We know we don't have to, but we want to. It'd be a meal,

just a few of us." He nodded then, and the tears slowly started to subside.

"Come on, let's get you cleaned up." I took him by the hand and led him into the kitchen, finding him a tissue and pouring him a glass of water.

"Oh, God. I couldn't have embarrassed myself anymore if I tried. I'm so sorry."

"What are you apologising for? You've every right to be upset if no one's bothered to do something like that for you. I'm glad that you'll let us. Ma's grown very fond of you, and seeing how you act with Ryan, you could be brothers you get on so well. You've fit in well here in such a short space of time."

"And what about you? How do you see me?" His question surprised me, and I was at a loss for words for a change. I floundered and turned away from him, hoping he couldn't see the hope in my eyes. I certainly didn't see him as a brother. In the short time I'd known him, I was starting to think I wanted more from him. I just didn't think he would see me that way, not after what had happened to him.

I schooled my expression and faced him. "I see you as a friend, one I'd like to get to know more, if you'd let me."

He tilted his head and looked at me. "A friend, huh? Not a brother?"

I shook my head. Definitely not a brother. The things that occasionally crossed my mind when I thought about Ziggy... I wouldn't be doing those to my brother any time soon.

"Nope, definitely not a brother." I hoped he'd understand the meaning in my words, that I wanted to be more with him.

"An interesting choice of words." He leaned against the counter and nibbled on his thumbnail. "You know, I think I'd like that. To be your friend, that is. Maybe in time, we could be good friends, go out and do stuff together, like good friends do."

"I think I'd like that a lot." Were we talking about being friends or something more? "But our food will be getting cold, so why don't we go back and eat. Ma will be worried you've run off unless you make an appearance."

"We can't have that now, can we? As for the party, meal or whatever you decide to do, I'm good with it, thank you." He looked unsure, and I didn't know why, but then he reached up and kissed me on the cheek. It must have taken a lot of nerve on his part to do that, knowing what had happened to him.

"That's a thank you. For everything you've done for me. Buying me clothes, finding me this place to stay and generally for being with me since I left the hospital and even before that. You are a good friend, Marc."

"I try to be. I want to do right by you, Ziggy. I don't think you've had it great in your life. From the little things you've said, your home life, what you've endured since leaving home and now this… I want to help you, help you see there are good people in this world. Not everyone is out to hurt you, certainly not me, anyway."

"Marc, is everything OK in there?" Ma shouted from the other room. "Your food's getting cold."

I rolled my eyes, and Ziggy laughed. "Come on, let's go eat. I've got my eye on that sweet and sour chicken if your brother hasn't eaten it all already."

We walked back in and took our seats at the table. Ma looked at me, a question in her eyes, and I nodded. Yes, he was fine. We'd be fine.

CHAPTER THIRTY-THREE

ZIGGY

I felt such a fool acting that way, crying at the table, but it was true, no one had ever done that for me before and no one had made me feel as welcome in their home as these people had done and I couldn't be more grateful.

When Marc and I had stood in the kitchen and he'd talked about me and Ryan being like brothers, the question just fell from my lips. I wanted to know how he saw me. I knew for a fact I didn't see him as a brother. If I did, the things that had been flitting through my mind would have belonged in a taboo book. I didn't think I'd ever start to have feelings for anyone ever again after Damian, but the time I'd spent with Marc, both in the hospital and since moving into his old house, I'd seen what a genuine person he was. Not at all like the sleazeball I'd lived with for almost four months, and that gave me hope that we could be something more.

The difference between the two of them was stark. One was the classic wolf in sheep's clothing and the other was the Good Samaritan. The comparison was laughable.

And now he and his family wanted to throw me a party, host a meal for my birthday, and I was so emotional and touched by their generosity, I couldn't stop the tears from falling.

Marc had to work the following couple of days, not nights this time, so I was going with Pat to her choir group. I'd practically begged to go with her. The other alternative was to sit in the house, and while I knew neither Damian nor Stuart knew where I lived, I was still uncertain about being there alone. The one time Pat had nipped to the shop, I'd been a wreck, jumping at every sound until eventually, I locked myself in the bathroom until she returned.

We arrived at midday and walked into the musty church hall. Why did they always smell the same? The old, rickety wooden chairs and a large trestle table complete with a hot water urn and mismatched cups and saucers. A variety pack of biscuits placed neatly on a plate; bourbons, custard creams and pink wafers. It was like a throwback to my very brief childhood, where I'd been allowed to go to a couple of children's parties.

"Pat," an elderly woman shouted, moving spritely across the floor. "And who is this handsome boy? Is this Ziggy?"

She grabbed my hand and led me over to a chair, settling me down next to her. I looked helplessly over to Pat, who shrugged and waved me off, walking towards the tea table.

"Pat's told us all about you, but her description did not do you justice. You look like a young Cary Grant." I had no idea who that was, so I smiled at her. "Oh, you wouldn't know who that was, would you? But that doesn't matter. You just have to know he was a handsome man. The women all loved him. Do you have a girlfriend, Ziggy? I reckon you could have the pick of any of them."

At that, Pat arrived with a cup of tea and a biscuit in the saucer.

"Leave him alone, Doris. He doesn't need the third degree. He's here to hear us sing, maybe join in. What do you say to that, Ziggy?"

I shook my head. I couldn't carry a tune in a bucket, no matter how much I used to think I could compete with Whitney. A memory of me singing with Duke came to mind, reminding me I needed to get in touch with him.

"I'll sit here and listen if that's OK? You would not want me to sing; I guarantee that."

A man in his forties called the ladies to order, and they went to stand on the stage, shorter people at the front, tallest at the back. After a few warm-up exercises, they started to sing, and I almost spat out my tea when they started on "Single Ladies". Seeing a bunch of middle- to old-aged ladies shaking their stuff to Beyoncé was hilarious, and I fought to control my laughter.

I could see Pat giving it her all, and in the break she came to sit with me.

"I'm glad you came with me. It does you good to get out of the house. Marc doesn't like you being there on your own, and I agree with him. You need to start getting out more. Maybe Marc could take you out? Movies perhaps, a meal here and there."

"You make them sound like dates, Pat. We're not going out, you know."

She nodded. "I know, but it'd do you both good, I think. He needs a friend, and so do you, so why not be friends together? He only really has Kyle, and I know there's been no one for him since Henry left him."

We sat for a while and watched as Norman, the choir master, put a couple more of the ladies through their paces, practising the moves. Hysterical did not cover what I was seeing right now.

"He thinks a lot of you, you know. He came to me that day, the day he brought you to the hospital."

I pricked my ears up at this, ignoring Beyoncé and concentrating on Pat's words.

"It affected him so much, and I knew then, had a feeling that he wouldn't let you go. Well, not you so much as your story, but then I think the more he got to know you, the more you made him see that there could be a life after Henry, a life outside of that job, that sometimes sucks him of all his joy.

"I think you could be the one to show him he can live again and can have happiness. I don't want to put pressure on you. I know you've been through a lot in your short life, have suffered at the hands of those cowardly wankers, excuse my French, but you could help him, as much as he's wanting to help you. That's all I'm saying."

"Break's over, ladies. Let's get onto our new piece, an Aretha Franklin medley."

Oh God, this was going to be fun. As the ladies sang, Pat's words ran through my head. I always thought Marc was so put together, but the more I got to know him and the more I heard about him, I realised that Henry had done a proper number on him, even more than I'd originally thought. Throw in the pressure from his job and taking me under his wing, and it was clear he had a lot on his plate.

But I didn't want to be the straw that broke the camel's back, the one that pushed him over the edge. Maybe after the party, I should look for somewhere to move to, give them all a break from my many, many problems.

A vibration in my coat pocket brought me out of my thoughts, and I checked the display, surprised to see Duke's number there.

I stepped out into the lobby and answered the call.

"Duke, how you doing, man?"

"Ziggy, where the fuck have you been? I know you sent a message to say you were alright, but you didn't follow up. Wondered where you were."

"Long fucking story, but I'm OK now. A two-week stay in hospital, but I'm out now, living with a friend's mum until I can get back on my feet. When are you next around? Can we catch up?"

"Yeah, of course. I can meet up anytime. I've got news too, so it'd be good to see you."

The doors to the hall banged open, and a gaggle of women spilled out into the lobby.

"Where the fuck are you? Why do I hear old women chattering?"

I laughed down the phone at him. "Part of the story, but I'll be in touch…soon."

We ended the call, and Pat grabbed hold of my arm, walking me out at a rapid pace.

"Quick, before Doris catches hold of you again. I think she's got a thing for you. At her age, you'd think she'd know better. Damn cougar. She's at least three times your age."

We sniggered together and ran for the bus, just managing to catch it, making our way up to the front of the top deck, where we chattered the whole way into the city. A brief stop in a local coffee shop and we were filled up on paninis and lattes. Pat was rapidly becoming a mother-like figure to me, and I realised that this was what mothers did, took their sons out for coffee, joked about things they saw and shared ridiculous videos on the internet. We did all these things and more. I was going to miss her when I left.

We got home around five, after shopping, to find Marc waiting on the driveway.

"Where've you been? I thought you were going to choir practice?"

"We were, but then we did a bit of shopping. I got new shoes and a beautiful new handbag. Ziggy has impeccable taste. I'll leave you boys to it, though. I'm dying for a cuppa."

I kicked the stones at my feet, feeling a little shy but having no clue why.

"How was your day?" I blurted out. "Hope it wasn't too stressful."

"It wasn't too bad today. Delivered a baby, that's always a good shift."

Marc looked as uncomfortable as I felt, and he leaned against his car, fidgeting with the keys in his hand.

"Would you, erm, like to go out for some food maybe or how about a takeaway?"

The takeaway sounded good, but I remembered what Pat had said about going out for meals, so I tucked away my tiredness and took the plunge.

"A meal out sounds great. Can I go and freshen up? I won't be long."

"Yes, yes. Of course, I'll come in and wait for you."

Was this a date? It felt like a date, one instigated by Pat perhaps? Either way, I was going to go out and enjoy myself, and I'd make sure to be the friend she wanted me to be for her son.

CHAPTER THIRTY-FOUR

ZIGGY

I rushed upstairs, deciding what I had in my wardrobe that would make me look good. All my other clothes had been lost, but thinking about what I'd had in my collection, it was probably a good job. They'd been street clothes; booty shorts and cropped tops, not suitable for going out to eat.

All I had now were skinny jeans and a couple of jumpers. I still needed that damn haircut, but I had hair gel, so I could at least do something with it. I dug around in the bathroom cabinet and found a bottle of fragrance. I wasn't sure if it was Ryan's or Pat's, but either way, it was going on. I had to try and remind myself this wasn't a date, as excited as I was.

Ten minutes later, we were in the car, driving to a local pizzeria. I loved pizza, the cheesier, the better, and it'd been a while since I'd had one. We were quiet on the drive over, and although I couldn't answer for Marc, I was feeling nervous. Pat's words about meals and movies made me overthink this. It did feel an awful lot like a date.

The pizzeria was a small place, tucked away down a back street in the middle of Liverpool. After parking, it took us a few minutes to walk there, and I was grateful we were seated at once.

Being out all day with Pat had left me feeling tired and a little weak. I'd not drunk half as much as I should have done, and a headache was starting to form at the base of my skull. I was determined to make the best of it, though, and enjoy myself.

"So, thanks for coming out with me. I know you were out all day, but I thought it'd be nice for us to have time alone again. I feel like I don't get much time with you at home."

"I feel the same way. You're my saviour and I feel I know little to nothing about you, only the few things you've mentioned and Henry. I'm sure there's more to you. You're a *Lord of the Rings* fan, so you need to tell me how you got into that. It's not everyone's cup of tea."

"No big mystery. Despite how I look now, I was a wimp at school, didn't fit in anywhere, hated sports. I was a walking cliché. I'd sit in the library, and I picked up the book one day and that was it; I was hooked.

"What about you? How was school for you?"

I didn't know if I wanted to answer that. School was horrible for me. I towered over everybody even when I was younger, and that made me a target for the bullies, especially when it was clear I didn't like the girls.

"School was a challenge. I didn't fit in anywhere. There was no welcoming gang of girls that all loved the gay boy. I was literally on my own from the time I stepped into high school until the day I officially left at sixteen. Shortly after that, I left home for good and came to Liverpool to try and find something to do.

"Here I am, four years later, not having made anything of myself other than selling myself to men who can't admit to themselves or their wives that they prefer men, or boys as I was when I started a couple of years ago."

Was Marc ready for the full story? He'd said he wanted to get to know me, and this story was me. It was what made me the person I was today. He looked at me with those gorgeous blue eyes, and I saw nothing but curiosity in them. I thought he'd understand me, understand why I'd left and why I'd done what I had when I left. It'd been a long time since I'd told anyone this story. Suzie didn't know the whole thing, and I know I'd told Duke a few things, but Marc just had a way that made you want to tell him everything.

Our pizzas arrived, and we were quiet for a while, savouring the taste of freshly made pizza. I moaned as the first burst of flavour hit me, closing my eyes in absolute bliss.

"I'm guessing it tastes good." I opened my eyes to see Marc smirking, that cheeky smile showing his dimples. Why had I never noticed them before?

"So fucking good. Where did you find this place?"

"I used to come here with Henry, but I'm not giving up the best pizza I've ever had because he used to bring me here. Too good to pass up."

"I agree completely. You did good."

Marc picked at his pizza, pulling off bits of meat and eating them.

"Tell me about your family." I knew it was only a matter of time until he asked, and I'd already decided I'd let him know what happened to me.

"Well, as I said before, school was a nightmare. I knew I was gay, didn't fit in with any of the groups and was bullied, not massively, just words and the occasional push and shove. The girls were worse than the boys, if you can believe that. I don't know why, but that's how it was.

"I managed, though. I had an older brother and sister, but they did nothing to help. My sister actually was in one of the groups that bullied me, so that tells you the sort of family I came from. Even at home she'd pick on me, but everyone turned a blind eye. She'd steal my stuff, blame me for shit that wasn't my fault. My brother ignored me for the most part, but he didn't do anything to stop his friends when they'd start on me. I started skipping school when I was about fourteen, didn't see the point in going."

I looked over to Marc and saw he was engrossed in my tale, his pizza untouched on his plate. I gestured for him to eat, and he picked up a slice, taking a bite.

"The school called in various officers to come visit me at home, threatened my parents, but nothing could make me go back there. I was already planning to leave home anyway, but just before my sixteenth birthday, a friend of my dad's started to take notice of me. I was naive; I had all these ideas that we'd run away together, live somewhere else as husbands."

I shook my head, remembering how it had all ended.

"God, I was stupid to think I meant anything to him. He was married, but I didn't know that at the time. I thought I was the one for him."

It dawned on me then that I had a pattern, falling for the wrong man and getting hurt. It happened time and time again. I had to stop being so stupid.

"What happened?" Marc's works shook me from my inner thoughts, and I continued.

"He used to take me to nice places, but never close to home, now I think about it. Always a little way from where we lived. I'm from a place across the Mersey and down a bit, not quite Chester. I wasn't old enough to drink yet, so it'd be the movies where we'd sit in the back row, sneak kisses, even a blow job or two. I didn't realise until now that he was technically a paedophile. I wasn't even sixteen, so underage, but I loved it, the thrill of almost getting caught and just the thought that someone loved me. Tall, gangly, skinny Ziggy that no one ever took notice of."

"That's fucked up, Ziggy. You don't have to tell me all this. I know it can't be easy for you." Marc was right. This wasn't easy for me, especially how it worked out, but now that I'd started, I found I couldn't stop. I needed to tell the rest of my story.

"I'm good. It doesn't upset me anymore. I've come to terms with it. I just want you to know the rest, then you'll have the full story about me. Poor little Ziggy, nothing ever goes right for him." I smiled then, a sad smile that made me wonder how I'd got this far in life. It'd been shitty from the start, but I wanted to make something of myself, so I tried to not let these things get me down.

"Anyway, we're almost done."

"Only if you're sure."

I nodded; I was sure.

"We messed around for a few months. We never had penetrative sex, I was never ready for that, and I think he knew maybe that was crossing a line we couldn't come back from, but sometime after my sixteenth birthday, I decided we needed to move it up a step. I knew where he lived and honestly thought he lived on his own. He never talked about anyone else, never wore a ring, so I went to visit him at his home. I was shocked as fuck I can tell you when I saw him with his wife and kids. He saw me across the street, and instead of running over to me, like I'd expected, he turned his back. I never heard from him again, but I decided to tell my mum about it. My dad had moved out a couple of months previous, said he'd had enough of her."

I knew I didn't need to continue. Marc would know where this was going, but I ploughed on.

"She didn't believe me, said I was lying, and when I threatened to go to the police with it, she told me not to be stupid, who would believe me, that I'd been nothing but trouble from the day she'd brought me home from hospital. That was it. My limit.

"I went upstairs, packed a bag, and left. I came to Liverpool, dossed around for a couple of years, sleeping in doorways, making a meagre living doing odd jobs here and there but never making enough money to get somewhere of my own. I met Suzie when I was eighteen. We hit it off from the start. She was smart and had a place of her own and had spare cash. The rest, you know."

By now I was tired of talking and drank greedily from my bottle of water.

Marc being Marc, did what he usually did and reached for my hand. I was used to his touch by now and was no longer afraid of him. I trusted his family and, more importantly, trusted him.

"I'm sorry you had to go through that, and I know I don't know you that well, but I think it's made you a stronger person. Look how you've come through this latest setback. I know you didn't come through it unscathed, but you're healing and doing something about it now. Reporting it to the police will help you, especially if we get justice. I'm always going to be here for you, Ziggy. You can count on me and the rest of the family. We've got your back."

As he spoke, he rubbed his thumb over my knuckles. The action soothed me. Nobody had ever touched me the way he did, with care and compassion. My dad's friend, Don, had only ever touched me in a sexual way. We'd never held hands. Punters just wanted sex, and Damian, well, he'd been gentle with me, but I now knew he hadn't meant it. Everything he'd ever done was for his own benefit and, ultimately, Stuart's.

Marc and I were building a friendship which was something I'd never had before, usually jumping straight in with both feet. I was trying to be cautious, trying not to fall head over heels, but he was making it damn difficult.

CHAPTER THIRTY-FIVE

MARC

Several days after our 'date', I still didn't have the numbers for his friends, and I was at a loss how I was going to get them. He kept his phone with him at all times. The only time he didn't have it was when he went for a shower. I also didn't know if he had a lock on it or a pin number. If he did, that was going to be another stumbling block. There wasn't long until the big day, his birthday only being eight days away.

I had to get creative and soon.

Since the night he'd told me his story, I'd started to look at him in a new light. I'd always known he was strong. He denied it, but to have endured so much, to be dismissed and shunned by his family, he was doing so fucking well.

Throw in a sexual assault and verbal and physical abuse at the hands of Damian and I was surprised he wasn't sitting in a corner rocking. Instead he was laughing and joking with Ma, helping her around the house and often when I came home, he was playing with Ryan on his Xbox. I'd not done that with him, so for Ryan, it was like having a younger brother.

I'd arranged another night out. I know, it was like I was quietly dating him, but I just thought he deserved to be spoilt for a change. He'd not really had a childhood, had never done things normal kids got to do, so I'd arranged for us to go Ten Pin bowling. During a conversation a week or more ago, he'd admitted that he'd never been.

I arrived at six to see him waiting on the sofa. He'd had a haircut, and now the bruising had faded from his face, his beauty took my breath. I knew not to mention it, though, he still wasn't there yet, but I'd been trying bit by bit to chip away at his insecurities, show him that I was someone he could trust.

"Wow, someone's been out for a haircut. It looks great."

I held him by the chin, turning his head from side to side, touching his hair as I did so. It was thick and baby soft. He said it was brown, but I could see flecks of auburn and gold in it, the colours shining in the light.

"You got everything you need?" He nodded and stood to his full height. He was only a couple of inches smaller than me, so he didn't need to raise his gaze too much to look into my eyes. God, but he had beautiful eyes too. I'd called them soulful before, and they were, but more recently, I'd seen a playful glint in them, making me want to see what mischief was held within them.

We continued to look at each other until a cough brought us back to earth.

"Are you guys going or just going to stand and make lovey-dovey eyes at each other all night?"

Trust Ryan to spoil the mood, but he had a point. We couldn't stay here all night. I broke the trance we were in and scratched my head, feeling slightly embarrassed at being caught just ogling the man before me.

I led the way out of the door and was shocked by a smack to my arse.

"Let's get going, Marc. There's balls to be thrown."

Yep, there was a mischievous person inside that often serious body, and I was determined to bring him out to play.

"Oh, you're on. Bring on the victory."

Two hours later and I was eating my words. Ziggy had either lied to me, or it was beginner's luck. His smug smile followed me all the way to the car, where he continued to gloat as we drove back home.

Ma was waiting for us as we stepped through the door, and we both laughed at Ziggy's antics. He was dancing around the lounge, pointing at me, making an 'L'-sign on his forehead.

"I take it you didn't win, Marc," she said with a giggle.

"No, I didn't. Either someone was lying, or it was awfully good beginner's luck."

Ziggy stopped dancing and stood in front of me, making the sign of a cross on his chest.

"Cross my heart and hope to die, I have never been Ten Pin bowling before." That mischievous look was in his eyes again, and his mouth quirked into a smile that showed his brilliant white teeth.

"Yeah, I'm not sure I believe you." I smiled at him but stepped back as the temptation to place my lips to his filled my head.

I swear he took a step forward as he was there again, as close as he could be, and I felt his hand graze mine. Was he feeling the same temptation I was?

His pinkie finger gripped mine, and we stood there, almost eye to eye. He reached up, his lips just touching mine, and I closed my eyes, tasting him, savouring him as he licked my lips. We moved closer, the gentle touch becoming a hard press.

Aware that I was standing in Ma's front room, I reluctantly took a step back, dropping my head to his. It was too much and not enough. My heart was pounding and my breathing turned ragged as I tried desperately to get myself under control.

"I'm sorry. I shouldn't have done that." Ziggy turned away from me, and I noticed then that we were alone in the room.

"Yes, you should have done that." I pulled him towards me and into my arms where he melted against me. We kissed again, small little kisses that heightened my desire for him, and when he tilted his head, opening his mouth, I didn't hesitate to take full advantage.

He groaned into my mouth, and I could feel the press of his hard cock against mine. I'd been waiting for this, and it seemed like he had too. Our mouths moved in perfect harmony, his tongue delving deeper into my mouth until he pulled away, nibbling on my bottom lip. I didn't want it to end and moved in again. His hands roamed up and under my shirt, and I shivered at his touch.

"Oh, God." He pulled away from me and walked to the other side of the room.

"What's wrong? I'm sorry. I shouldn't have done that. I feel like I took advantage."

"No, no, you didn't do anything of the sort. If anything, it was me that started it."

He faced me then, and I could see the conflict on his face.

"It was good. Too good! I can't help but think it was too soon. I'm trying so fucking hard not to fall again, hard and fast like I usually do, but you're testing my resolve so much, Marc."

OK, so it wasn't that he didn't want to or regretted it then. That made me feel better, but if we were going to take this anywhere, we would do it at his pace.

"Your rules, Ziggy. Your pace. I'll go as quickly or slowly as you want right now."

"What I want is to take you upstairs and have you fuck my brains out." He looked to the ceiling as if contemplating his next words. "I really, really want that, just not yet. Is that OK? Can we work towards that?"

We could definitely work towards that. I walked to the sofa and sat down, patting the space next to me.

"Come sit. Let's slow it down a little."

He sat away from me, but I pulled him closer, tucking him beneath my arm.

"We'll just sit here and watch a little TV. We never have to do anything until you're ready to, OK?"

There was no response from him, but he snuggled closer, laying his head on my chest. Ma came back in, a satisfied smile on her lips. She'd said before in passing that she thought we'd make a cute couple, but I'd always shut her down, telling her it wasn't like that between us. Since bringing him here, the attraction I felt towards him had grown to the point I was fantasising about him when I was at home, imagining him there.

A little while later, he moved from my side, saying he needed to use the bathroom. He jogged upstairs, and it was then I noticed his phone had fallen from his pocket. Now would be an ideal time with him being upstairs. I snatched it up, quickly swiping my finger across the screen, releasing it. Thank God there was no pin.

I told Ma to watch out for him while I quickly accessed his contacts, hurriedly making a note of the numbers I needed.

A cushion to the head told me I needed to hurry. I just had one number to get when Ziggy walked into the room, and that's when all hell broke loose.

"What the fuck do you think you're doing?" He reached across and ripped the phone from my hand. "I should have known better. I thought you were different, but you're all the same. Why won't you trust me?"

He turned to Ma, tears streaming down his face. "How could you do this to me? I thought we were friends, but I was wrong."

I tried to explain, but before I could, he stormed back up the stairs, and moments later he came down with a small bag, his only coat draped over his arm.

"I've called a taxi. I'll just wait outside." His indifference to me was worse than his tears, and I reached for him, his arm slipping through my grasp.

"Don't fucking touch me, and don't bother coming to look for me. I want nothing more to do with either of you, ever."

The beeping of a car horn let us know his taxi arrived, and he swept out of the house, down the driveway and into the waiting car.

I watched as it drove away, not knowing what the fuck had just happened. What I did know was that I'd let the one thing that mattered to me walk out of my life. I just hoped it wasn't forever.

CHAPTER THIRTY-SIX

ZIGGY

I should have known better. I was so fucking stupid. Every. Single. Time. I got taken in by a good-looking man, and look where I ended up. On the streets with nowhere to stay. Well, not again. I wasn't going to be sucked in again. I was done.

As the taxi pulled away, I looked forward, refusing to look back on the one thing I thought I'd got right this time. Marc.

"Where to, mate?" Shit, I had no idea where I was going to go. I couldn't go to Suzie's. She lived over in North Wales, and it'd cost an absolute fortune to get there. The only place I could think of was Duke's, and I'd have to hope he was in so I could borrow the fare from him when we got there.

I gave the taxi driver the address and watched as the city went by, haunted by thoughts of what had happened earlier in the night, the kisses we'd shared, the hardness of his cock against mine. But it had all been a damn lie. I'd never meant anything to him. If I had, he wouldn't have been snooping on my phone. That day when I'd lost my phone at Damian's, I'd found it later downstairs in the kitchen. I knew for a fact I hadn't left it there, and when I'd broached the subject with Damian, he said he'd found it under the bed and took it downstairs for me to put on charge.

When I thought about it now, it must have been him. He'd taken my phone and had probably done the same thing that Marc was doing. Checking up on me. He'd said I could have my independence, and I'd believed him.

"Everything all right, dude? You're crying, bad break up?"

I touched my face, and there were indeed tears. I was so sick of crying. I needed to be stronger, be better, learn to stand on my own two feet, and flitting from man to man wasn't going to help me do that.

"Something like that, yeah. But I'm OK." I took my phone out, intent on calling Duke. It was only best I called him to let him know I was on my way.

He answered almost immediately.

"Ziggy, is everything OK? It's late." I checked my phone only now realising it was almost 11 p.m.

"Sorry, I didn't see the time. Look, this thing with my friend's mum, it's not working out. Is there any chance I could bunk with you for a couple of nights, just until I can find something else?"

"Of course, you know where I am. I'll set up the sofa again for you."

As we pulled up outside Duke's house, I asked the driver to wait for me while I went inside to get his cash. Duke handed me twenty quid, and I paid him, telling him to keep the change.

"So what happened this time?"

"You make it sound like it's always a drama with me, and it honestly isn't."

"No?" He asked the question, his one eyebrow raised. I'd not known Duke for too long, but he'd been there for me last time with Damian, and here he was again, helping me out. I had a lot to thank him for. He was a good-looking guy too, and if you didn't look too closely, you'd think he was a young Lenny Kravitz, complete with piercings. No wonder he always did good trade.

"Ok, maybe a little bit of drama. You got a drink, though? I'm dying here."

"Sure, sit down, and I'll bring them over."

Several beers later and I'd brought him up to speed on what had happened with Damian and now Marc.

"Jesus, you sure can pick 'em, Ziggy. First the psycho and now this one. What's happening with the police anyway? Have they found Liam?"

"I went to the police, gave them a DNA sample and finished off my statement, but I've not heard anything. I almost forgot too, but when Liam first started coming around, I mentioned to Damian that he looked young and he said that the clubs usually checked stuff like that. Perhaps Stuart found him at a club. Not sure what sort. Would it be a BDSM club, or do they have clubs where you can find a Daddy?"

"No idea, mate, but I could ask around if you wanted me to, find out."

"That could be good. I could take a look at them, see if Liam's there or if anyone knows him. How soon could you find out for me.?"

"I have a friend. Let me shoot a text off to him now. They probably only open at night, but we can visit together."

He was quiet for a while, and I stood up, going to the bathroom. How did I get myself into these messes? Duke must think I was a proper drama queen.

"OK, so there's only a couple of clubs that are into that sort of thing, and they're open all day. We could go tomorrow if you've nothing else to do."

Wow, that was quick, but I had to ask, why wasn't Duke out working?

"You not working tonight? I never thought that you might be out and about."

"I was going to tell you. I'm not doing that anymore. Didn't you notice there was only us two here tonight? I've been doing more of my day job, massaging. The place where I was working part-time offered me a full-time position. Means I can earn enough money to keep me afloat without having to sell my arse every day of the week.

"What about you? What are you going to do?"

I hadn't given it much thought, but I supposed I needed to find another job.

"I don't know. I can't go back to the cafe. I was only there for one shift, and I don't feel comfortable going back to Crosby. I know they've cleared out of the house but, I don't know, I just don't think I'd feel happy there."

"I feel you, man. I wouldn't go back there either. You can stay here as long as you want, Ziggy. I'm happy to help you out, but I'm off to bed. I was up early this morning."

He came in for a side hug, and I hugged him back; this was Duke. He was a good friend, and I knew him I could trust.

As I lay there on the sofa, my arm beneath my head, I thought back to just a few hours ago and the kiss Marc and I had shared. Had it only been tonight we'd done that? It seemed like days ago, and I felt sad it had all ended that way.

I decided there and then, I was off men for good. No matter how handsome they were, how charming they were, it was going to be a no from me from now on.

Despite the hour, my phone began to ring, and I knew exactly who it'd be, but when I looked at the display, I saw it was Ryan. What was he doing up this late? He'd need to be at work in a few hours, so this didn't make sense.

I debated not answering it but knew one or the other of them would just keep ringing until I answered.

I knew it wasn't his fault, but I couldn't stop the "What" that fell from my mouth as I answered.

"Don't shoot the messenger, Ziggy. Marc asked me to call you."

"He getting you to do his dirty work now? Not man enough

to call me himself? I'm not interested in anything he has to say. Don't contact me again, Ryan. Delete my number, every one of you. I won't be answering again."

I hit 'end call' and turned it off, tucking it into my bag. I had no wish to talk to Marc again, his actions had tarnished my opinion of him and I was fucking livid with him. I was sad I'd no longer be living with Pat and Ryan. They'd become like family to me in the short time I'd lived there and I'd miss them dreadfully, especially Pat. Her generosity, taking me in when I had nowhere else to go, treating me like a son, it made me sad I might never see them again.

I tossed and turned all night, and when Duke came in the following morning, I was surprised I'd got any sleep at all. My eyes were sore, as was my throat, but that was soon remedied when Duke handed me a hot cup of tea.

"So, what's the plan for today? Are you ready to visit these clubs? I guarantee you won't have seen anything like them before. That's even if we get inside the door. We might not yet."

"I'm ready. Do I need to wear anything special?"

"What, like a sleepsuit or a nappy?" Duke laughed. "No, I think you'll be alright in jeans and a T-shirt. Jesus man, for a sex worker, you really don't know a lot, do you?"

The comment stung a little. I knew enough to get me the money I needed. I didn't get involved in things I wasn't interested in, and after seeing Liam, I knew I didn't want to do that, and the spanking also wasn't my thing.

Call me vanilla if you must, but sex didn't have to be kinky to be good.

"I just know what I like, and it isn't that, nor was the spanking Damian gave me."

"Jeez, defensive much, Ziggy?"

He lit a cigarette, taking a deep drag before blowing the smoke out through an open window.

"Go get dressed. I have to be at work later."

CHAPTER THIRTY-SEVEN

ZIGGY

The first club we visited gave us nothing. No one knew any 'littles' by the name of Liam, and his description matched numerous boys apparently. We only had the address of one more, and I wasn't holding out hope for this one either.

We were admitted into the second one and led into a small room off to the side.

"Duke, how lovely to see you again." The blonde woman sitting on the couch offered us tea and a seat, and I was tempted to ask Duke how he knew her. I didn't think he was bi, so there had to be another reason. It made me wonder who the friend was he'd called last night to find the information we needed.

"Likewise, Sal. Haven't seen you for a while. My friend here has a few questions, if that's OK."

"I'm looking for a friend. I haven't seen him for a while, and I'm worried about him. His name's Liam. I know it's not much to go on, and I think once I describe him, it won't be much more for you.

"He's small, said he was eighteen but only looked about twelve. He's slight with dark-brown hair and eyes to match. He likes being a little. The last time I saw him, he was more like a toddler and was with a guy called Stuart. Again, no last name, sorry."

I wasn't sure if I saw recognition in her eyes, but if she did know him, she hid it well.

"I don't know him myself, but I can ask around. We're not the only club to offer this type of entertainment. Have you tried the place on Hart Street?" Her question was addressed to Duke, and he nodded. We'd just come from there.

"Well, leave me your number, and if I hear of anything, I'll let you know. How worried about him are you?"

"Very, so if you do know him, I would appreciate a call. I need his help."

We stood to leave, and Sal shook both of our hands, bringing Duke in for a tight hug.

"Don't leave it so long next time, Duke. People miss you, you know."

I think I could guess how they knew each other, but it was their business. We stepped into the bright sunshine, and Duke put on his sunglasses, looking as cool as ever. I walked beside him, again the tall, gangly boy that no one noticed.

"So, what do you want to do now?" he asked as we walked.

"I've no money, so we'd best go back to your place. I need to try and find a job so I can pay you some rent at least."

"We can look when we get home, but we'll grab some coffees to go. My treat until you can pay me back."

The bus ride home took longer—it was later in the day and the traffic was worse—but as we walked up to the door of Duke's house, I recognised the car parked outside. It was Marc's.

"What the fuck, Duke? There's only one way he could have found me and that's you telling him. I thought I could trust you, but clearly everyone I think is a friend is just out to deceive me."

"Just listen to him, Ziggy. I think you'll find out it's not what you think." He grabbed my arm and hustled me in through the open door, closely followed by Marc.

I must admit he looked as bad as I felt, dark circles under his eyes and hair that looked like he hadn't put a comb through it.

"I'll be in the bedroom, but stay and listen. I'm warning you."

I sat sullenly on the sofa and crossed my arms.

"Well," I said, addressing Marc. "What weak-ass explanation are you going to give me now?"

"I'm here to tell you the truth. If you'd have stayed around last night instead of storming out, this whole spectacle could have been avoided."

Who the fuck did he think he was, coming into Duke's house talking to me like that?

"If you're going to be like that, you can fuck off right now. I don't have to sit here and listen to this."

"Yes, yes you do, Ziggy. Sometimes you act all mature, then other times, you're like a little boy that doesn't get his own way and throws a tantrum. Whilst it's adorable, it's also fucking annoying. You wouldn't let me explain last night, but now, you'll sit and listen. Ma was distraught last night, and even Ryan's skipped work today."

Shit, now I felt bad and began to regret how I'd handled it. To think I'd put them all through that, but it wasn't my fault Marc had taken my phone and looked through it. It was the kind of thing I was sure Damian did and the memories it evoked brought out the defensive side of me.

"Well, you'd best have a fucking good explanation why you were in my phone, and if not you can just leave."

"How many days until your birthday now, Ziggy?"

"A week today, why?"

"I was looking through your phone so I could get the numbers of your friends: Duke, Suzie and Beau. So I could invite them to your party. No other reason. Not because I don't trust you, not because I want to control you, but because I wanted to do something nice for you. But now? I'm not sure you're worth the effort."

Aw, shit. Now I did feel bad, and I opened my mouth to speak.

"Don't say anything right now. I'm so fucking cross with you, and I'm seriously considering whether your childish behaviour is worth the bother. Ma opened her house to you, looked after you. She's sorry for what we did, and yes, maybe we could have handled it better, but you could have too."

I didn't know what to say to that. I'd never had a relationship before either with a woman who cared enough to be my mother nor with a man that genuinely wanted to be with me, and I'd fucked up, again.

"I don't know what to say to you. I am sorry. The only thing I've ever known is people letting me down when I've put my trust in them. My mum, my brother and sister, Damian and then I thought you were the same. I see now that you were just trying to do a good thing, but all I saw was you looking through my phone. That was the sort of shit that Damian pulled. At least try and see it from my point of view."

He sat next to me on the sofa but leaned forward to rest his elbows on his knees.

"Where do we stand, Ziggy? Ma and Ryan think a lot of you."

He didn't say anything about himself, so I had to ask.

"And what about you, Marc? How do you feel about me?"

He laughed then, but there was no humour in the sound.

"If you'd have asked me a week ago, I'd have said you were a good friend, one that I was starting to have feelings for."

That sounded good, but what did he think now?

"But now, after last night, I'd have said you were someone I have feelings for, someone that I want to try and have a proper relationship with. Someone I can see me going out on dates with, sharing kisses, walks in the park, then coming home and spending nights in bed with, making love all night long. That's how I feel about you, Ziggy."

He turned to look at me, and I was lost for words. Did he still want that now after me storming out?

"What do you want, Ziggy? Because at the moment, where we go from here depends on your answer."

And what did I want? That was the million-dollar question. Was it too soon to jump into something with Marc? Of course it was, it'd only been a matter of weeks since we'd met, but we had taken it slowly, had become friends, and looking back, I'd moved in with Damian far sooner than with Marc. But I couldn't deny the attraction I felt for him, the flutters I felt every time he was near, the way my heart beat a little quicker when he looked at me just the right way.

But he wasn't asking me to move in with him, he just wanted to know how I felt about him. He was kind, considerate and had never done anything to make me not trust him—until last night, and even then, it'd been a misunderstanding.

But before I could speak and tell him exactly what I wanted, he continued.

"I'll tell you what, Ziggy. Here's what we'll do. If Duke will have you here, I want you to stay here with him, and then in a week, on your birthday, we'll have the party. We still want to do that for you, even if all you can be is my friend. It's what we do for each other. But if you decide you want something more with me, tell me then. Maybe being with each other almost every day has clouded both our judgments and what we need is time away from each other. To think about what we want."

He stood and moved towards the door before I could even answer him.

"You have my number. If you don't want the party, let me know by this evening, and we'll call it quits, the party, you and me, everything. I can't say I won't be disappointed, and I hope you won't do that, but knowing what you've been through, maybe I'm the one making unreasonable demands of you."

The door closed behind him, and Duke came out of the bedroom, a resigned look on his face.

"You don't half know how to pick 'em, Ziggy. I've said it before, and I'll say it again. What are you going to do?"

I didn't know, but I was going to take the week to think about it, and maybe by the time my birthday came around, I'd have my answer either way.

I didn't message Marc later that evening, but Duke did, saying yes to the party and if he could send over the details, he'd make sure I was there. I knew I should have done it, but if I started texting him, I might never stop.

Two days later I received a call from Sal. She'd found Liam and had given him my number. When I asked if he was alright, she hesitated, saying she'd left it up to him to call me. It wasn't what I wanted to hear, but it was better than nothing. If all else failed, I could pass the information on to the police and they could follow it up. I hoped he'd call. I wanted to speak to him first, so all I could do was wait.

CHAPTER THIRTY-EIGHT

MARC

The following week dragged on. After meeting with Ziggy at Duke's house, if I thought it'd do any good, I'd have put him over my knee and spanked him myself. I was so annoyed with him, upsetting Ma like that, but I knew we were as much to blame as he was.

After getting the text from Duke to say the party was going ahead, I'd messaged him asking why Ziggy hadn't called. His reply was that Ziggy was a stubborn arse, but his best guess was that he'd cave if we started talking again and he believed we needed time apart.

I couldn't believe how Ziggy had got under my skin in such a short space of time, and in a way, I knew this separation would be good for us both as much as I hated it. Ma was excited about the party when I told her and threw herself into the preparations. We were only having it at the house so nothing too big. Suzie had said she'd definitely be there, and Beau was surprised to have been asked, seeing how he didn't know Ziggy that well.

My thinking was that he needed people there of his own age, people he felt comfortable with and they were that for him.

I missed him, though, and every time I went to Ma's house, I expected to see him either sitting on the sofa with Ryan or with Ma in the kitchen or garden. We all agreed the house seemed a little quieter, a little emptier without him in it. Every day I hoped he'd see things my way and want to make a go of it, and Kyle wouldn't stop ribbing me about it every chance he got.

I'd asked him to come along too so he could see for himself how well Ziggy was doing and also give Ziggy a chance to thank him personally. He'd mentioned to me more than once how he'd like to do that.

Each night in bed, the one and only kiss we'd shared played on repeat in my head. I was sad to think I might never experience one of them again, but I jacked off more than once as I also remembered the thickness of his erect cock against mine and to thoughts of how delicious they'd be rubbing together, both of us coming with pants and gasps.

The night before the party, the images just wouldn't go away, and as I lay in bed, I got my fleshlight out of the drawer next to my bed, making sure to lube it well. It didn't beat the real thing, but it was a close second.

I closed my eyes, slipping the sleeve over my stiff cock, and I groaned as I moved it up and down. I imagined it was Ziggy's arse, hot and tight. I remembered the view I'd had of it in the hospital, and my hand sped up. I twisted it on the upstroke, and my cock responded, leaking copious amounts of precum. This wasn't going to take long, but that didn't matter. Stroking myself faster and faster, my orgasm built until I came with a shout. My muscles tensed and as my breathing finally returned to normal, I thought about Ziggy and how we could be so right together if he'd only give us a chance.

The following day, I was early at the party house. I'd offered to help with food prep. Ryan had made him a cake, and I knew he'd cry when he saw it. He was such an emotional person and tried to hide it behind a facade of strength, but deep down, I knew he just wanted someone to love him.

After Henry, I didn't think I'd ever find anyone again but meeting Ziggy had changed my outlook, and now, I wanted to be that person, the one to look after him like he deserved, the one to love him. I'd thought I wasn't worthy either. Henry's treatment of me had made me wary of most men, but Ziggy wasn't most men. He was funny, perfectly flawed and uniquely Ziggy and the man I loved.

Fuck, that surprised me, but the more I thought about it, the more I knew it was true. Could you love someone in such a short space of time? I asked Ma the exact same question, and she nodded, saying she knew Dad was the one after only two dates. That it didn't matter how long you'd been together. When the heart knew, it knew.

At seven on the dot, all of Ziggy's friends arrived, all except Duke. He and Ziggy were due around seven thirty. It wasn't a surprise party per se, but we wanted everyone there for his grand entrance. Duke had said not to worry; everything was under control. He'd lent him some clothes and Ziggy was excited, not just for the party but to see me too. He'd apparently talked non-stop about whether I'd like his outfit, would I like his hair and he'd even painted his nails a dusky blue.

I didn't particularly care about any of that; I just wanted to see him.

At seven forty-five, they still hadn't arrived, and I was getting nervous. What if he'd changed his mind? What if he didn't think I was the one for him? But I needn't have worried. We'd left the front door open so he could just walk in when he arrived, and arrive he did in a flurry of sparkles. He looked magnificent, dressed in a pair of pink sparkly trainers, very skinny black jeans that left nothing to the imagination and a purple button-up shirt. A touch of glitter shone in his hair, and I'd never been happier to see anyone in my life.

Our eyes met, and I swear time stood still. His brilliant smile lit up the room as he greeted his friends with hugs and kisses before finally walking towards me. The room went quiet as everyone stood to watch.

"Wow, you scrub up well, Marc. I love you in this." I looked down at what I was wearing. I had jeans on, the same as him, but I wore a fitted short-sleeved, dark-blue button-up shirt that clung to every muscle. I was playing to my advantage here. I knew he liked them. He'd stared at them enough when he'd thought I wasn't looking.

"You don't look so bad yourself, Ziggy. I'm liking the sparkles." The people around us had started talking again, so I didn't feel so self-conscious.

"Can we talk, privately?" He motioned towards the laundry room, and I followed him, not knowing what he was going to say.

He closed the door behind us, and the noise in the other room dulled, giving us peace and quiet.

"So, I've spent this week thinking a lot. About you and me and whether there should be a you and me." He paused as if thinking of what to say, and I began to get nervous. From his actions when he'd walked into the house, I'd been hoping for a good outcome, but now he picked at his lip with his teeth, seemingly as nervous as I was.

"It was horrible not seeing you this week, and I missed you, so fucking much. I know we haven't known each other long, but is it too soon? Can we be an us? Would Pat have me back here? I can't believe I fucked up so badly. Will she forgive me? Will Ryan forgive me? Can you forgive me, Marc?"

My kiss was his answer, and I wrapped my arms around his waist, pulling him in closer to me. I peppered his face and lips with kisses, telling him in my way that he was forgiven.

He wrapped his long arms around my neck and kissed me back, a frantic kiss of tongues and teeth and wandering hands. His hands gripped my hair, and I hauled him in, gripping his arse. I lifted him with ease, and he wrapped his legs around me; the sensual rub of his hard dick against mine was tantalising, the friction rubbing me in all the right places.

He dropped his head to my shoulder and continued to rut shamelessly against me, but I wasn't going to stop him. It was all kinds of glorious, and I thrust against him in return. Not much longer and I'd be coming, and I'm sure Ziggy had the same idea.

"Oh my God, not here, not here. I want to come so bad, Marc." He placed his feet back on the floor and dropped to his knees, nuzzling into my cock through my jeans.

"I need this in my mouth now." He breathed deeply, inhaling my scent. Fuck, that was hot. I was in danger of losing it there and then.

"Jesus, Ziggy, we need to stop. There's getting on for twenty people out there, and they'll know exactly what we've been doing if we don't go out there soon. It is your party, after all."

"I know, I know. Let's go socialise," he said with a sigh. "but I really can't wait to go back to your place." He stood up then and faced me, the biggest pout on his face.

I kissed his lips, happy that I got to do it. "Come on then.We can go back to my place later if you still want to. No pressure, but I'd love nothing more than to peel you out of those extremely tight jeans."

"I'd love nothing more than for you to do that. I've thought of little else lately." He stroked my face lovingly. "You're a breath of fresh air to me. I'm not used to this kind of attention."

He kissed me again, a promise of what was to come but we kept it tender, sweet loving touches. We broke apart at the same time though as a knock on the door shocked us both.

"Are you ever coming out of there? There's people here to see you, Ziggy."

"Coming, Pat."

"Well, I did think you were, but I didn't want to interrupt too soon."

"Jesus, Ma. Did you have to go there?" I shouted, shaking my head. She was incorrigible.

Raucous laughter gradually faded away as she moved from the door.

"Guess that's our cue to leave then."

We both straightened our clothing, and after a quick peck to the lips, we walked out into the party, both of us as happy as we could be. We'd found each other in the strangest of circumstances, but at long last, we were together.

CHAPTER THIRTY-NINE

ZIGGY

The party was amazing. Seeing Suzie again and even Beau made my night. They gathered round as I told my story, Suzie swearing like a sailor as usual, threatening Damian and Stuart's balls if she ever got hold of them. Duke already knew what had happened, so he mingled with the rest of the guests. I had a quiet word with Beau, and he agreed to speak to the police if and when they ever caught the two brothers.

Meeting Kyle brought on the tears yet again, and I couldn't thank him enough for what he'd done for me, but he kept saying it was his job, it was what he did. I was never more grateful to the two of them, and in my eyes, they were the heroes of this party. Without them, I wouldn't be here celebrating. His girlfriend, Gemma, was pregnant with their first child, which they announced a little later on into the night. Everyone applauded and cheered, and Kyle got embarrassed by all the attention.

All in all, it was a brilliant do, and when Ryan brought out the cake, I cried again. It was understated, unlike me, but beautiful in whites and greys, a lit sparkler in the top making it the best cake I'd ever seen.

I looked over at Marc after a few hours of chatting and a little bit of dancing, and he knew what I wanted. I wanted to go back to his place where we could be alone to show each other just how much we needed one another, but before we left, I needed to thank Pat. I'd been a brat, and I needed to apologise for my behaviour.

I was getting better with touch, especially with those I knew, and I took her to one side and gave her a hug.

"I'm so sorry I acted like a dick that night, Pat. Will you ever forgive me?"

She pulled back so she could look me in the eye, no mean feat as she was about a foot shorter than I was.

"You're forgiven for everything. We should have told you what we wanted instead of going behind your back, but we wanted it to be a surprise. I'm not cross at you. I could never be that, not when I see the smile you've put on Marc's face. The way he looks at you, the way I see you look at him… It warms my heart, child."

At this rate, I'd be crying again, so I held her close. "Thank you. You don't know how much this has meant to me. Having somewhere I can call home, a place where I feel safe, and it's all down to you, Marc and Ryan. Is it OK if I come back? I've missed you, and I promise, I'll get a job so I can start paying you some rent."

I felt her nod against my chest, and she reached into the pocket of her dress, bringing out a tissue and blowing her nose.

"I knew I'd cry, and I'm so happy right now. But I can see Marc watching you, I think he's ready to go home. So, off with you, and I'll see you back here tomorrow, not too early mind. I think I'll be having a lie-in. Don't you worry about paying me either, child. You'll always have a home here."

We said our goodbyes and I walked across the room to Marc, noticing the lustful look in his eyes as I approached.

"Are you ready to go?" I asked. I was more than ready and hoped he was too.

"I've been ready for the past two hours. Do you know how difficult it's been to control this permanent hard-on I seem to have?"

"Well, very soon, you won't need to, and I, for one, can't wait to see it."

I did the rounds, promising to keep in touch with people, my friends especially. Beau said he'd put a good word in with Sandy about getting my old job back. I wasn't sure how I felt about that. For a start, it was way out in Crosby, and also, I didn't know if I could be there with all the memories it held.

Finally, we were sitting in Marc's car, on our way to his house. He promised it wasn't far, and I hoped he was telling the truth. I was dying to see him naked, positively gagging to have his cock in my mouth and tasting his come. The heated looks he was throwing my way, I reckoned we were in for a good night.

Walking through the door, we were assaulted by a ginger ball of fur; I guessed this was Smeagol. He wove himself between our legs until Marc reached down to pick him up.

"This is Smeagol. Say hello to Ziggy, precious. He's come to stay with us tonight, but you will need to sleep down here. We've got things we want to do, and cats aren't invited."

It was such a sweet cat, and the way Marc was with him was so cute, but he was right. What we planned to do was not for his kitty's eyes.

He put him down on the floor, and Smeagol ran to his basket, snuggling down and closing his eyes. Marc pinned me with his gaze, and I knew that this was it. We were completely alone for the first time, both of us knowing this was a turning point in our relationship.

"Now, what was it you said earlier? You've been dreaming about my cock?" His lips moved to my ear, and he whispered his next words. "I've fantasised about your arse and how it would feel, me sliding inside, your hot, tight hole, taking me. But first, I want to lick you, taste you, gently stretch you, one finger at a time until you're begging for me." He kissed the sensitive skin beneath my ear, and I shuddered, imagining him doing all he'd said. I was so turned on I collapsed against him.

"Oh, God, Marc. Yes," I panted. I wanted him to do all that and more, and I rubbed his cock through his jeans. "Fuck, I need you now."

And I did. I needed him naked; I wanted to see him in all his glory. I wanted to lick him all over, bite his nipples, caress his balls. I fumbled with the buttons on his shirt, but he pushed me away.

"I want you to undress for me. I want to see you." At his words, I thought about the scars that littered my body. Would he still find me attractive when he saw them? I hesitated. I'd never once been ashamed of my body, but now, doubts surfaced in my mind. What if he didn't like what he saw? What if he was disgusted by me?

As if reading my mind, he brushed the hair from my face and bent down, kissing me gently.

"I don't care about your scars, Ziggy. I just want you. They make you who you are, don't ever be ashamed of that."

I bowed my head and slowly started to undress, taking care not to fall over as I removed my jeans. I stood before him in my underwear, feeling very self-conscious.

"All of it, Ziggy, I need to see you." I stepped out of my tight boxers and stood before him, my arms by my side.

"Beautiful," he whispered, "just beautiful." I stiffened at his words and moved my hands in front of me.

"Don't say that. Please don't use that word."

"Why not? It's true, you are."

"Damian used to call me beautiful."

"Ah, I see." He moved my hands to my sides and gazed at my naked body. "Exquisite. There, that's a better word. You truly are exquisite." He brushed his lips over my skin, making me shiver with need.

He traced the scars on my stomach with his fingers and dropped to his knees. He ran his tongue along each one, kissing it before moving on to the next. My cock was already hard, and with each lick, each kiss, it pulsed with need. I was eager for his touch. Finally sensing my need, he slowly licked a stripe from base to tip, and a drop of precum gathered at the end.

"Mmm, just so ready for me." He licked the slit and suckled the head into his hot mouth.

"Fuuucckk." The sensation was indescribable. It'd been years since anyone had paid my dick so much lavish attention, and I almost came there and then.

"You need to stop, and you also need to get naked too."

He chuckled and stood, undoing the buttons of his shirt. As his toned, tattooed body came into view, my mouth went dry. He was a vision of masculinity, the hair on his chest settled neatly between his pecs, and when I spied the single bar piercing each nipple, my cock dripped, pools of precum gathering on the hard, tiled floor.

"Jesus, I think you're trying to kill me here."

He stayed silent but continued removing his clothing until all that remained were his briefs. His large, uncut cock leaked, creating a wet patch.

I traced the outline with my thumb, paying special attention to the head. I knelt in front of him and placed noisy kisses along its length. He threw his head back and whimpered. I continued my adoration of his perfect cock, removing it from the confines of his briefs. It bounced free, and now it was my turn to whine. It was long and veiny and not too thick, but the thought of having that up my arse turned me into a quivering mess.

I edged towards it as it hovered in front of my face, and the image of another, smaller cock came to mind. I battled with the image. I wouldn't let Stuart ruin this for me, but the more I tried to forget, the more I remembered. I couldn't do it. Those fuckers had ruined me.

I sat back on the floor, my hands covering my face and sobbed, tears flowing from my eyes. What would Marc think? I'd thought I was ready, wanted to be ready, but here I was, poor damaged Ziggy. I continued to cry, heaving sobs that hurt my chest. A soothing voice I vaguely remembered whispered soft words of comfort and arms brought me into a hug, offering solace and safety.

I was broken…damaged, and the thought that no one would ever love me like this brought a fresh round of tears. I was lifted by strong arms and placed onto the sofa, a warm blanket covering my shaking body. This was not how I'd seen this evening going, but here I was, alone once again. Poor fucking Ziggy, the boy that no one could love.

CHAPTER FORTY

MARC

I wasn't sure what had happened, but one moment, Ziggy was ready to swallow my cock and the next, he was sobbing on the floor. I could only think it had something to do with his assault, and as I tried to comfort him, he fought back. I did what I'd done before, though, and spoke what I hoped were gentle, comforting words.

After laying him on the sofa and covering him with a throw, I redressed and went to get water from the kitchen. I sat at the end of the sofa and offered him the glass. I didn't want to get too close to him, unsure of what his reaction would be, but he took the glass, clutching it to his naked chest.

We sat in silence as he finally got himself under control. I wouldn't push him, knowing that he'd tell me in his own time. I wanted so much to reach out to him, let him know I was there for him, but now wasn't the right time.

"I'm sorry." Just two words from him conveying so much emotion and hurt.

"It's not your fault, Ziggy. I understand; I really do." In our job, Kyle and I had come across victims of domestic violence and assault many times. Often they thought it was their fault, that they deserved what happened to them, and then there were those who thought they were fine—until they weren't.

I was guessing Ziggy fell into the latter category. He'd been so happy earlier, eager to move things forward in our very fragile relationship only to find that the ghosts of those two bastards were still hanging around, threatening what we had before it had properly started.

I wouldn't let that happen. We'd get through this together. There was no doubt in my mind I'd be sticking around. Ziggy, on the other hand, I knew he'd try to push me away, tell me he wasn't worth the bother. But he was worth every moment of my time, and I'd do whatever I could to make him see that.

"Maybe I should just go. I don't even know why you want to try with me. I'm broken, incapable of love."

And there it was, the doubt, the feeling of worthlessness that I knew was in there. There was no way I was letting him get away with it.

"No, I don't think you should go at all. I think you should try to tell me what happened. Help me understand, and together we can find a way around this."

He stared off into the distance, his jaw tense.

"I'll never be away from them. What they did to me, it'll always be with me. How can I ever have a normal relationship if all I'll ever see is them?"

He turned to me, and I saw the pain in his eyes. I didn't have an answer for him right now, but I thought he'd need to talk to someone, try to work through these issues. I had no doubt he'd get through it, but at this moment, I knew he'd think it was all over.

"I ruined our evening. It could have been so good tonight. I thought I was ready for it, that I'd be able to make you feel good, but all I've done is let you down. Maybe you're better off without me. You should find someone else."

He went to stand, realising at the last moment that he was still naked. He sat back on the sofa, covering himself with the throw.

"Here, let me get your clothes, and if you want, I'll take you back to Ma's house."

I handed him his clothes, and he put on his shirt and boxers, turning his back to me as he dressed. He didn't put on his jeans, and that gave me hope he intended to stay.

"All I saw was him, his pathetic dick coming towards me. That's what he did, you know." I could see the anger in his face now. "He put his dirty, useless, minuscule dick in my mouth and made me take it, every measly inch. He kept thrusting, hurting my throat, making me gag, and when he came, I puked. All over him and me, and that's when he punched me, time and time again until Damian made him stop.

"He was livid, psychotic even. I thought I was going to die, Marc." His voice broke, and the tears started again. I wanted to pull him close, but in the end, I didn't need to. He lay down, his knees to his chest, his head in my lap.

"I'm so tired. Tired of pretending I'm OK, tired of seeing them, over and over, tired of watching my every move, wondering if they'll find me and finish the job they started."

I stroked his hair, not knowing what else to do, but I refused to say it had ruined our night. The party had been a huge success, and Ziggy had enjoyed himself, catching up with his friends, and when we'd been alone, it was as if a fire had been lit inside of me. I wanted him like no other, and I refused to allow them to spoil it.

"Do you want to stay here? I can make up the spare room if you'd like."

"Would you mind? But I don't want to sleep alone. Can I sleep with you? In your bed?" His voice was so small. How could I say no to him?

"Come on, let's go." He stood and followed me as I made my way upstairs. I pulled the covers back and stripped, digging out a couple of pairs of pyjamas and T-shirts for us to wear. This time, he didn't hide, climbing into bed in just the pants, the T-shirt lying unused on the chair.

Turning off the light, I lay next to him, listening to him breathe. I could tell he wasn't sleeping and wondered if he still wanted to talk.

"Are you OK?"

"I think so, just tired now and sad. Sad that we didn't get to do what we wanted. I'm not sure how I'm going to get over this, but I think if we're going to make a go of this, I have to try. I want to give you everything, Marc. I wasn't lying about that."

He moved over to my side of the bed, turned on his side and threw his arm across my stomach, cuddling close.

"Here, lift up." He lifted his head so I could place my arm around him, and we lay there, snuggled into each other. "We'll get through this. You'll get through this. Just remember, I'm still not going anywhere."

He said nothing, and it was then I realised he'd gone to sleep. I lay awake for a while, reliving the past few hours and thinking how best I could help him get through this, but in time, my head hurt and I needed to sleep. I'd booked a few days from work, hoping that Ziggy and I would be celebrating not only his birthday but our fledgling relationship. Little did I think I'd be consoling him, reminding him yet again that he was never alone.

I woke alone the next morning, but the space next to me was still warm. I worried that he'd got up and left, but when I heard the cupboards banging downstairs, I realised he must be in the kitchen.

Walking down into the open plan kitchen, I heard Ziggy talking and wondered if he was on the phone, but as I listened closer, I laughed quietly.

"So, Smeagol, my little precious. Where does your Daddy keep the coffee? Does he drink coffee in the morning, or does he drink tea? What? No answer? You're not a very helpful kitty, are you?"

I heard the sound of more cupboards opening and closing and decided to put him out of his misery.

"The cupboard just to the right of the kettle."

He spun to face me, smiling from ear to ear.

"Hey, you're up. Did you sleep well? I had the best sleep ever and feel like a new person this morning."

"I slept well, thanks, if a little warm. Someone's a cuddler, I see."

"I am a little. Suzie always used to moan at me and when I was with Damian..." He trailed off, not finishing his sentence.

"Well, that doesn't matter now, does it," he continued. "But yes, I like to cuddle."

While we'd been talking, he'd been making tea. We moved to the small table and chairs and sat. I smiled at him across the table, barely able to believe he was here in my house. I knew things hadn't gone to plan last night, but this morning... This was what I'd wanted, having him here in my kitchen every morning.

"What do you want to do today? I know Ma said she was having a lie-in, and as it's only"—I looked over to the clock on the microwave—"fuck, Ziggy, it's only 7 a.m. Why are we up this early?"

"Seven? Shit, I thought it was about nine." He picked up his cup of tea and marched towards the stairs. "I'm going back to bed. You joining me?"

Damn right I was joining him. I picked up my own cup and stepped into my bedroom to see him snuggling under the duvet, a sweet smile on his face.

I pulled the covers back to find him completely naked. I dropped them back in place, then lifted them again.

"Erm, you're naked, Ziggy. Where are your clothes?"

"I might have taken them off. I want to test a theory, whether it was being naked or the thought of, you know, sucking your cock that got to me."

"Do you want me naked too?" He nodded enthusiastically, that mischievous look in his eyes again.

"OK then, if you're sure." I didn't know how this was going to go, but my no longer soft dick had decided being naked in a bed with Ziggy was a fantastic idea, and as I dropped my pyjamas to the floor, it sprung upwards, hitting my stomach, a string of precum connecting the two.

Ziggy's eyes lit up, and he squirmed in the bed. I could see him rubbing himself beneath the covers and wished I could do that for him. I climbed in with him and lay on my back, wondering what we were going to do.

"Do you mind?" He reached across and placed a tentative hand on my cock. "I figured if I couldn't see it, it might be OK."

"We don't have to do anything, Ziggy. I'd be happy to wait until you feel better about this."

"I know, but I want to at least try and feel you now, all hard and sticky in my hand. I want to do something with it. I thrust gently in his hand, showing him just how much I wanted him to continue.

CHAPTER FORTY-ONE

ZIGGY

The feel of his cock beneath my hands was so good, and after last night, I was desperate to make it up to him and see how far I *could* go. I felt like I'd let him down. I knew I hadn't, that the images of Stuart and his pathetic dick had set me off.

My own cock responded, growing as I rubbed myself, and I closed my eyes, feeling the tension building. I hadn't had the urge to do anything remotely sexual since the attack. The odd hard-on, mainly when I'd thought of Marc, but other than that, nothing.

Feeling brave, I sat up in bed and moved over to him, straddling his thick thighs. He really didn't like to skip leg day, and I loved the feel of the hard muscles beneath me. I gripped us both in my hand and moved backwards and forward, gyrating while I rubbed.

"Fuck, Ziggy. That feels amazing."

I loved the feel of his skin against mine, and it'd been so long since I'd had an orgasm, I didn't think it was going to take long at all. I continued to rub and grind, watching as he closed his eyes and threw his head back. Fuck he was sexy, and this sight of him, nipples pierced, tattoos covering his chest, it was all too much.

"Shit, I'm gonna come already," I grunted and erupted over my hand, continuing to stroke Marc's dick, then watching as he too reached his release, pumping spurt after spurt of creamy spunk over us both.

I collapsed on top of him and nestled into his neck, my smooth chest tickled by his wiry chest hair.

As our breathing returned to normal, I felt an overwhelming sense of relief that I'd not freaked out. At least I knew how far I could go before that happened.

I rolled onto my side of the bed and looked over at Marc, smiling at the blissful look on his face. He, too, turned to face me, reaching across to stroke my now sweaty face.

"That was hot, and thank you. I know how much that must have taken, but I'm very, very grateful you did it. Let's shower and then come back to bed for a nap. I'm exhausted."

He leaned across me, dropping a kiss to the end of my nose. "Let's go, gorgeous."

I followed him into the bathroom and eventually back to bed. The water had cooled by the time we managed to leave the shower, our heated kisses not enough to keep it warm. We didn't bother getting dressed and slipped back under the covers, cuddling into each other.

We woke around eleven to the sound of my phone. I hopped out of bed and ran downstairs, answering before it could stop.

"Hi, this is Ziggy." Silence. "Hello, is anyone there?" I panicked for a moment, thinking Damian or Stuart were calling, but a small voice on the other end stopped me in my tracks.

"It's Liam. You wanted to speak to me."

"God, yes, I wanted to know if you were OK. Are you? OK, that is." I waited to see if he would answer.

"Can we meet up? We need to talk. I can meet with you in about an hour if that suits." He sounded brusque and to the point.

"That'd be great." He mentioned a coffee shop, and we agreed to meet there at twelve thirty. It suited me as it was only about twenty minutes from where Marc lived.

After ending the call, I ran upstairs to Marc, jumping on the bed.

"That was Liam. He wants to meet up in about an hour and a half. Will you come with me? We need to try and persuade him to help us put those wankers behind bars."

"Of course, but you haven't told me how you found him. We've got time before we need to leave."

I remembered I'd never got the chance to tell him, so as we lay in bed, our fingers entwined, I told him about Duke's friend and how he'd put us in touch with Sal and how I'd left my number in the hopes he'd get in touch.

"Let's just hope he can help then. His testimony could be what we need to put those bastards behind bars for a long time." I hoped so, but after spending time with him, I wasn't convinced.

After a quick brunch, Marc drove us to the coffee shop. He offered to wait in the car, but I insisted he came in. I didn't want to meet with Liam on my own, my nerves getting the better of me. What if this was a set up and Damian, or worse, Stuart, were there too?

He agreed, and just before twelve thirty, we walked inside. I almost didn't recognise Liam. He was sitting at a small round table looking skinnier than I remembered. His hair was shaved on one side, black stitches stark against his pale skull, his arm in a cast and sling. What the fuck had happened to him?

Marc went to the counter, and I sat opposite Liam, no doubt a look of complete shock on my face.

"I know, I look terrible, but it could have been worse. I could be dead, but if you're going to ask me what happened, well, there might be a bit of a problem there." He tapped his head, then dropped his hand to his lap. "Because of this, I can't remember anything. The doctors think my memory might come back in time, but they can't say either way."

"What do you remember? Was it Damian or Stuart that did this to you?" I was desperate to know.

"The last thing I remember was sitting at home, waiting for Stuart to come home. He was late as usual. He'd been staying out later and later, and I'd already accused him a week or so earlier about having another 'little' on the side. He'd denied it, but I didn't believe him." He stopped talking as Marc approached the table, sitting next to me.

"Oh, this is Marc. He's the paramedic that saved my life after Damian and Stuart almost killed me too. He's been helping me since I left the hospital." I turned to smile at him as he reached across to hold my hand.

"And he's a bit more than that, I can see, but good for you. I'd always been torn about speaking to you about Damian and Stuart. I didn't know exactly what was going on with them, but I'd occasionally hear them talking about you, about how Stuart didn't think Damian was moving quickly enough, that you'd lose interest and move on. I should have told you, and I'm sorry now that I didn't."

"I'm OK now. It doesn't matter. Carry on, maybe if we can put enough of a story together, we can go to the police."

Liam looked horrified. "No, I'm not going to the police. I agreed to talk to you, not them. What if he comes back and finishes the job?"

"That's exactly what I was thinking, but it was because of you that I did go to the police." I debated how much to tell him but decided full disclosure was needed.

"Just before they attacked me, Stuart mentioned about having 'shut you up' because you were a bratty, smart-mouthed little and that you'd deserved everything you'd got. I couldn't get those words out of my head, and when I was torn about reporting the attack, Marc reminded me that they could have done it to someone else. The thought that you could have been lying somewhere in the same state I was made me do the right thing.

"I think between us, we could give the police enough evidence to arrest them. They just need to find them."

"What? You mean you don't know where they are?" Liam looked surprised when I shook my head.

"No. Why would I? Do you know where they are?" Liam laughed then. "Of course I do. Didn't you ever hear Damian talk about Georgie?"

"Damian's wife, she walked out on him with his daughter, Daisy, six years ago."

"Georgie's their sister, not Damian's wife. He must have told you that to make you feel sorry for him. She used to come to the house. A nasty piece of work, used to smack them around all the time when they thought I wasn't watching. I never said anything, of course. When I was 'little Liam', they'd talk all the time, not bothering if I was in the room or not, but she was the boss, and when she said jump, they asked how high."

"Well, fuck me." Marc's voice surprised me. I'd forgotten he was there.

"Yeah, exactly. She has a place about an hour outside of Liverpool. I reckon they're all there, lying low."

The only thing still playing on my mind was why Liam hadn't reported the attack.

"Why did you leave it? Why not say anything?"

"For starters, I can't say for sure. I don't remember much after Stuart came home. I know that probably means he did it, but I have no proof. I just know I was picked up by the police, walking the streets, rambling. I was taken to the hospital, and I eventually remembered my name but nothing else. Things are still a little unclear. I remember you, remember the house in Crosby and up to the actual assault."

I sat quietly for a while, thinking about what we could do. My first and only thought was that if we both went to the police and told them everything we knew, and with the extra bits of information that Liam had, perhaps it'd be enough to pick them up and arrest them. Surely it was that simple. I just had to convince Liam it was a good idea.

"Where are you staying now?" I was assuming he hadn't moved back in with Stuart.

"I moved back home. My parents have been very understanding, so at least I have somewhere to stay, even if it's not a permanent solution. They've never been accepting of my kink, shall we say, nor the fact that I'm gay."

Marc had been quiet through the whole conversation but spoke now.

"I know you don't want to, but with two statements naming Stuart in two and Damian in at least one of these attacks, I think you have a good case. Isn't it better to not have to keep looking over your shoulder to see if they're going to be coming for you? It has to take a toll, Liam, both physically and mentally." His eyes found mine, and an understanding passed between us then. He knew what that attack had done to me, not just the physical scars, but the mental ones too.

"Please, Liam. I can't move on with my life until I know they can't hurt me anymore, and I need to move on. I have hope and a future waiting for me, and I need closure." I squeezed Marc's hand. He was my hope *and* my future.

Liam sat quietly for a while, and I could almost see the cogs turning inside his head. I knew it was a hard decision to make. Hell, I'd had the same misgivings he was having now, but how to get across to him that this was the right thing to do? How many others would suffer at their hands? And now knowing that their sister was the instigator, that just made matters worse.

Finally he spoke. "OK, I'll think about coming to the police with you. I won't put myself through any more unnecessary pain. I've been through enough, Ziggy, as you have. But I don't have what you have. I don't have anyone to help me through this, only my parents."

"That's all I ask, Liam, and I'm grateful, I really am. I do think with both our accounts we can get them put away."

"I can't promise anything, Ziggy. I'll call you, though, let you know."

He stood to leave, and I watched as he walked away, a slight limp where he didn't have one before. It could have been so much worse for both of us, and hopefully, he'd find someone that would love him, kinks and all.

CHAPTER FORTY-TWO

MARC

I could tell by Ziggy's expression he was disappointed. I think he'd thought Liam was going to jump right in and dash to the police station with him with a story of how Stuart had tried to kill him, the same as he'd almost done to Ziggy.

As it was, that wasn't going to happen, and it had taken some persuasion on both our parts to get Ziggy to even think about reporting the incident. I tried to distract Ziggy for the rest of the day with a walk into the city, shopping and a nice meal, but I could tell he wasn't happy with the way it had turned out.

I only had tonight and tomorrow before I had to return to work, and we agreed Ziggy would stay with me until then. Before my shift started tomorrow, we planned on collecting his few belongings from Duke's place and dropping him off with Ma.

Returning home after our day out, Ziggy sat on the sofa; his earlier good mood had vanished, and the fear that he'd never be done with Damian and his brother was making him miserable.

"Hey, do you want to watch a movie? Chill out a little."

"Maybe? Do you have snacks? I feel like I need cheering up tonight." He sat on the sofa, his head resting on the back and turned to look at me as I got our food together. "I thought meeting with Liam would help, but all it did was make me more depressed about the whole thing. What if he won't go, Marc? I don't know where they're living at the moment, only Liam does. Can I give Liam up to the police just so they get arrested?"

"I think you have to do what's right for you. I know it's hard, but do you actually owe Liam anything? He said himself he'd heard Damian and Stuart talking about you but didn't do anything about it. He could have told you, Ziggy. So, as to whether you should protect him, I think only you can make that decision."

I sat next to him on the sofa, putting a bowl of popcorn in his lap and my arm around his shoulder.

"Let's just watch the movie and forget about it for a while. We can have another talk tomorrow. Who knows, Liam might do the right thing."

He placed his head on my shoulder and sighed, feeding piece after piece of popcorn into his mouth.

"Play the movie, Marc. Let's get lost in a world of hobbits and elves."

I started the movie but could hardly concentrate. Ziggy would feed me popcorn, and after a while, his fingers lingered in my mouth. The little shit was taunting me, and the swell of my cock inside my jeans was becoming decidedly uncomfortable. I'm sure he noticed too, as with each piece, he would drag his buttery fingers along my lips.

If he wanted to tease, I could too, so the next time he did it, I sucked on his finger, swirling my tongue around the tip.

I saw him trying to hide his erection beneath the bowl, but if I was uncomfortable, he would be too. I placed my hand on his leg and started to stroke and realised that neither of us was watching the movie. Ziggy squirmed beneath my touch, but I knew it was up to him to make the next move. If he couldn't do that, then I was prepared to wait as long as it took to ensure he was ready.

"Fuck this." Ziggy removed his finger from my mouth, put

the bowl on the floor and turned to smash his lips to mine, climbing into my lap.

We groaned in unison as Ziggy attacked my mouth, licking and biting, his hands fisting my hair, tugging and pulling on the ends. I squeezed his arse and pulled him against me, his hard length rubbing against mine.

I wanted him in my bed, and I wanted him now, more than I'd ever wanted anything before.

"Bed, now," I managed to get out between kisses, and Ziggy hopped off my lap, pulling me up, leading me by the hand to the stairs. We didn't make it very far before he slammed me against the wall, assaulting my mouth with voracious kisses, our breathing loud in the now quiet room.

Step by step, we made our way upstairs, eventually reaching the top and my bedroom door. I flicked the light on, picking him up and throwing him on the bed. I was ready for him, but I wouldn't force him. Without breaking eye contact, he started to undress, ripping his shirt over his head and slipping his trousers over his slim hips. He leaned back on his elbows, his eyes hooded as he licked his lips.

I quickly stripped, standing naked in front of him, my cock hard and hurting. Beads of precum formed, and in one movement, Ziggy was there, thumbing the droplets and sucking them into his mouth.

Such a fucking turn on.

I crawled up the bed, forcing him onto his back, kissing a trail up his body until I reached his lips, swollen from our previous kisses. I hesitated, unsure whether to continue, but he reached up, chasing my mouth. I found his cock with my hand, moving my hand up and down with languid strokes, the silky skin encasing the hardness beneath.

He arched his back, thrusting into my hand, his head thrown back in blind ecstasy. I moved down his body, licking and biting his nipples, lavishing attention on them as he writhed beneath me.

"Fuck, that's good. Bite me, make it hurt, Marc." I bit harder on his nipple, and a spurt of precum leaked from him, giving me the lubrication to work him harder. His foreskin was pulled right back now, and his mushroom head was engorged. I needed to taste him, and, opening my throat, I swallowed his cock.

His groans filled the room as I devoured him, taking him to the root time after time. I pressed my nose against his pubic hair, inhaling his scent and swallowed, his cock hitting the back of my throat. I kneaded his balls, rolling them in my hand, and slowly moved my fingers to his crease, edging closer to his hole.

I wasn't sure how far to take this, but from his shouts and the fact he wasn't moving away, he was into this as much as I was. I pulled off his cock with a pop and glanced at him; his eyes were closed. He was beautiful, and right now, he was all mine.

"What do you want, Ziggy? I can stop right now if you need me to."

He opened his eyes; his pupils were wide with lust.

"I want you to fuck me, Marc." His voice was hoarse from his shouts of pleasure, and I swooped in again for another round of kisses.

I needed supplies, though, and they weren't here in my bedroom. I got off the bed and walked towards the door.

"Where are you going?" A whine accompanied his question.

"Supplies, Ziggy. They're in the bathroom." My cock bounced as I ran to the bathroom, grabbing what I needed from the cabinet.

Walking back into the bedroom, I was met by the sight of Ziggy stroking his long cock, and for a moment, I just stood and stared.

He slowly opened his eyes and smiled. "Get over here. I was getting lonely." He didn't need to ask twice, and I lay on the bed next to him, coating my fingers in lube.

"Remember what I said to you before?" I asked and his eyes widened, I turned him gently onto his stomach and moved down the bed to his arse, spreading his cheeks, licking his crack from his hole to his balls time after time. His unique taste was intoxicating as I speared his hole with my tongue.

As I inserted a finger, he lost the use of his words, and all I could hear were mumbled curses. I loosened him up with another finger and then another until I thought he could take me. I wasn't thick, but I had length.

He picked up a condom and expertly rolled it down my painfully hard dick, snagging the lube from the bed, slathering it on my cock.

I was surprised we'd got this far to be honest, and he still seemed to be on board with the whole thing. He turned onto his stomach again, reaching back to plunge his lube drenched fingers into his waiting hole. It was my turn to groan, watching him work himself open and inserting a fourth finger. Fuck, he'd have no problem taking me.

"Shit, Ziggy, I can't wait any longer. Move your fingers."

He did as I asked and raised himself onto his hands and knees, presenting me with his gorgeous arse.

I used both hands to spread his cheeks and spat on his hole, rubbing my saliva into his pucker before slipping my thumb inside.

"Now, Marc." I didn't need telling twice, and I lined up with his hole, pushing slowly, watching how he opened up for me. I slid in, inch by inch, keeping his cheeks spread. I'd never felt anything like it. He clenched his arse, squeezing around my cock, and I stilled, waiting for the sensation to pass.

"More, I need more," he said, his voice strained.

I pulled out, then slammed back in, eliciting a wild shout from him. "More." His pained voice belying his command, but I carried on, trusting that he knew what he wanted.

I could see his hand moving beneath him, and he hung his head, grunting.

Gripping him around his chest, I hauled him up, his back to my front, changing the angle. A gasp left his mouth, and I put my hand around his throat, my other hand working his cock as I pumped him from behind.

Suddenly he froze, and I wondered what had gone wrong.

"Ziggy? Do you want me to stop?"

He hung his head, and I felt a wetness on my hand, realising at the last moment that he was crying.

I tried to pull out, but he stopped me.

"No, wait. I'll be OK, just, just…not my neck."

Fuck, I should have thought, remembering now back to the marks he'd had around his throat when he was in the hospital. I removed my hand, my cock starting to soften inside him.

"Don't stop, please Marc, I need you to finish. I need you."

He turned his head, capturing my lips in a kiss, and I started to thrust again. I wrapped my arm around his chest, setting a punishing pace as I chased my orgasm, helping him reach his.

Moments, minutes, hours later, I had no idea how long it was, but I felt my balls tighten as I finally came, filling the condom. It was so strong my vision went dark. The feel of Ziggy's release spilling over my fist brought me back to reality, and we both fell forward, desperately trying to catch our breath.

My cock slipped out of him, and a small cry left his lips. I stroked his back, moving down to his cheeks, caressing the soft skin.

"Marc, please." I wasn't sure what he wanted, but I took a guess and gently inserted my fingers inside him. He hummed a quiet 'thank you'.

I settled in behind him and wrapped my other arm around him, the condom hanging from my now limp dick. I had no desire to move, and I don't think Ziggy did either. I wiggled my fingers inside of him, and he pushed back, relaxing against me.

We lay like that for a while, both of us sated and worn out. The sex had been just as amazing as I'd thought it would be, but I couldn't help wonder at what cost. Had he done this just to please me, or had he wanted it as much as I did? I didn't want to ask, but I knew we'd be having that conversation.

CHAPTER FORTY-THREE

ZIGGY

I couldn't believe how sex with the right person could change you. Having Marc pound into me from behind was just about the best thing I'd ever experienced. I'd thought sex with Damian was good, but it paled in comparison.

When he'd gripped my throat, though, I'd panicked and frozen, my mind thrown back to the attack, Damian clutching at my neck.

But I'd come this far, and I wouldn't let it spoil what we had. I'd centred my mind and blocked out the memories, pleading with Marc to continue, to help me obliterate the images and feelings of helplessness. I'd thought he was going to stop, but he started again.

The emotions he evoked in me were like none I'd felt before, but my old insecurities began to surface again. He'd tire of me, everybody did, and when the memories of the assault hit again, he'd start to hate me.

I'd make the best of tonight, lying here with him holding me, freshly showered and snuggled under the covers. Tomorrow I'd be back at Pat's place, but no doubt he'd visit less and less, not wanting to hurt me. I was expecting it, felt sure it was going to happen.

The next morning, he woke me with tender kisses to my back and neck. He was being nice, letting me down gently. He'd got what he wanted, and now I'd be cast aside, no longer worth his time.

I climbed out of bed and started to dress. He'd need to rest today and would need me out of his hair.

"Hey, what's wrong?" He grasped my hand. "Where are you going? Come back to bed, baby. It's early."

"You have to rest, and I need to get back to your Ma's place. She'll be expecting me. I should go."

I pulled out of his hold and continued dressing, tears forming in my eyes.

"Stop. Just stop for a moment, will you? What's got into you? I thought we had this all worked out, and now you're acting as if it was just a one-night thing for you. Is that what I was? Just another 'trick'?"

No, and that was the problem. He was more than that, but how could he ever want me? I'd tried with Damian, but it had come to nothing. It always came to nothing.

I sat on the edge of the bed and stared aimlessly at the floor, waiting for the words I knew were coming.

"Last night meant everything to me, Ziggy, and I need to know what it was to you. Was it just a one-off? I thought we were on the same page, that you wanted me as much as I do you, but the way you're acting now?" His voice shook as he spoke. "It's like it meant nothing."

"Of course it meant something. It was the best thing that has ever happened to me."

"So why the change of heart now?"

"Because."

"Because what? You're going to have to explain this to me because I thought what we shared last night, what we've done the past few days, what we've been through the past however many weeks, was us getting to know each other and us deciding to be together."

"But how can you? How can you want to be with me when I'm like this? I froze last night, Marc, right in the middle of sex. What if it happens again? What if I can't continue next time? You'll start to hate me, you'll want someone that can be with you all the time, and I can't promise you that at the moment."

"God, Ziggy. Don't tell me what you think I need. What I need is you, my perfectly flawed Ziggy. The man I can't forget, who has refused to leave my every waking thought for the last God knows how long. The man I love."

I turned to look at him then. What was he saying? It couldn't be true, could it?

"Tell me again," I demanded, getting lost in his beautiful blue eyes.

"I love you." I moved closer to Marc.

"Tell me again," I said, softer this time, the words getting caught in my throat.

Marc held my face and kissed me softly on the lips. "I. Love. You."

I threw my arms around his neck, not believing we could both feel this way after such a short time. I could never say the words to Damian, they just never felt right, but with Marc, there was no doubt.

"Oh my God, I love you, too, so fucking much. I thought it was too soon, but it's not."

He hugged me back, and we fell onto the bed in a flurry of kisses.

After a couple of moments of intense making out, I pulled back. I did need to have a serious talk with him. I didn't want to fall into the same pattern as I did with Damian.

"I still want to go back to your Ma's. I want to stay there for as long as she'll have me. I don't want to rush into moving in here with you and ruining this before we've even got started." The next part was hard for me to admit, but I knew it needed to be done.

"I also need to go and see a professional, talk about the assault and hopefully, they can help me work through it. It could take weeks, months or fucking years, but I think I need that."

He nodded and held onto my hands. "I think it's a good idea, and I'll be with you every step of the way. As for staying with Ma? I agree, moving in together now would be too soon, but I won't wait long. I want you here, with me, every day. Waking up next to me." He nuzzled into my neck, almost making me forget my words.

"That's fine with me but stop. There's more," I panted.

"I also want to find a job and be independent. Damian never wanted that, needing to control my every move, my every thought even, but I need you to know that's not OK. I'm my own person. I'm Ziggy."

"I'll never do that to you. You want a job? Fine with me. You want to go out with your friends? Also fine with me. As long as you come back to me, I'm good with that."

"Then I think we have everything sorted."

He laid me on my back and covered me with his body, intense kisses making me weak at the knees. My stomach started to grumble, breakfast was needed, and Smeagol would be wanting his food. It was while we were eating, that my phone rang.

It was Liam.

"I'll do it," he said, not waiting for me to speak. "I'll talk to the police and report the whole thing. You were right. We can't have this hanging over us. Can we go today? If I think too much about it, I may never get there."

"We could pick you up in an hour and go straight there. I'll make sure I'm with you when you speak to them."

"Thank you. I think that'll help. I don't want to be on my own."

"Hey, you're never on your own, Liam. I'll always be here."

We quickly finished our meal, and an hour later, Marc and I picked him up from one of the more affluent parts of Liverpool. A quick word at the front desk of the police station and we took a seat, waiting for the two detectives that had interviewed me.

Half an hour later, and we were still waiting, getting more and more impatient as the moments passed.

Liam couldn't stop fidgeting, unable to sit still until eventually, we were called through to an interview room.

Detective Woods, whom we'd met before, sat down opposite us, his partner, Detective Palmer, standing as usual.

"So, this is Liam," Wood said, smiling at Liam and glancing at the wound on his head. "Looks like you've been in the wars, son. Why don't you tell us what happened?"

Liam retold the story he'd told Marc and me, the detectives taking notes. When Liam got to the part about Georgie being their sister, the detective paused, looking over to me.

"I didn't know, I swear. He told me they were married." He nodded to Liam to continue.

"It's true. Damian used to tell everyone she was his wife, but she's the person that bullies them both. They do everything she says."

"Do you know why? Did you ever hear anything?"

Liam shook his head. "I never heard much, but I think it's something they've been doing a while. They see it as a game, I think, enticing people like me and Ziggy, hoping we'll obey them, not fight back. Unfortunately, with me and Ziggy, they picked on the wrong people and this"—he pointed to his head—"this is the result. We both almost died at their hands. It took a while for me to get on board with this, but Ziggy's right. We can't let them do this to someone else. They need to be stopped."

This was the most I'd heard Liam say, and the courage he had to speak up, well, I was proud of him.

"OK, I think we have more than enough to bring these people

in. We managed to match the blood at the house in Crosby to you, Ziggy, and if you can leave us with a sample too, Liam, we can search the other property you mentioned." He stood from the table, putting his notebook away. "We'll be in touch."

Detective Palmer had been quiet throughout all of this, but I'd seen the looks he was giving Liam. At first, I'd thought he was being his usual annoying self, but when he made sure to give Liam his card before we left, a small smile on his face, I wasn't entirely sure what to make of it...but I had an idea.

CHAPTER FORTY-FOUR

ZIGGY

After our talk, Marc and I had taken things steady, neither of us wanting to rush what we had. We knew it was something special, but it was also new and fragile.

I'd returned to the hospital for a check-up and had spoken about the problems that had been plaguing me since the attack, the flashbacks, the occasional nightmares, and how it had been affecting my relationship with Marc. They'd referred me to a therapist who could see me as a private patient, Pat insisting on paying for the sessions. I agreed on the understanding I *would* pay her back. Charity wasn't something I could accept readily but this I could accept.

The sessions were hard, forcing me to confront things that had happened in the past; Don, Damian and Stuart. How their actions had affected my life and could still affect me in the future. She gave me coping mechanisms to use but I declined the medication, using a more holistic approach to the treatment.

The therapist agreed that what I had with Marc, how we were taking it slowly, was good for me. That this was the right way forward. I was starting to feel better about things, feeling more settled, and our relationship, both physical and emotional, was improving.

That is until I got the call from Detective Woods. Marc had wanted to come with me but had to work. I arranged to meet Liam there, and Pat came along for moral support.

There was no waiting this time when we arrived, and we were taken immediately through to a conference room, not an interview room this time.

Both detectives met us, and again Palmer couldn't take his eyes off Liam.

After sitting, Detective Woods spoke.

"So after your last visit, we went to the first house you mentioned, Liam, the one you'd been living at, but unfortunately, we found no trace of Stuart nor of you there. As with the house in Crosby, it was empty. We did a thorough forensic search but came up empty-handed."

This was not the news we'd wanted, but he continued.

"The other house, however, the one you mentioned where you thought they might be staying, we did in fact find Georgie but no Damian or Stuart. We brought her in for questioning, and she had no qualms about turning them both in. We were unable to detain her, as according to you both, she did nothing to either one of you."

Liam and I looked at each other, hoping that they'd been able to find them.

"We eventually took both Damian and Stuart into custody. After hours of questioning and the presentation of evidence, they finally confessed to the assault on Ziggy. They'll both be charged with Grievous Bodily Harm with intent. If they're found guilty, they could find themselves in prison for a long time, maybe even life."

Woods turned to Liam.

"In your case, it's a little more difficult as we have no physical evidence, and with your amnesia, we can't prove it was Stuart who hurt you. In the absence of a confession, your case may go untried."

Liam squeezed my hand. We'd known it might come to this, but at least they could be tried and hopefully convicted for the attack on me.

"So, what's next?" Pat had stayed quiet, but I could see she was quietly fuming, her eyes flashing with anger.

"They'll be charged and will go to prison until a trial date is set. There will be a preliminary hearing first, and it'll be up to you whether or not you attend. We understand that it could be difficult for you, Ziggy."

He wasn't wrong, but if I could be there, I would, especially for the main trial anyway, even though it could be months away.

"We'll obviously keep you updated, but at least now you can maybe start to move on, build a life without the fear they may come after you again."

This was the news I'd wanted to hear, and although it might not give closure for Liam, as long as they ended up behind bars for my attack, I'd be happy.

We left the station, Liam nor I knowing how to feel about the whole thing. Pat decided we needed coffee and took us to a local cafe. We ordered coffees and sat waiting for our order.

"How do you feel, boys?"

Liam shrugged. "It's what we thought, but I'll try and move on now. I'm hoping to move out of my parents' home soon, find a place in the city to rent. I lost my job as a barber after I ended up in hospital, so I'll need to try and find something else. I'd love to find another Daddy too, but looking like this, that's not going to happen any time soon." His hair was growing back slowly, and although the cast had been removed from his arm, he still walked with a limp.

Pat turned to look at me, but we'd already discussed what would happen in the case of either outcome. She knew how I felt that them being arrested and tried was the best possible thing to happen.

"I can move on now. I feel like it'll help with the therapist sessions too. I just need to get a job. I need to tell Marc, though. He'll be waiting to hear." I stood, waggling my phone in my hand.

"Go call him then, but don't be too long. Your coffee will get cold."

I hoped he wasn't on a call, but when he answered on the first ring, I was relieved.

"Hey, babe. How did it go?"

I told him the highlights, feeling tearful as I finally realised I was free from them.

"Will you be staying with me tonight? I want to know everything, and I think we might have some celebrating to do. Is that OK?"

"Yeah, I'd like that. I'll go home with Pat first and pack a bag, then meet you at yours around six."

"I'm looking forward to it, gorgeous." Since that one time he'd called me beautiful, when I'd told him that was what Damian had called me, he'd made sure to never use that word again and gorgeous was fast becoming my favourite.

I walked back into the cafe and sat with Pat and Liam, a sudden rush of emotion hitting me.

"I can't believe it's over. I know we still have the trial but, I don't know, I feel like we should celebrate. Sod the coffee. Let's go find a wine bar."

Pat clapped her hands enthusiastically. "I'm in." She turned to look at Liam. "What about you, sweetheart? Are you in? I hope you have your ID with you."

Liam rolled his eyes. "Yes, I'm in, and I always carry my ID."

We guzzled down our coffees, and even though it was only midday, we found the nearest wine bar, ordering their most outlandish cocktails, full of umbrellas and fruit.

We toasted each other, and with each subsequent cocktail,

toasted all the people that entered the bar. We giggled, we laughed and when "Single Ladies" played, Pat showed us her moves and sang it out loud.

By 3 p.m. we were shitfaced and we needed food. Liam knew of a good burger joint, not your usual one, but one that sold fat greasy burgers with all the toppings, plus we could eat in.

We ate in silence, broken only by the occasional hum of appreciation as we devoured the burgers and fries, the food going someway to soak up the alcohol we'd consumed. Even after eating, we were still feeling a little tipsy.

"Hey, how about this bar?" Pat dragged us through the door, and Liam started to laugh.

"This is a sex shop, Pat." She glanced around, her eyes wide at the goods on display.

"It is? Oh, well, let's take a look. I might be able to find something for those lonely nights." OMG, that was not an image I wanted, but Pat thought it was hilarious and her schoolgirl giggles filled the store.

"Maybe you could find something for you and Marc? I'll tell you what, you find it and I'll buy it. My treat. In fact, Liam, I'll buy you a gift too." She wandered around the store, breaking into uncontrollable laughter at each new item.

She picked up a huge dildo, shouting across the store, waving it in her hand. "Liam, do you want this? 'Cos if you don't, I think I might buy it." She looked at it appreciatively, fitting her hand around the thick girth.

Liam and I looked at each other. If we didn't get her out of here soon, we'd be kicked out. We hurried over to her, prying the dildo out of her hands and placing it back on the shelf before the shop assistant could come over.

"Let's pick something, quick, then we can leave." Liam hurried over to the butt plugs, picking up a set of three silver, jewelled plugs. I had no clue what to buy, so I grabbed the first things to hand without even looking. This was not a shopping trip I wanted to experience again.

We trailed Pat to the counter where she had indeed gone back for the dildo she'd been waving around. The cashier was suitably amused when Pat admitted she'd be having fun with that later and packed our purchases into separate bags, handing them to each of us.

By now, it was getting on for 5 p.m., and Marc would be home at seven. I still had to grab a bag from Pat's place, but as I stepped out into the fresh air, the alcohol hit me again.

I couldn't remember the last time I'd been this drunk, but before I knew it, we were inside another bar, Liam having bought a round of shots.

"To dickheads everywhere." Pat's toast brought a few stares, and a couple of drinkers joined in with the toast. Before I knew it, we had another round in front of us, courtesy of a businessman at the end of the bar.

Pat saluted him with her glass and swallowed the shot in one, encouraging us to follow suit. My head was spinning, but I drank it down anyway. We were having far too much fun, and I needed to make this my last.

It was Liam who decided to leave first.

"Shit, I need to go. I have an interview at the job centre in the morning." He took out his phone and made a call, telling us he was being picked up in about five minutes. He declined our offer to wait with him, saying he'd be fine.

"Pat," I slurred, "I need to go too. I'm staying the night at Marc's."

She nodded. "Let's go then. I think I might have overdone it a little bit."

We tumbled out of the bar, and I waved down a taxi for Pat. I'd have to go straight to Marc's; I didn't have time to make two journeys.

I finally arrived at his house and leaned on the doorbell. What was taking so long?

CHAPTER FORTY-FIVE

MARC

What the hell?

I opened the front door, not knowing what to expect. Who was leaning on the doorbell? I wasn't expecting anyone, just Ziggy, but he had a key.

When I opened the door, a very drunk Ziggy fell through it. What on earth had he been doing? Knowing that he'd gone to see the police with Ma, I could guess what had happened, though.

I shook my head as I picked him up from the floor, a huge, glassy-eyed smile on his face.

"Hey, babe. I went out with Pat and Liam. We had a few drinks and ended up in a sex shop." He sniggered and thrust a paper carrier bag into my hand. "This is for you, my love. I love you, have I told you? I really love you. Can we go to bed now? I think I might be sick."

I didn't doubt for one moment that he was going to be sick; his face was turning a funny shade of green. I hauled him to his feet and guided him to the downstairs bathroom, just about getting him to the toilet before he threw up.

I'd never seen him like this before, and I'd be having words with Ma, knowing full well this was her influence. Ziggy wasn't usually a big drinker.

I sat with him, stroking his back as he continued to be sick until he eventually stopped, slumping over the toilet bowl, finally asleep.

So much for our night of celebration. It seemed he'd started early and without me, but I knew we had plenty of time. I lifted him gently and carried him to the sofa, covering him with the throw. I knew he'd probably sleep all night now and the food I'd bought would need to be put in the fridge.

As I walked to the kitchen, I tripped over the bag Ziggy had handed to me. Curious to see what was inside, I pulled out the parcel, barking out a laugh as I pulled out a prostate massager and a couple of cock rings. Seriously?

I had no idea what had possessed him to buy them. In his state, I was not surprised, though. The thought that he'd gone out with Ma had me groaning in dismay. Not only would she know what he'd bought, but there was every chance she'd bought something too, knowing her.

I settled myself on the other end of the sofa, Ziggy's feet on my lap and turned on the TV. I guess I'd be waiting until he woke up. I started to watch a programme Kyle had told me about, and as it starred Henry Cavill, I'd be watching every episode.

After a couple of hours, I needed to pee and get a drink. I lifted Ziggy's feet as carefully as I could, did my business, and grabbed water and painkillers for him and a beer for me.

When I got back to the sofa, Ziggy was sitting up, bleary-eyed, his hair sticking up in all directions.

"Here, babe, take these." I handed him the pills and water, and he swallowed them, chasing them down with the glass of water.

"Better?" I asked.

"No. What happened?" He was still slurring his words, and I shook my head, a small smile on my face. He was going to have a rotten hangover tomorrow.

"You tell me, babe. Last thing I knew, you were going to the police station, then over to Ma's to pack and bag, and then here to wait for me. I don't think that's what happened, is it?"

He shook his head, then cringed. "Shit, that fucking hurts. This is all your ma's fault. She started it."

I'd no doubt about that, but I was sure no one had forced him to drink.

"Was it wine, prosecco?"

"Cocktail and shots." He turned green again at the thought. Jesus, no wonder he was drunk. I couldn't be mad, though. Today had been the day he'd learned that those two bastards would be going to trial. I just wished he'd waited for me.

He started to fall asleep again, this time with his head snuggled in my lap.

"Baby, let's get you up to bed. You'll sleep better there. Let me carry you."

I hoisted him up into my arms and started to carry him upstairs.

Looking into my eyes, he started to giggle.

"Something funny?"

"You. You're funny. And you're lovely." He poked me in the cheek, then put his fingers on either side of my mouth, squishing my cheeks. "You're very lovely, and all those naughty nurses in the hospital wanted in your pants." Drunk Ziggy was a funny Ziggy.

"But I got your pants." He leaned towards my ear and whispered. "I got your dick too. It's all mine. I'm gonna take a picture and take it to those nurses and show them. This is my dick, not yours. Well, not my dick, your dick, but my dick."

Honestly, I had no idea what he was talking about, and I reckoned he'd have no clue either in the morning.

Laying him on the bed, I started to undress him, shoes and socks first, until he was just down to his underwear.

"Come lie with me, Marc. Did I tell you you were lovely?

You're very handsome. Can I have your dick? Can we have a dog? I want a dog called Honey. I want to walk along the beach with you and Honey. Can we do that? We can take Smeagol too. Can we walk a cat?"

I hardly heard the final words as he fell back asleep, but the smile on his face told me he'd be having sweet dreams. I just hoped it was about my dick. He'd be getting that in the morning. I'd give him tonight, but tomorrow, he was mine.

The next morning, Ziggy woke with a groan.

"What the fuck happened yesterday, and why have I got such a hangover? Oh my God, I'm dying."

He was awake then and no doubt feeling like shit.

There was only one cure for a hangover, and that was a strong cup of tea and a bacon sandwich.

"Morning, Ziggy. I would imagine you and Ma are feeling a little worse for wear today. I'll go grab tea and breakfast. You'll be right as rain soon."

He groaned again, throwing a pillow over his head.

"No food. I can't eat anything."

"Yes, you can and you'll feel much better."

I went down to the kitchen and stood cooking his bacon, a strong pot of tea on the go. I was about to take it up to him when he made his way gingerly down the stairs. He still looked a little green, but at least he wasn't rushing to the toilet.

"Sit, take these and drink this." More painkillers and more tea, he'd be fine.

I placed his bacon buttie in front of him, urging him to eat. "Come on, eat up. You'll be fine. You can go back to sleep when you're done. This'll help."

He nodded and nibbled at his sandwich, taking an age to eat it. By the time he'd finished, I'd already cleared up.

"I'll just lie on the sofa. Join me?" He slumped on the sofa, patting the seat next to him.

I sat on the sofa, encouraging him to lie down. "Here, put your head in my lap and take a rest."

"Did I say anything stupid last night?" he asked, looking up at me.

"Mm, maybe a few things, but I do want to know why we have a prostate massager and some cock rings? I thought if we were going to have sex toys, we'd buy them together."

"Oh, fuck. I forgot about that. Please don't ask me what Ma bought. It was so embarrassing. She was waving it around in the shop."

I wouldn't ask, but no doubt I'd find out sooner or later.

"You told me I was lovely, that you had my dick, were going to show all the nurses said dick and that you wanted a dog called Honey."

"I did? I told you about Honey?"

"You did. Why is Honey so special? Who's Honey?"

"Honey's the dog that got me through the assault. She was a Golden Retriever. When they were, you know…" I wondered if he could continue, given the subject matter, but he ploughed on.

"When they were forcing me and beating me, I went to my happy place. Honey was always there and my lover. He never had a face, or I could never see it anyway. When I was in the hospital, dreaming, it was your face I saw. You were my lover. You were there with Honey. You were in my happy place, Marc. You are my happy place."

I leaned down and kissed him softly. We were definitely going to get the dog. How could I not now after hearing that?

I could see him starting to drift off, but I needed to say one thing before he did. He needed to know.

"You are too, Ziggy. You're my happy place. You'll always be my happy place."

And he was and always would be. His happy place was in my heart, and mine would always be in his.

EPILOGUE
ZIGGY

Two Years Later

"Marc, quick grab Honey," I shouted as he ran after the dog, and I watched as he and Honey fell into the wet sand and surf, laughing as she shook herself all over him. God, how I loved that man and the fact that he'd bought me Honey, a Golden Retriever no less, just made me love him more.

We'd decided to head to the beach today to take both of our minds off this anniversary, two years to the day that Marc had found me almost dead in the street.

Damian and Stuart had both got their comeuppance for the near-fatal beating and were serving twenty years each in prison for what they'd done to me. As we'd thought, they couldn't be tried for the attack on Liam, but justice had been done and we'd both benefited. Why they'd done what they did to us both was still a bit of a mystery. The police had since obtained evidence that they'd suffered abuse at the hands of their parents and sister, and that it had progressed from there. If it hadn't happened, though, I'd have never met Marc.

He was the best thing to ever happen to me. His unconditional love and devotion were what got me through those first six months after leaving the hospital. At times I'd been downright horrible to him, but he'd stuck with me, taking it all in his stride. His family and friends had welcomed me with open arms and made me feel wanted, which was more than my own family had ever done.

My friends had come through for me too, Suzie, Duke, Liam and even Beau had helped me recover and regain myself, and for that, I'd be ever grateful. We'd met up at times, gone out on the town and not once had Marc complained. Hell, he'd even joined us at times.

After the trial, Marc had taken me away, somewhere there were no reminders of what I'd been through. He'd taken a month from his job, and we'd travelled around Europe, visiting city after city and experiencing so many countries, it made my head spin.

I still worried, still had moments during our lovemaking when I froze if he touched me the wrong way. At first, it had caused problems. I'd feared our relationship wouldn't survive, but Marc was nothing if not patient, and he always gave me the time I needed to come back to him. There were times I'd been sure he'd leave me, having had enough of the broken and damaged boy, but that had never happened, and I was so glad he'd stuck by me.

We lived apart for a while until his ma started dropping not-so-subtle hints that we belonged together almost every day, and she'd been absolutely right. We did belong together. He understood me and I understood him.

Many times, Marc would return home after a particularly hard shift, mad at the world for what he'd seen, what he'd had to deal with. Unlike his time with Henry, I was always there offering a shoulder to cry on. I'd run him a bath and wash away his worries, bathing him, taking care of him, and often on these nights, our lovemaking would be fierce, him needing to exorcise the demons that lived in his head.

But despite all these setbacks, we loved each other deeply. I knew that and he did too. We'd vowed never to be apart. And let's face it, since that fateful day that had rarely happened. When I moved in with his Ma, he visited every day until eventually we couldn't deny what had grown between us any longer.

I watched now as he ran towards me, a huge smile on his beautiful face but a look in his eye that told me he was planning something, Honey hot on his trail.

I stood my ground, ready for anything but I wasn't ready for him to lift me into the air, Honey trying her best to jump up us both, barking excitedly.

Squealing, I half-heartedly smacked his back as he ran up the beach towards the car.

"Put me down before you drop me." I felt the laugh vibrate through his body, his usual deep chuckle reaching deep into my gut, stirring feelings in my groin. The vibration plus the friction of his body against mine had my cock hardening in my shorts.

He slowly slid me down the front of his body, and the groan that left my mouth was pure filth.

"Fuck, Marc, that feels so good."

"I know, gorgeous, I feel it too. Perhaps we should make our way home."

I slipped my arms around his neck, and he gripped my arse. I wrapped my legs around his waist, causing all kinds of sensations that were becoming hard to ignore.

He rested his forehead against mine and closed his eyes, breathing deeply.

"I love you so much, Ziggy. I can't put it into words just how much. As much as I hate this day, hate what could have happened, this day also means so much to me, to both of us."

We kissed then, a slow, passionate kiss that made my toes curl and my dick leak, and as we continued, his tongue stroked and tasted mine. To think a couple of years ago, I'd hated being kissed, but Marc's kisses were from the devil himself, potent and sinful, and I loved every one of them.

He pulled away, and I whimpered, instantly missing his mouth.

"Let's go. I need to finish this, and here on the beach is not the place to give you the best orgasm you've ever had."

"Yep, I'm in total agreement." Marc dropped me to my feet and hugged me close. I knew today was bad for him. I hardly remembered it, but he and Kyle had told me about how they'd found me and Marc's reaction from the moment he laid eyes on me.

We walked slowly to the car, Honey trotting by my side. She was definitely my dog, rarely leaving my side, and when I came in from work, the kisses I'd get were almost as good as Marc's.

Last year, we'd spent the anniversary in bed, but this year, we'd decided to leave the house, and thinking about it now, today was a celebration, not a sad day. I'd said this to Marc a few days ago, and he'd agreed and the more we'd talked about it, the more willing he was to see it as a good thing.

And now, with a good fucking on the cards, I was more than happy to go home and spend the day in bed. I broke into a jog, not wanting to wait any longer, and I heard him laughing behind me.

"Come on, hurry up," I shouted back at him, eager to leave this beach that held so many memories for me.

Since returning from Europe, we'd moved to Crosby, and as ridiculous as it sounded, it had helped me to see that the threat had gone, that I was safe, and with Marc by my side, I'd always *be* safe. He'd make sure of that. Marc had managed to secure a job working as a Senior Paramedic Team Leader, a promotion, and the job was closer to where we lived now. It meant moving a little further away from his family but they loved coming to visit us, joining us on our walks along the seafront.

He finally joined me at the car, loading Honey into the back. I couldn't wait to get home now, and my balls tingled with the thought of what was definitely going to happen as soon as we stepped through the door.

For some reason, Marc didn't seem in as much of a rush as before, and I sighed and tutted all the way home.

"For fuck's sake, Marc, are you channelling Miss Daisy here? I could have walked home quicker than this."

"Patience, Ziggy. We'll be home soon enough, and the night is young. It's not even five." He patted my knee, and I flinched, memories of a night that seemed so long ago now coming into my head. The night that had started this mad journey we'd been on.

"Hey, I'm sorry. I forget sometimes." He put his hand back on the steering wheel, but I reached across and took it, bringing it to my lips for a kiss. His hand was cold, and another memory stirred, but this time, I shoved it away. I had to remind myself this was a day for celebrating, not for dwelling on the past and certainly not for giving Damian or Stuart any more of my time that they in no way deserved.

"It's OK, baby. I know it's you and not him. I just sometimes forget. I know you'd never hurt me."

We pulled up outside our house, a beautiful home with a garden for Honey and a place where I was able to explore my love of flowers. Gardening was my haven, my getaway when I felt things crowding in, and I admired the view, thinking that I had a few bare patches I needed to fill.

A touch to my shoulder woke me from my daydream, and I looked across at the man who had stolen my heart.

"Shall we?"

"Yes, we shall."

I walked up to the house, and Marc went to let Honey out of the car, but what was taking him so long? I didn't have the keys, and it was getting a little cool.

Finally joining me at the front door, he let us in, him walking in front of me. I couldn't resist and squeezed his arse, loving the firmness I felt beneath my hand.

"Nice arse, Marc."

A cough to my left and I looked around the room we'd stepped into, surprised as fuck to see everyone I loved. Marc's family, my friends, Kyle and a very pregnant Gemma, again.

"What's going on? Why is everyone here?" I was gobsmacked.

Marc turned towards me, an excited Honey at his side, a bright purple ribbon around her neck.

"I thought about what you said the other day, about this being a day of celebration, not a day to be sad." He scrubbed his hands across his face, then continued. "I've been wanting to do this for a while now, so why not today? Why not make this day a day we remember for the right reasons?"

I was at a loss for words and even more so when Marc dropped to one knee. I heard a sniffle and looked across at Pat, who had tears in her eyes and a handkerchief clutched to her face.

"Ziggy, you came into my life at the best possible time but for the worst possible reason. I think it's safe to say it's been eventful, but it's a journey I would take time and time again if it led me to you, every single time.

"You are my world, my sun and my moon. I want to grow old with you, want to have a family with you. Hell, we'll even have another dog if that's what you want, but I don't think I can live my life without you in it."

He untied the ribbon from Honey's neck, and she licked his face, expecting a treat for being such a good girl.

"Ziggy Coleman. Will you marry me?"

There was never any doubt that my answer would be yes, and I held out my hand as he slipped the simple gold band on my finger. It was a perfect fit, just as we were.

"I can't do this without you either." I pulled him to his feet and reached up to caress his face. "The answer's yes, Marc. It will always be yes."

A cheer went up around the room as we kissed, and my world fell into place. Marc had done his job, and he'd done it well.

I really do think it was the one he was put on this earth to do, and that job was…saving Ziggy.

THE END

ACKNOWLEDGMENTS

Another book! Who would have expected that? Certainly not me but here we are again.

Thanks go to all those who've supported me through writing this book. It was a tough one and at times, I almost gave up on Ziggy, but we got there in the end.

I want to start by thanking Marianne and Joanne for reading as I wrote, giving feedback and offering their unwavering support.

Karen as usual for her amazing editing skills, Wynter Adams for a gorgeous cover and Jae Atal for proofing for me at short notice. You all did a brilliant job, making this book what it is.

Huge thanks once again to Tom. Yes, he's still here, still putting up with my ranting and raving, my tears and tantrums when the words won't come, being my absolute voice of reason and just getting me through it every day. Not sure quite what I'd do without him.

My brilliant group, The Nava Dancers and the Dancing Divas street team for getting Ziggy in front of you all. They've done an amazing job and I appreciate each and every one of them.

Lastly, the hubby and the boys. Letting me write when the story hits and sharing videos and memes when the words deserted me, keeping me at least partway sane.

Finally, to you readers, many of whom will be picking my books up for the first time but a lot of you having followed me since the start, reading and reviewing.

If you enjoyed this book, please leave a review. It means the world.

Alex x

ABOUT THE AUTHOR

Alex is married and has three grown boys and two fluffy dogs. She lives in the UK and when she's not writing about her dancing men, she can be found sitting down with cup of tea and a good book.

She would love to write full time and dreams of the day she can sit in the South of France, overlooking the sea writing about love and happy ever afters.

If you want to follow Alex, she has an active Facebook group – Alex J. Adams - The Nava Dancers | Facebook

Goodreads: Alex J. Adams| Goodreads
Bookbub: Alex J. Adams Books - BookBub
Instagram: Alex J. Adams (@alex.j.adams)

WANT MORE BOOKS BY ALEX J. ADAMS?

Nava Dance Studios Series
Dance With Me
Poles Apart
Book Three coming soon

Liverpool Boys Series
Saving Ziggy
Book Two coming soon

DANCE WITH ME
NAVA DANCE STUDIOS, BOOK ONE

Joe has twelve weeks and counting until he marries the woman of his dreams. Or is she?

After meeting with Seb, their sexy dance tutor, he's not so sure anymore. This has him questioning his choices. Is marriage to Clare really what he wants?

Is he prepared to give it all up for the man he wants or should he let him go?

Daniel's death left Seb a mess.

Unable to form any meaningful relationships since, a veil of sadness covers him. And then he meets Joe, with his dimpled smile and two left feet.

Against his better judgement, he's falling for the very engaged, very straight guy.

Finding Joe was easy, but someone from Seb's past is out to get him, threatening his career and his very future.

Can Joe and Seb overcome their very real problems to get their happy ever after, or will it all come crashing down?

Dance With Me is a slow burn MM contemporary romance featuring a sexy dance tutor, an accountant, who's anything but boring, and an adorable dog. HEA guaranteed. Features mention of drug abuse, overdose (off page) and kidnapping.

http://mybook.to/DanceNavaStudios

POLES APART
NAVA DANCE STUDIOS, BOOK TWO

Passion, that's what Dom had, passion for pole dancing, and nothing would stop him following his dream

But a call in the middle of the night, had him running home, leaving the life he loved. His brother needed him and to Dom, family was always important.

So here he was, back where it all began and where it had all ended.

A chance meeting, a reconnection with the one he thought he'd lost forever.

He'd been sent to tempt him that was for sure and he didn't think this was ever going to be enough for Jacob, he needed and wanted it all from him again. Tears pricked his eyes as he remembered how he'd almost lost him, had almost had to live his life without him.

Yes, he wanted everything, his mind, his soul and most importantly his heart. He just hoped he was willing to give it

Poles Apart is the second in the Nava Dance Studios series and whilst it can be read as a standalone, it would be advantageous to read book one, Dance With Me, first.

This is a story of second chances, lost loves and reconnection. A story that will warm your heart and is guaranteed to leave you smiling. Trigger warnings: homophobia and attempted sexual assault

http://mybook.to/PolesNavaStudios

Printed in Great Britain
by Amazon